D0735373

WEST OF WHERE YOU LIVE

Craig Miles Miller

"We kill what we cherish and cherish what we kill"
William Kittredge

ONE

Fort Collins

He woke in the cab of his pickup at the Cenex station in Sterling, Colorado. Outside the sky was still black and starless, with only the thin line of predawn to the east.

He got out of the truck ands stretched beneath the lights of the gas station's eaves. The white lights of the pumps were on. There was the singular light of a pay phone by the street. He walked behind the truck and dropped its tailgate and sat upon it, shook out a cigarette and smoked.

It was almost June but he felt cold here and he tightened the denim jacket around his chest. The coat was old, bleached by sun and washings, its padded lining full of circumspect stitching. It had been his father's. Again he looked at the black sky to the west, at the rising light on the flat horizon to the east. Again at the pay phone. He smelled the air: gasoline, cattle, rain somewhere. Some early morning traffic began to gather now on Highway 14, cars and trucks with plates from Colorado and South Dakota, Nebraska and Wyoming. It meant something to him.

By the time he pumped gas into the truck the lights popped off in groups. Gray clouds took up the whole of the western sky. Near the phone, numerous sparrows pecked at spilled wheat chaff along the curb.

Inside the station he paid for the gas, for coffee, for a small pack of Hostess Donettes. Outside he set the coffee on top of the cab and ate. The wind came in with the heavy smell of dung and wet earth. It was a Monday. He watched the cars and the birds, then looked at the phone. The sparrows peppered the sky when he walked to it. He used coins from his pocket to make the call.

Hello? she said.

He hesitated. He thought she would be at work, that he would only leave a message on the machine. He had called the house phone, not her cell.

Hello, she said again.

It was Monday, he was certain.

Trevor? Is that you . . ?

He wondered if it was it a holiday. Or if, maybe, she was unable to go to work because of him.

Cass, he said.

She was silent for a second.

Trev. Where are you? I can't believe it. I don't understand the note you left. She paused. He could hear her breathing. Where are you?

He touched the cigarettes in his coat pocket, looked at his blue Silverado along the gas pumps.

Where do you think I am?

Think you are? I don't know. Key West? Down the block? I don't know . . . You're not in New Orleans are you?

No. Not there.

This time he took a cigarette, lit it. Neither spoke.

Say something, Trevor, she finally said.

I told you I'd call.

No, you wrote you would call. You never told me anything, Trev. Never.

He smoked. It was no longer dawn and a mist began to gather, beading the phone, his hands, his hair with moisture.

Tell me where you are. Tell me you're coming home. Say you'll be back in Fort Lauderdale tomorrow. Tell me that.

He watched the water begin to collect in the depressions of the pavement.

Trevor?

I'm sorry, Cass. I can't tell you anything.

I know things were . . . No, I didn't know it was this bad, between us, for you to just up and leave. How could I know? You never . . . If it's what we talked about, argued about weeks ago—a month ago, Trevor— you never . . .

He took the phone away from his ear and looked across the street where two small girls in hooded jackets were playing along the sidewalk, pulling weeds that had grown between the cracks and then tossing them into traffic. He saw no parent. Slowly he brought the receiver back to his ear.

But she was quiet now. No voice or even the sound of breath. It began to rain then and he turned his back to it, hunched his shoulders. He threw out the wet cigarette.

I called to say hello. To let you know I'm okay, he said and she began to speak again. Cass, he said. Cassandra. It's raining. I can't talk.

She stopped and Trevor imagined her looking out the window, into the back yard.

I'll call again, he told her. It's not your fault, Cass, only me. I'm sorry. It's only me. And he hung up.

He took Highway 14 out of town, heading west with his wipers on. He turned on the radio, low, country music out of Greely. He tried not to think of Cass as he passed the open land: cottonwoods, barbed wire, tumbleweeds, windbreaks of pine around homesteads. The sky a constant gray. He was headed for Fort Collins, planning to stay only a couple of days. Then he'd go to Cheyenne and then Douglas— the high plains of Wyoming—to the ranch that belonged to his family. All of them places he had not seen in over twenty years.

The outskirts of Fort Collins were filled with chain stores and it wasn't until he neared the university that he felt he recognized the area. The motel he pulled into was now a Best Western, it was across from the university and a place where he had often met Darcie. Trevor had not consciously thought of Darcie for a long time, just as he had—determinedly—not thought of his father. Yet, in many ways, he had never stopped thinking of them.

In the lobby, after paying in cash for two nights, he told the clerk he might extend the stay.

We're all booked Friday and Saturday, the man said.

I'll probably be in Cheyenne by then.

Really? Well, you shouldn't have any trouble finding a room in Cheyenne.

It was still too early to get into his room so he left his truck in the motel lot and crossed the street to the university. It felt odd to him to be walking the concrete paths inside the campus, seeing the pines and deep grass, the brick buildings in the damp and grey light. He had attended Colorado State. Had graduated from the School of Agriculture. But that was in a different life and the memory of it brought an unwelcome feeling within him. So he left the campus, heading down a side street until he came to an intersection with a cluster of shops.

He remembered the old buildings but not what businesses used to be in them. Everything was very quiet. The spring semester was over and most students were gone. Anyway, it wasn't even noon yet. Trevor realized that he was very hungry. He had driven three days straight, eating little, sleeping little, following only a map in his head and the road signs along the Interstate. He had driven long and hard to get to Fort Collins, a place he never thought he would return to.

He entered a small cafe for coffee and eggs.

After eating, he sat with his coffee and let himself finally think for a bit about what he had just done. The leaving of Cass back in Florida, the quick packing of his tools, a few clothes, the old jacket from the back of their bedroom closet. Soap and toothbrush and toothpaste. Shaving cream and razors. He needed a shave now, he thought. He also thought how he had cashed his last paycheck. How he had cut up his debit card so that he would not be tempted to use it. He did not bring checks or any information to access the savings account—a joint account. That was for Cass. Everything he had left behind was for Cass. And then he had written the note. And he had left.

Trevor, in the cafe, quit drinking the coffee and paid his bill. Left a tip. Even after three days, he still wasn't ready to consider all of the consequences, the ramifications, of what he had done.

Down the block from the café was a western wear store. He had not packed much clothing and so he entered the doors. Inside there was an arid smell. The smells of hay and leather and wood. Familiar smells, childhood ones, like that of feed stores and barns and corrals. He was the only one inside besides the saleswoman, whose help he declined.

Walking past the racks of shirts and coats, he went to a wall where the jeans were and picked out two pair of boot-cut Wranglers. Then he picked out two blue denim shirts with snap buttons. The saleswoman, young and short-skirted, watched him as he carried the new clothes to a back room where the boots and hats were.

He set his items down and studied the boots. He had not shopped for clothes—these kinds of clothes—in so long and he wanted them to be basic, to wear well and be authentic in their way. He wanted new clothes so that they would last. He finally chose a pair of Nocona boots, brown with a simple stitch pattern, rounded toes, a low heel.

There were many hats: Detsons, Henschels, Stetsons. Cloths and straws. He took his time before picking out a grey Stetson and trying it on. Trevor looked in the mirror and felt foolish. He had rarely worn a cowboy hat, as had his father. Only his grandfather and older brother seemed natural in them, able to keep them on their heads in all weather. But he kept the gray Stetson. He told himself he would get used to it.

At the cash register the saleswoman smiled and asked if he had found everything he wanted and Trevor only nodded. The total was much more than he had expected. He looked at the cash in his wallet and he hesitated before deciding to use the credit card. He had more than enough money, but he did not know when he would have hard cash again. Anyway, it was only a single expenditure and he would not be in Colorado for long. The woman smiled at him and Trevor did not smile back as she returned the card and he put it away. Everything but the hat was put into a large plastic bag.

At the Best Western he was given a key to room 215, a smoking room. Inside, Trevor threw his duffle of gear on the bed and set the hat and plastic bag of new clothes beside it. He drew open the curtains and looked out to see the motel's sign, his dark blue Silverado in the lot, the busy street and the brick Chemistry Building across it. The sky was still a matte of clouds, everything muted and drizzly, and he could not see the mountains.

He closed the drapes. Sat on the bed. He told himself he should get up, drive downtown. He should drive up the Poudre and visit Gus and Frida—his godparents—if they were still there. If they were still alive. But he could not bring himself to do it. Not yet. No one knew that he was back. No one knew anything about him, not since he had left at the age of twenty-two.

Trevor stood up and undressed. He opened the plastic bag and put on the new denim shirt, the new jeans, the boots and hat. He flipped on the harsh bathroom light and looked at himself in the mirror there. Everything felt tight, looked silvery in their newness. He removed the hat and boots. The clothes. Decided he would wash them—the jeans and shirts—to rid them of their shine and stiffness.

When he turned off the light, bringing the small room back to shadows and darkness, he thought again of Darcie, then of Cass back in Florida. He looked at the black telephone on the desk and then looked away. A great fatigue rose up within him and he swept the bags from the bed and laid on it. He felt cold but didn't get under the covers. He needed sleep, he knew. The three days of driving with only catnaps were catching up to him now. He closed his eyes and began to drift into a half-sleep and then, within that half-sleep, he heard his father calling his name.

It was his father's voice, clear and unmistakable, calling from the front door of the house in Cheyenne, his heavy voice saying Trevor's name, calling him inside from the neighborhood when Trevor was a boy.

Trevor sat up quickly and sat on the side of the bed. He lit a cigarette. He stood up and began to pace. Smoked. Stayed in the dim room. Later he took a long shower and did not turn on any lights until he was dry and ready to shave.

He wore his work jeans, a white t-shirt. He wore his new boots and the Stetson. The jacket that had been his father's. The dirty clothes from the drive he put in the plastic bag with the new and he went out the door and to his truck. He drove to the Ram Laundromat, north of the university, a place still there and under the same name despite the years.

Inside it was uncluttered and clean. Though there were maybe seven other people attending to their clothes, it looked empty to Trevor. He realized that this was only his perception, because in South Florida there were always people everywhere at every hour. Perhaps for Northern Colorado, seven or eight was a crowd.

He went through the usual motions—a little pack of detergent, quarters from the change machine, the run of water and starting of the machine. There was a television on, which Trevor made a point to ignore. He looked about the room, at a woman with a young boy, at a man older than him reading a magazine, a lone woman with long black hair folding her clothes--a student, no doubt. She was alone. She looked to be, most likely, Indian or Pakistani. The young woman suddenly took her eyes from her folding and looked directly at him. Her eyes were large, dark. She gazed at him shamelessly and he averted his eyes. He felt conspicuous in his hat and boots and he turned and walked to the front window of the Laundromat.

The sun had come out. Trevor took out his cigarettes and lighter then removed his coat, draped it on a plastic chair. He went outside and lit up. It was chilly but the dry air felt good. He looked up at the breaking clouds over Horsetooth Reservoir, the light needling down in rays. A God sky, his mother had always called it, both seriously and as a joke. My sky, his grandfather would say.

Trevor, alone out front, heard the Laundromat door open. He heard footsteps, then felt the presence of another. He turned his head enough to see the young woman who had looked at him. She spoke to him, asking if he was from Fort Collins.

No, Trevor said and he did not look at her.

Are you only a pretend cowboy?

He turned his head slightly to her. Looked at her face, which was attractive, inscrutable. She had a British accent.

I'm sorry?

I was wondering if you were a real cowboy.

Trevor tossed the cigarette. He assumed she was making fun of him. He was much older than her, and though he had been told he was a handsome man, had become more handsome with age, he thought that she was only amusing herself.

No.

You're very tan, she said, now looking at his bare arms.

Just last week Trevor had been working in west Broward County, out near the edge of the Everglades.

I work outdoors.

Her own skin was a dark olive, smooth. She had rounded hips and heavy breasts.

It's just . . . The boots and hat. That lovely jacket. She looked momentarily inside the big window. Your face. Quite like a cowboy come to town.

She was staring at him again, her eyes direct and unabashed. And amused. He could tell that she wanted him to play along. And he returned her stare, kept his face flat, an expression—or lack of one—that he had once practiced as a young man but had perfected in New Orleans, where he had met Cass. In Fort Lauderdale it became just his face, without practice or pretense.

There, she said. Right now. You look like a cowboy. That face.

No, he said and he turned his head. He reached for another cigarette but had smoked the last one. He squeezed the empty packet and put it in his pocket.

Then you *are* pretending.

He met her eyes again, which held a feigned innocence. Her plucked brows arched. Lips full. She smiled at him.

My wash is done, he told her and excused himself. She turned her body as he walked past her.

Trevor carried the wet wad of clothes to the dryer. Fished his pockets for change. The young woman came back inside. Trevor felt her eyes upon him but he did not look at her. He started the machine and watched his new and old clothes tumble within the eye of the dryer. When he turned she was, indeed, looking at him. She was by the front door where Trevor wanted to go.

As he walked past her he could not ignore her presence.

Yes, he said to her, I'm only pretending.

This appeared to please her. She smiled. Her eyes smiled. She seemed to want more from him but he walked past her and out the glass door. He went to his truck and got a pack of cigarettes from the carton of Marlboros he kept in the glove box. He did not look back but went to the sidewalk and began to walk beneath the trees. When he did look back he saw her. She was still watching, a deliberate stare, and so he nodded before going off, into a neighborhood where he had once lived as a student.

When he returned his clothes were long dry and the young woman was gone. So was his jacket.

Trevor looked on the floor and around the room. Checked to see if there was a lost and found box. He asked a few people if they had seen it but no one had.

He folded his laundry—now cool to the touch—and told himself that the loss of the jacket was unimportant. It was nothing. But he did not believe himself. It was the only item in his possession from when he had left Wyoming and that he'd kept through his days in New Orleans and the many years in Fort Lauderdale. And now it was gone.

When he carried his clothes out to the truck, he saw the note. A handwritten piece of paper trapped beneath the wiper blade:

> *You left your coat. Such an interesting coat. A person might nick it. You can reclaim it, if you like, at the Copper Horn tonight. When the sun is down, I should think.*

By nightfall the sky was cloudless and a creamy afterglow hung along the mountains west of town. All the streetlights were on, the lights of store windows, the headlights of other cars as Trevor drove down College Avenue and parked downtown.

As he walked he felt cold. He had no other coat than the jacket. He had his new jeans, the boots and hat, a t-shirt beneath the new shirt, but it was not warm enough for him. He would have to re-adapt to the chill of night, eventually to the brutal cold of winter. He took his mind off it by looking at the changes in Fort Collins. Downtown was cleaner, more lively. Gone were the hardware store, the boot repair shop, grocery and housewares. Gone was the old Cache Hotel. Now restaurants and boutiques, taverns, outfitters and the usual chain stores dominated the refurbished buildings. He walked past it all, feeling no press of nostalgia, no rim of sweet sadness to acknowledge the passing of time and sense of loss. There was too much change for him to feel it. College Avenue was, in a fashion, not unlike Duvall Street in Key West or Las Olas in Fort Lauderdale, it was Bourbon Street. Every main street in every gentrified downtown was a version of Bourbon Street now, Trevor thought, authentic and inauthentic at the same time. But he held out hope for Cheyenne. How much could a place like Cheyenne change? Ultimately, he was more interested in Douglas, and, really, only in the ranchland his family owned outside of Douglas. And even then, within that land, was the parcel he coveted and that he planned to make his own. That was all he needed or desired, he reminded himself. The other changes mattered not at all.

At the corner of College and Mountain there was a pedestrian mall. Everything was done in dark brick. There was a fountain. There was a bronze statue of a deer. And there was the Copper Horn Saloon.

Directly inside was a sitting area with a fireplace, then a bar and a main area with pool tables, dartboards and arcade games. There were lighted signs advertising American beers. A jukebox played music he didn't know. There were not many people. It was dark.

Trevor did not look for the young woman. He went to the bar and sat alone with empty seats next to him. He rested his arms on the false copper-plated counter and looked for an ashtray. He saw none. Saw no one smoking inside the bar and guessed that it was not allowed. When the bartender came Trevor ordered ginger ale; he did not drink alcohol.

He was thinking of going outside to smoke when she appeared in the seat next to him.

You must think I'm rash, she said.

She was wearing his jacket.

I was cold, he said.

She looked down at the coat as if it were a surprise, then slid her apple-colored hands along the ragged lapel. She wrapped it tight along herself.

It is an attractive coat. Warm. Full of character. I'm sure someone would have pinched it. I saved it for you, really. She smiled. Her hair was long and straight, black. She made no offer to return the jacket. I saw you sitting here, so alone. I saw your hat. Her eyes lit up at the mention of the hat. It makes me think you're not really pretending.

Trevor made no comment and she leaned back into the barstool. She then asked him how old he was.

Older than you, he said. Older than this bar.

And you really are a cowboy of some sort, admit it.

She reached to touch his hand but Trevor withdrew it.

I grew up on a ranch.

In Florida?

Trevor was surprised. He tried not to show it.

Wyoming, he said.

I saw the plates on your lorry. I thought: Oh! A Florida cowboy.

Trevor shrugged. He was unsure what to make of her, unsure of what she wanted.

You even talk like a cowboy.

He raised his head and regarded her beneath the brim of the Stetson.

Not much, she said and laughed.

It was a guileless laugh, reminding Trevor how very young she was. Not as young as him when he left home, maybe, but young enough to laugh honestly at her own joke.

The bartender came over and asked if she needed anything. She shook her head and waved him away and turned her attention back to Trevor. She watched him, waiting for him to speak, but he would not fill the space with words. So she did.

I'm from London—Hoxton—but my parents are both from Mumbai, originally. I won an essay contest to study in New York, at university. I never had much interest in the States, you know, but I won the contest. So I wrote more essays then I wrote poetry, which was more appealing than the bloody essays. Now I write fiction. Stories, mainly . . . She paused, as if to see if Trevor was listening. He was. He wondered if she was drunk, or high on something, but he didn't think so . . . New York is unorganized, wicked, often ugly—don't you think?—but it's exactly what I needed. Yet, it's not really the States, is it? Not America the beautiful. So I applied for graduate school, to study the fine, *very fine*, art of writing, and ended up out here. Mountains, sky, charming people. Fresh and clean. Cowboys . . . Trevor nodded this time when she paused. He was being polite, but he did not understand why she was talking to him, telling him her story . . . But I'm done with that. School, that is. I'm going to quit. I mean, it's still only studying. It's still but an apprenticeship. What's life if you don't dirty your nose in it? Classrooms are for writing, not telling stories. You understand the difference? It's piffle.

Piffle, Trevor said.

She stopped then. Looked away for the first time as if embarrassed. She wrapped her arms around herself again, around the jacket. Gathered her thoughts.

And you're from Wyoming, but your truck is from Florida? You may or may not have been a cowboy in the past, but now you are a . . .

Carpenter.

A carpenter. Good. But you've come all the way to Fort Collins to . . .

Do my laundry.

Oh! He does have a sense of humor after all. You do your laundry here but you're from a ranch . . .

Trevor realized he was playing her game now. He wasn't sure why or how it had come about.

Around Douglas, Wyoming, he told her. My grandfather has a ranch there. I lived there and in Cheyenne.

And Trevor considered that his grandfather was no doubt dead. Had to be dead. Dead and gone like his father. Like Darcie. The ranch was no doubt being run by his brother. His mother would be there—unless she too had died. And suddenly Trevor could not fathom seeing his mother again. What would she look like? What could he say to her? What if she really was dead and gone?

And . . . you went to Colorado State?

He was surprised by the question. He didn't answer her.

It was a logical assumption from what you've told me. Why else would you be in Fort Collins?

I have family here. Godparents.

And you live in Florida?

Trevor did not answer.

You're staying with your Godparents?

No. They live up the Poudre.

You're staying in Cheyenne then?

Trevor was tired of the questions. He reminded himself that he had come for only one thing.

I came here to get my jacket.

Don't change the subject, she said quickly and smiled. I told you about myself, now we're talking about you.

He could see that she was enjoying herself. Maybe it was only fodder for poetry or fiction—a story—but he could not tell. She was bright, intelligent, aggressive. She was attractive. She had a thing for cowboys maybe. But there was an insecurity about her, too. Something affected in her manner.

I'm just visiting.

She nodded.

And you're drinking . . . She reached for Trevor's glass and drank from it. Made a face . . . Ginger ale?

Look. It was nice talking to you. I hope you get everything straightened out—school, writing, cowboys.

My name is Bisma, she told him. She extended her hand. Bisma Patel.

He hesitated, then took her hand. It was warm, soft. He shook it quickly.

Trevor. Trevor Kallengaard.

Kallengaard? What's that, Norwegian?

My family came from Sweden.

Interesting, she said. Mister Trevor Kallengaard, the Swedish cowboy.

He reminded himself again that he had had enough. That he wanted to leave. To have a cigarette. He did not understand why he was still talking to her, unless he was lonely, or because he was tired of talking to himself.

I'd like my jacket, please, he said.

It's cold, she said and made no move to relinquish the coat. You won't take it from me, will you? I have no car and have to walk.

Trevor held his face steady. Said nothing.

Listen, she said. When you go to the Poudre tomorrow, give me a lift. I'll give it to you then.

I don't think . . .

Just a ride. I love to get out in the canyon but have no car.

I don't want . . .

You won't have to bring me back. I'll hitch.

Trevor did not see himself as rude, any more than he saw himself as gregarious. He realized that he could not just take the coat off of her, though he wanted to.

You can't, he started then started again. You just can't . . .

Oh, but I can, she said and smiled and her dark eyes smiled too. You're quite wrong: I can. She took out a cell phone. Here, I'll call you so you'll have my number. What's your cell?

I don't have one, he said.

No number? You don't have to be shy.

No phone, he told her.

Really?

Trevor nodded.

The young woman—Bisma Patel—took a napkin from the bar. She removed a pen that was not his from a pocket of the jacket. She wrote down an address. A phone number.

Tomorrow? she asked and held out the napkin.

Trevor regarded her, didn't want to answer her but then did as he took the napkin.

In the morning. Early.

Ten?

Seven, or earlier.

Eleven, then.

Trevor said nothing. It was another game.

Very well, I win. We'll make it ten. Call me first. She smiled—her teeth milk-white. It was nice to meet you, Mister Trevor Kallengaard.

Trevor folded the napkin and placed it in his front shirt pocket, next to his cigarettes. He did not look back when he went out the door.

Outside the air came down from the mountains and cut through his layer of clothes. He walked quickly to the truck, started it, sat there with the heater running. He took out a cigarette and lit it, cracked the window to let some of the smoke out. He touched the napkin in the shirt pocket.

Trevor wondered why he had put up with the girl—the young woman. Why had he listened to her, bantered with her, let her engage him. Why had he been truthful in his answers? Was it, simply, because she was young and attractive? Was it that he missed Cass but would not admit it to himself? He was not seeking sex or companionship. Certainly not love.

He had loved Cass. Probably still loved her but that love had become untenable. He had loved another woman before Cass and Cass herself had loved another man in New Orleans, a man who was killed. That was how they—he and Cass—fell in with each other. The other people they had loved had died. And now tonight, his talking with the woman, seemed to have had little to do with an article of clothing.

If he could so readily leave Cass, Trevor thought, and leave his mother, brother and grandfather—his godparents--and never contacted them again, leave the people who claimed to love him and who he could claim to love in return, if he could do that, why couldn't he just abandon a jacket? Even if it had been his father's?

He finished his cigarette. He drove back to the motel.

TWO

Cache La Poudre

Cassandra Tipton had just passed Opa Locka Boulevard when she was caught in a bottleneck of traffic. She worked in Miami but had not been in all week, and now this would make her late. She listened to her car's air conditioner, to the muffled traffic moving freely in the opposing lanes. She looked at the soft blue sky, the bright sun above the Atlantic, thought about how the boil of heat and humidity was right beyond the thin glass of her window. She could turn on the radio or her iPhone for music—but she did not really enjoy music when she drove. She liked to think. And all she could think about, despite trying to distract herself, was Trevor.

She realized, now, that it had been coming. She had seen it coming, had seen the change—a shift—in him, something small but powerful. Cass knew his weak spots and had duly poked them. Then she had moved on to larger issues: she had started drinking again, socially and at home, after years of abstinence; she had expressed a need for friendships, a desire to go out with other couples; she wanted to get married, though they had lived together for over ten years, and she wanted to start a family, one last chance to have a child. She had been patient—first having to convince herself she wanted these things, then trying to convince Trevor—but she had seen it coming. His resistance. His concealed anger. His unmitigated silence. Still, these were the things she wanted. They were not wild or outlandish things. They were normal.

But she knew he might leave her. Had even wondered if such a separation wouldn't prove to be a good thing. A necessary thing. They had both carefully avoided anything that hinted at a life beyond themselves, at anything momentous. Since leaving New Orleans they had both been such quiet and timid people—social hermits. Both guilty of this long bland march into the middle of their lives.

But Cass had not foreseen that he would leave her so abruptly. So callously. And that this abandonment would make her so angry. That his absence would hurt so much.

A van slipped into the space in front of her. Her lane was going no faster than the others, yet the van had pushed its way in, her vision now blocked by the wide metal of the vehicle's back. Cass touched the horn but then did not press it. There was no point. All she could do was back off a bit, allow some space, keep moving forward. And, she realized, it was in traffic like this, returning from a trip to Key West, when she knew Trevor might leave her.

She had finally said out loud what they both knew she had wanted for years: a child. She had told him. She was forty years old and life was boring and empty and she wanted a baby. It was direct. It was concrete. It could not be construed as anything else.

Trevor, I want a baby.

And he had said nothing. But his face became bare and flat, his jaw set itself tight and he only looked out the windshield. She said nothing in return, waited, and finally he turned his head and looked at her, just his handsome face, intransigent in its blankness. And that was his answer. Just the face. No words. Only his silence for the remainder of the trip.

And then, weeks later, he had left her.

Traffic was picking up speed. She could see the city ahead, Miami a stack of sun-struck buildings. She did not really want to go to work, had not gone to work since Trevor left her. But after the cryptic phone call, after enough days to let it sink in, she needed to go to work. What else could she do?

She slid into the right lane, a slower one, delaying her arrival into the city. She let her mind fall away from the commute and into memories of Trevor: how he had shown up in New Orleans, in the Marigny, Marcus being the first to befriend him and, because she and Marcus were lovers, Cass then met and befriended him too. And he started working at the restaurant in the Quarter where Cass worked. He had been so quiet, so young looking. Girls liked him, teased him, asked if he were still in high school. Nobody knew much about him . . . And when Marcus died—when he was killed, robbed and senselessly run over by the people who robbed him—Trevor was there, close by but still silent. And when Cass could no longer stand being in

New Orleans and moved to Fort Lauderdale, it was Trevor who came to assist, to help her pack, then to drive, then to move into one of Cass' mother's properties near the beach. And he had stayed. And Cass had been glad he had stayed—as she didn't know anyone there, really, and did not get along with her mother.

It was her mother who made a point about *how handsome* Trevor was, as if that was Cass' motivation for returning to Florida, as if Marcus—who was African-American and who her mother more than disapproved of—had not been killed and Cass had only come to her senses and brought Trevor along as proof. But it was after that and after a month of living together that she slept with him.

And it was enjoyable. Not just the sex but the touching, the being close to a man. She was surprised that Trevor was such a capable lover. Had expected him to be inexperienced, clumsy. But that was not the case. Somewhere within him was a confident and passionate man. It was surprising. And she remembered that: the first time making love, the intimacy they shared after Marcus' death.

In the car, exiting onto SW 8th Street, Cass realized that it had not been as she had thought—that she had chosen Trevor. No. Trevor, in New Orleans, before Cass even knew it, had made up his own mind. He had chosen her.

Cass felt a sudden pool of emotion inside her, of affection and loss, a deep longing, all gathering up in the pit of her stomach.

She did love him. And she wanted him back.

Trevor sat in his truck in the motel parking lot at eight-thirty in the morning. Windows up. Heater on. He sipped black coffee and ate a banana—both taken from the lobby. He was bareheaded, having left the Stetson in the room. He had slept hard and dreamless and had been awake since six, spending that time working up the courage to visit his godparents, Gus and Frida Sorenson, whom he called uncle and aunt. Gus Sorenson had originally worked the ranch, along with Trevor's father, Trig. Frida was from Douglas and had dated Trevor's father for a while--though she married Gus--before his father met and married Anna, Trevor's mother.

But having convinced himself to drive up the Poudre Canyon, now, in the truck, he was thinking of the woman who had his jacket. He told himself, yet again, that the jacket didn't matter. All he really wanted was the ranchland. Everything else—the jacket, his godparents, his brother and even mother, let alone the young woman from London—were inconsequential. Yes, he had an emotional attachment to the jacket, as he did to his truck and some of his tools, but it was only an attachment. Replaceable objects. Clothing, a vehicle, hammer and saw and such. Even a human being was, potentially, only an object and attachment. Things among millions of things, people among millions of people. Billions, really. Weren't they, ultimately, replaceable? All of them?

He did not want the woman—Bisma—with him, any more than he wanted Cass to be by his side. He didn't trust the girl to return the coat, to do what she had promised. He expected only more wordplay and questions from her.

Yes, it was cold. Yes, he would like to have the jacket. But he could buy another. And until then, he'd just have to get used to it.

Trevor put the truck in gear.

He drove north through town on 287. At Laport he could see the Cache la Poudre River, running flat and calm on its way to the South Platte. Here there were a few pastures and empty lots, weeds and sunflowers growing along the unmowed fence lines, as he turned left onto Highway 14.

When the asphalt began to climb there were pines along the hillsides. Further up Trevor saw the peaks of the Rockies, distant and white, unmistakable on the horizon. The sight of them caught him for a moment, these mountains once so common and now so striking. But after sighting them for a while, he did not look for them again.

The river ran on the right now, its water rushing along a boulder-strew path, as the road climbed with turns and curves. Some cars were already parked along the pullouts, people in colorful clothing, wetsuits, people with backpacks and kayaks. The highway was newly paved and there was little traffic.

Trevor knew this route, even after twenty years. He recognized what was old and what was new. He kept his feelings for the land, for the place, in check as the walls of the canyon rose tighter, higher, the river now thin and silver, a faster cascade. And then the square tunnel—a sign that the turn to Uncle Gus' would come soon—a small but rough tunnel looking almost hand-carved from the rock. He passed through it, a short but dark passage, into the sunlight again, the sparse trees and rocky cliffs and the river now far below. One more curve and then the side road—CR 27—was there just as he knew it would be and he slowed and he turned and then he stopped, just off the main highway.

Trevor put his truck in park and sat there, atop a small wooden bridge that traversed Young Gulch Creek. The highway and river behind him, the gravel county road rose into the trees ahead of him, beyond a cattle guard. He rolled down the window. Turned off the ignition. Took out a cigarette. Lit it and smoked. His nerves hit him then, a tremor in the shoulders and hands, jittering the cigarette. He thought that maybe he should not do it, just show up at Uncle Gus and Aunt Frida's house. Show up like a ghost in grey sheets and a bloody past. He did not know if they would accept him. If they would, possibly, not even remember him. Maybe they were no longer there. Maybe they were old and had moved into town and he would only find an empty house or someone else living on their property . . . But, no, he doubted that. They would be there.

He tried to negate the large emotions he felt within. He finished his cigarette and listened to the ticking of the truck, to the river behind him, the insects and unseen birds. He watched mud dauber wasps work the creek bottom and thought of their paper hives that no doubt hung below the bridge. Trevor watched the wasps and stayed very still until the feelings of fear and doubt, the potential of joy in seeing people he knew, seeing family, subsided. Then he started the truck again and drove over the bridge and over a cattle guard—the ring of tires over the metal a familiar sound. The truck raising dust until he hit the hill where the road had been oiled.

Trevor stopped again, this time at the mouth of a long gravel drive with fields of Johnson grass around it. The drive led upwards and into a copse of larch and aspen. Behind it, he knew, were spruce and pine and the house, all hidden from the road. There was a mailbox, old, pocked with buckshot. The name SORENSON in faded paint along it. Trevor eased his truck past the mailbox and onto the drive, which was not oiled or graded. Dust rose like a fine smoke behind him.

The house sat in the shadow of pines. It was two stories with shakes, its eaves matted with brown pine needles. Its white paint was faded, almost grey, and still had dark green shutters. The front door now painted red. Concrete steps and pathway led from the door towards the parking area beneath the blue spruce, a tree large and wide where the branches had been cut to accommodate vehicles.

Behind the house was green pasture. A creek ran through the property there, a place Trevor had played much when he was a boy, and two Appaloosa ponies were visible, cropping the grass beneath the early leaves of cottonwoods. And beyond that was mountain—pines and scree and granite outcroppings, patches of snow in the shadows.

He parked in the mix of bare dirt and needles beneath the spruce. He turned off the ignition and listened through the open window to the wind in the trees, to the clatter of chickens somewhere. He lit a cigarette before getting out and putting his boots on his godparents' property once again.

Uncle Gus, Aunt Frida were a childless couple—Trevor's mother had said they couldn't conceive—who, for a time, had treated Trevor and his older brother, Ross, as children of their own. Ana and Trig's kids also Gus and Frida's.

When Trevor closed the truck's door, a large yellow dog appeared. It rounded the corner of the house, barking, and Trevor stopped in his tracks. He let the dog approach. It kept its eyes on his and showed its teeth, its barks sharp and strong. It stopped a yard shy, hunching its shoulders, blocking the path to the house. It was an older dog.

Betsy, Trevor said to it.

The dog only moved in closer.

Betsy girl. It's only me, girl. Betsy girl.

It would not stop barking.

Then the red door opened. A man stood in the threshold, hand on the knob, looking.

Betsy, Trevor said again, loud enough for the man to hear. You know me.

The man stepped out into the sunlight and it was Uncle Gus. He appeared shorter, heavier, hair going to gone. A white beard. There was still authority in his stance, in his stare. The dog did not look back, did not stop barking. Gus did not call it off.

Trevor threw his cigarette into the dirt, snuffed it with the toe of his boot. The dog reared up, bayed at a higher pitch. Trevor looked at the dog's eyes again.

It's only me, Betsy.

His uncle came down the short steps and down the pathway, walking with his elbows out, a short-stepped gait that Trevor now remembered. He was deliberate in his slowness, did not drop his gaze, had that subtle contempt and defiance that mountain people had. That ranch people had. An automatic defensiveness and distrust of outsiders.

Trevor looked square at his uncle. His godfather. He held spurious emotions in tight, the dual feelings of dread and elation, the worry of scorn or love. Uncle Gus came and stood just behind the barking dog.

She doesn't remember me, was all Trevor could think to say.

His godfather glanced at the dog and gave a single sharp call. The dog fell silent. It sat on its haunches now. Still, he did not send it away.

Not a she, he said.

It's not Betsy?

Uncle Gus eyed Trevor. There was a hint of confusion, of curiosity now.

Son of Betsy, he said. But we call him S.O.B., mainly.

He gave Trevor another close inspection, then looked down to the dog. Go on. Kennel up, boy. Kennel up.

The dog got to its feet, still looking at Trevor, and trotted off, around the house where it had come from.

Uncle Gus stepped forward, studied Trevor's face, took a look at the truck and then back. He rounded his shoulders and Trevor saw the man's eyes soften.

There was a sudden slackness in his godfather's knees, as if he were dipping like a mud dauber wasp.

It's not you, is it?

Trevor smiled, short, tight, controlled. The only smile he had.

It can't be you.

Trevor took a step back and leaned against his truck. He crossed his arms along his chest, holding everything in. He could feel his heart. Could feel the quiver in his smile so that he dropped it.

It's me, he said.

He held Trevor by the wrist, rushing him through the parlor and into the living room, calling Frida's name. Trevor, in the almost sunless rooms, saw the photographs upon the walls. Faces of the living and dead and potentially dead. Of people he had pretended to no longer know, a family that had not existed for years. He was led quickly into the kitchen with its mallow light and flowered wallpaper. Wooden cabinets and Linoleum. And Aunt Frida was there. She looked at him and saw him and brought spiderlike hands to her face.

She knows me, Trevor thought, felt. She knows who I am.

Uncle Gus let go of his arm and moved to the side. Under the kitchen lights Trevor said nothing as Aunt Frida put her face close to his, an aged face mapped with wrinkles but holding the same clear eyes, and she touched his cheeks.

Oh, Trevor, she said. Trevor Kallengaard.

She brought her hands down and wiped her eyes. She then embraced him.

Sit. Sit down, she said as she let go and looked for a chair at the table, pulled it out and sat down in it herself. Trevor pulled his own chair and sat. Gus stood by the stove, watching. I knew it was something when I heard the dog, Frida told him, and Gus went out. But I was afraid to look . . . I dreamt about you just last week, Trevor. Last week. And here you are. I was afraid to look.

His uncle snuffled from the stove.

You dream about everyone, he said.

Trevor smiled a little and looked down at the floor. Then all three of them were looking at the floor. All silent. The kitchen warm and sunlit. Some curtain had been drawn between them and Trevor could sense the shift, the rise of memory. Memories not yet ready to be disturbed or discussed.

Hey now, his godfather said, let's put on an early supper. A brunch, they call it. We'll kill a chicken, got some early spinach in the garden, some red potatoes.

I'll kill a young hen, Frida said.

No, Trevor told them. It's all right. It's too early. I'm not here for . . .

Come on now, Gus said.

No . . .

Frida reached across the table, took his chin in her hand.

You'll stay with us, she said. What are you thinking? We've got a spare room, two really. We'll feed you. She pulled her hand away, stood up and looked at him again. You've grown so handsome.

Please, Trevor said but she did not hear or want to hear and then she was gone, away from the table and into the mudroom and then out the back door.

Let it be, Gus said, waving his hand. She wouldn't feel right, not feeding you. He came and sat across from Trevor at the table.

Well now, Gus said then paused. I can't believe it. Then he said nothing and looked out the small window for a while. You want a beer? He stood abruptly. Or a whiskey? I'd say we should have a snort.

I don't drink.

Drink a little beer, don't you?

Trevor shook his head.

That's right. You never did drink much.

I did.

You did? And his godfather cocked his head, seeming to remember when Trevor did drink, had drunk, and then he stopped. He put his hands in his pockets. He sat back down.

Where you staying?

In town.

Gus nodded.

Been up to Douglas?

Not yet.

There was silence.

You know, Gus said, I always thought if I ever saw you again, I'd have a lot to tell you. Too much maybe. But right now, I can't think of a thing.

How's my mom?

Annie? . . . You know, Trevor, you did your mother a great disservice. Never writing or calling or coming back. Broke her heart after it was already broke. No one knew where you went, where you've been. Good as dead, we all thought.

She isn't . . .

Dead? No, she's alive. But she's not in Douglas. She's in Glenrock, down the road. He stopped. Raked his beard with his fingers. Now, Thor—your grandfather— he's passed and gone. Maybe you expected that.

Trevor nodded.

Though a lot of people thought he would never let go. He was working right up till he had a stroke, you know, he still played pretty rough till that. A smile came briefly to Gus' lips. But after that, well, he went about two years ago. Your brother buried him on the ranch, with the others.

Trevor didn't comment. Didn't ask about Thor's stroke or how he had died. Did not ask about his brother. He wanted to ask about the land—the ranch—and, now that Thor's death had been broached, ask if there had been a will. But he could not bring himself to do it. He did not want to push, nor did he want to let anyone know of his intentions concerning the land.

Why Glenrock? he asked.

Annie, she's in a home, Trevor. We, your aunt and I, used to go up there a lot, but not so much lately. We're getting old. We got Frida's pension from the County. I keep a few ponies here, some mules for the Cache and Comanche outfitters. Gus gave the window another look but Trevor did not look with him. Fact is, Trevor, not much point in visiting. She has Alzheimer's.

His godfather cleared his throat, rubbed his neck. Trevor stayed stiff in the wooden chair.

Does Ross visit?

Don't think so, anymore. Not that it'd matter. He's never been the same after your dad, after Darcie died. Definitely not since Thor.

Trevor felt something give in his expression. He could not stop it or help it. His uncle saw it, his own face reddening.

I'm sorry, Trev. It was such a long time ago. No one's forgotten but no one blames you. You just made it worse by running away. You got it wrong. No one blames you.

Ross did.

Okay. Fair enough. Your brother did. But you should have known he would. You were what, twenty years old? Twenty-two? You'd lived with him long enough not to let him scare you off. Ross was like Thor, no one could tell him different even if the truth was staring him in the face . . . You going up to see him?

Trevor did not answer. He let the question hang in the white kitchen with the flowered walls. He could hear the sound of a hand pump somewhere.

If you're going up there, you'd better let him know. He's not the best of company . . . Are you going up there?

Trevor still did not answer. He kept his hands to himself. Looked out the window. Thought of his mother.

I have to leave now, he said.

What? . . . Come on now, Trev.

Trevor stood up. He looked for his hat but remembered he had not brought it.

I've got to go. I'll be around.

Where? . . . Where'd you say you were staying?

In town.

Where in town?

Trevor slid his chair back to the table.

Come on, Trevor. Gus stood also. Have something to eat. I know it's early, but what's Frida going to say? You're going to make her feel bad. She'll think it's her fault.

Trevor did not sit back down. He only said that he was sorry. That it couldn't be helped.

Don't be a damned fool, Gus said. Your father, that girl . . . It was an accident. Neither of them are on your hands.

No, was all Trevor could say.

I don't know where you've been, but you only made it worse, acting like you were the one who was killed. Can't you see it? See beyond yourself?

I didn't come here for that. I don't want to talk about that.

Why? Gus asked. It happened. It's over and done with. Why not talk about it?

Then they both heard it, a soft crying from the mudroom. She was there, looking back at them when they looked at her. A dead chicken, headless, bare of feathers, in her left hand.

Frida, Gus said.

Trevor could not look her in the face. He stared at the fresh bird, plucked and pump-washed, its skin white as the moon. A thick rivulet of blood trickled from the stump of its neck. It ran down the pimpled flesh to the knuckles of his godmother's hand, pooling at the wedding band.

I'm sorry, Aunt Frida, Trevor said. He backed up and looked at both of them again. I only came to visit. I'm sorry.

Then he turned and left the way he had come, through the living room and past the photographs and to the parlor, to the door. He could hear his uncle call to him. He went out the door to the sunlit yard. Everything was sharp and particular, the grass and spruce trees, the shade, his sense of everything. He went to his truck, got in, saw the dog come to the corner of the house, silent this time. He started the engine.

Uncle Gus. Aunt Frida. They were at the steps when he pulled away.

Trevor found himself going faster as he descended the county road. The tires clipped over the oiled and pressed gravel, loose stones pinging on the undercarriage. He was thinking of Darcie and his father, of the twin pines at the bottom of Boxelder Creek along Harriman Road, he thought of the blood on his face and hands and clothes . . . He took shallow, rapid breaths. He could not understand why he was going faster. He didn't want to go. He saw the end of the road with its cattle guard and bridge, the black paved main highway with its cross traffic and the canyon beyond it. He heard his tires over the cattle guard, felt it, then he was on the bridge, saw the faded stop sign for Highway 14 and the deep, collected gravel at the county road's end. Travis hit the breaks.

He put his weight into it. Felt the new boots slip on the pedal, felt the bump and slush of the gravel through the pedal and the boots, the truck fishtailing, the front wheels crushing to a stop just as they hit the blacktop of 14.

His foot was still pressed to the brake when the cloud of dust came from behind. It balled around the Silverado, filtered into the open windows and settled like a fine ash upon the dash and seats, his clothes and skin. He watched the remaining dust pass over the highway and disperse over the gulf of the river.

He crossed his arms on the steering wheel. Everything was still, quiet. A photograph. Until a car came along and gave an extended horn, passing inches from his front bumper. Trevor sat up and backed his truck up a bit. Put it in park. Put a cigarette in his mouth and found his hand shaking when he lit it.

Cass had wanted to meet the man tomorrow and give herself another day to think it over. At least meet him somewhere public, like the lobby of the Riverside Hotel or Lester's Diner, somewhere in Fort Lauderdale. If not that, then at his office—which was in Hialeah. But no. He said that he would be gone the next few days, so that—if possible—today would be best. And would she meet him in Opa Locka, at a house, not his office? . . . It had been Tina, her co-worker, who recommended the man, the detective. She had prodded Cass and went so far as to dial his number and hand her the phone. Cass had confided in Tina—in lieu of telling Mava, her mother—told her that Trevor had left, told her how she wanted to find him. And now here she was in Opa Locka—driving along littered side streets, following the GPS on her phone and beginning to get the creeps.

The detective's name was Collis Mudd. Tina said he was honest, had references, was inexpensive. He was a little unorthodox but did good work. An ex-cop. He had tracked down Tina's niece a year ago, all the way out in California. Cass trusted Tina, who was, she supposed, her closest friend. And the man, Collis Mudd, had sounded pleasant enough, professional enough, on the phone. Yet, the neighborhood she was driving through now didn't exactly inspire confidence. Opa Locka was done in faux Moorish architecture—onion domes and turrets, minarets painted in garish purples, golds and reds. And now there were low rent apartments and duplexes, black bars on their windows. There were cardboard boxes and malt liquor cans. Plastic bags stuck in tree branches. Signs mainly in Spanish and Creole. And the people in the streets loitering, walking, adult men on bicycles.

But then Cass was ashamed of herself.

They were only people. The world outside her car window wasn't much different than the Marigny or Bywater in New Orleans. These people were her neighbors back then, her friends. They were no different than Marcus, her lover, no different than herself. She had forgotten. She had been ensconced in her part of Fort Lauderdale for too long. Another symptom of living a reclusive life with Trevor.

Trevor . . . She again asked herself if she wanted him back. Why she wanted him back. Was he really worth all this trouble—actually hiring a private detective to look for him? Wasn't he just a coward and she was better off without him? . . . She didn't know. Not yet. She would find him first, see him again, and then make that decision.

Cass checked her phone again, turned east on Fourth, saw the residential neighborhood of bungalows and grassy yards, gravel driveways. Citrus and banana and abundant flowers, tall Poinciana trees in red bloom. Collis Mudd's street was Southwest Fifteenth. She turned on it and saw the house: a well-maintained stucco of coral pink with white bahama shutters and solid wood door. A concrete drive held an older model Mercedes sedan. She pulled up behind it and parked.

This was all too soon, she thought again, standing in front of the door. She had let Tina push her into this. She didn't know this man from Adam, yet here she was on his doorstep. Maybe she should wait a few more days, give herself more time to think it over, more time for ... For what? she asked herself. For indecisiveness. More time for Trevor to escape even the memory of her, of them as a couple?

She rang the bell. A small child answered. A boy of maybe seven.

Is Mister Mudd home?

My dad?

Yes. I'm Cassandra Tipton and I think he's expecting me.

It felt odd speaking so formally to this young boy. It felt odd saying her own surname, as if she should have taken Trevor's: Cassandra Kallengaard. Or Marcus': Cassandra Underwood. Cass Underwood, Mr. and Mrs. Underwood. She would have taken his name, she thought on the doorstep of Mr. Mudd, she would have married Marcus. But he had been killed.

Just a minute, the boy told her and left the door open as he wandered back into the house. Cass could hear a television from inside; cartoons. She could see some toys—plastic dinosaurs mainly—scattered on the tiled floor. The boy returned.

Dad said to come in ... to please come in.

Thank you.

She followed the boy inside, past the dinosaurs and into a kitchen. The television was then turned off. The boy pulled out a chair for her to sit in at a table along the wall. The kitchen was small, clean, tidy. Using a stepstool, the boy got out two glasses from a cupboard. He then took a jar of iced tea from a refrigerator—the refrigerator had many small fingerprints on its surface—and poured it without spilling. One for her and one opposite. Cass said thank you and the boy nodded and then left.

Cass waited. She was uncertain what she would say, how she would frame Trevor's disappearance.

Then a large man entered. Tall and big boned and slightly overweight. She could not determine his age, other than he was older than her. He had very black skin—darker than the boy—and short hair. He wore a rumpled white dress shirt and dark slacks. Cass thought he looked more like a jazz musician than a private investigator. The man met her eyes, smiled, stretched out a large hand. He had a gold wedding band on the other.

Collis Mudd, he said.

They shook and he sat down across from her. They drank some tea.

Thanks for coming to the house, Mrs. Tipton. I apologize, but the kids are sick—or so they say—and there wasn't anyone else . . . You have kids?

No. How many do you have?

Four. Two girls and two boys.

Oh.

So, Mrs. Tipton, you have someone missing? You said on the phone, your husband?

My husband. Did I say that? No. It's Miss Tipton, Cassandra. We never married.

I see.

But we've been together for many years. Twelve years. So he's, essentially, my husband. His last name is Kallengaard.

Twelve years.

Yes, she said and then she told Collis Mudd a little about Trevor Kallengaard. She said that they'd met in New Orleans but hadn't lived together until they came to Fort Lauderdale. She said that he was a carpenter. She then told him about how Trevor had up and left without warning, only leaving the handwritten note. Cass had called his employer but they knew nothing, other than that he'd been paid on Friday and he'd left early. She had considered calling the police, but there was the note and then there was the phone call.

The detective sat and listened and did not interrupt. Cass thought that she was talking too much, that maybe this was not the proper procedure, but it was nice to tell someone other than Tina. It was nice to have someone listen. He only nodded his head, looked over at the entryway twice as if looking for his kids, in case they too were listening, but there was no one.

And this note? he asked.

She hesitated, then opened her purse, took out the small square piece of notepaper that she had kept with her since Sunday. She had not shown Tina the note. She handed it over to Collis Mudd.

Dear Cass,

I'm sorry. It's for the best that I go and I won't be back. I realize it won't make sense to you but understand that it has to be done. I'll call.

Trevor

Whereof one cannot speak . . . Thereof one must be silent

He handed the note back to her without comment. She placed it back in the side pocket of her purse.

And the phone call?

That was three days later. He said he was sorry but wouldn't tell me where he was. He said it was raining there.

He nodded.

Well, Miss Tipton, I can work for you on this. I have to go to Everglades City tomorrow, finish a job there, but after that I'm open. He looked at her and must have seen some uncertainty in her face. It doesn't sound too difficult, he told her, though you never know. If you decide to hire me, we have to talk about my fees and expenses. You'll have to sign a contract.

Okay. Yes. But I haven't thought it all out yet.

That's fine. I'll show my license and give you some references. But you were referred by Mr. and Mrs. Sanchez?

Sanchez? No, the sister of Mrs. Sanchez, actually. A co-worker of mine.

Where do you work?

Cass was a freelance copywriter for a large department store. She named the store.

I'll get you the documents, the references, and can answer anything before you sign. I only take one case at a time, usually. I work a little slow, a little old-fashioned. I like to be here for the kids when need be, like today.

Oh, your wife works then?

He paused for a moment.

This is her house. We're separated. Getting divorced.

Cass felt a little embarrassed, though she didn't know why.

It's not the references. It's more that, that I'm not sure I'm ready . . . I thought this would be more exploratory. Get some ideas of the plausibility.

Okay. Since you're here and assuming you'll want to hire me, let me ask some questions. Simple ones, Miss Tipton.

Cass, please.

Cass, he said. First, let me ask, did he take anything of yours when he left?

No, no.

Credit cards?

Mine? No.

But he has some?

He has one, I think. His own.

Okay. But let me ask about money. You have a joint account? Savings? Checking?

Both. Yes. Joint accounts.

And he didn't . . .

Oh, no. No. I admit I checked but he didn't touch it. He only cashed his paycheck, I think.

No valuables missing? No stocks, bonds, retirement accounts?

No, Cass said.

The reason I'm asking is to see what his options are, moneywise, and to figure out a motive. Some of them take everything. It happens.

Cass nodded.

So the credit card is his own, you said, not in both your names? Not the same number?

It's his own. Separate.

But, as far as you know, the bill would come to your address, a shared address.

Yes, I think it would. It would, unless he's changed his address.

If he's changed his address then it would be very easy to find him.

Yes?

But you can't guess where he's gone to?

No. At first I thought the Keys. We go there a few times a year. He likes islands: Key West, Cedar Key, Amelia Island.

Those are all in-state. Does he have a passport?

No. Not that I know of.

I thought maybe he'd be in New Orleans, but I don't think so now. He said he wasn't in any of those place, on the phone. He sounded far away.

I'm guessing he doesn't use a cell phone, or you would have tracked him.

That's right. He never had a phone, barely uses a computer—has no laptop.

Collis Mudd nodded. He drank more tea.

I'm sorry to ask, Miss Tipton, but would he be involved in anything criminal? Drugs? Money laundering? Something like that?

Oh, no. Not at all.

Do you think there's someone else? Would he have run off with another woman? It's usually money or another person, with adults. Sometimes both.

Cass was going to answer no, but a child, a small girl, wandered into the kitchen. She looked about five and carried a hairbrush and a handful of colorful ribbons. Her eyes were bright but her nose was runny.

Daddy, the girl said, James won't do my hair.

Excuse me, Collis Mudd said to Cass as he took the brush and ribbons from the girl. I'm sorry. You think about that question.

Go ahead, Cass told him. It's all right. She smiled but the girl only looked at her father and Cass watched as the big man easily tied pink and yellow and red ribbons while brushing out fingerfulls of his daughter's dark hair.

This is Keena, Collis Mudd said. Keena this is Miss Tipton.

The girl now looked at Cass with big eyes.

That's a pretty name, Cass said.

I named the boys—Todd and James. Their mother named the girls—Lakeesha and Keena.

While Collis Mudd continued to work his daughter's hair, Cass considered the question—did Trevor have another woman. Her immediate reaction was no. Trevor was no romantic. He was handsome and women liked him but he was not a pursuer of women. He was shy and internal and did not easily connect with people, did not attach himself to others.

No. I don't think so, Cass said and both Collis Mudd and the girl looked at her. Cass put her hand to her mouth.

There, he said to his daughter. Go back to your room. And tell James he should be reading, not playing games or anything.

The girl said okay and left, wiping her runny nose.

Sorry, Collis Mudd said.

She's cute.

Thank you . . . So, no one else.

Cass shook her head.

Doesn't sound like it. From the note, the call. Must be something else that made him run . . . Where's he from? I mean, where was Mr. Kallengaard born? Is he from this country?

Oh, yes, he's from the U. S.

Kallengaard? Is that German or something?

It's a Danish name, I think. No, Swedish. His family was Swedish immigrants somewhere down the line.

I see, and he's from where? Where did he grow up?

Cass was embarrassed that she didn't know much more. She was uncertain about Travis' history, about where he had come from. He had never revealed much to her and she had not pried. After Marcus had been killed and they had come to Fort Lauderdale, it was like a new life. Day one. Neither of them talked about things previous to that. But thinking of it, Cass remembered when Trevor first showed up in New Orleans, how he knew nothing of the city, of its food or music or festivals. Marcus was the one who got him the job at the restaurant that they worked at, she and Marcus helped him find a better place to rent. They had all laughed at him, at his innocence and clothes—his boots, his haircut—how he sweated all the time yet would never wear shorts . . . But—she recalled now—it was his jacket. Even in the heat he wore a denim jacket that he hung on the coat rack that no one else used, in the storage room. And she walked past it and always smelled something, something different above the usual smells of crab boil and shellfish, of pepper and roux, and one time she tracked that smell down, to his jacket, and realized that it smelled of straw and sage and of things she had not smelled before. It smelled of open land, she remembered herself thinking. And she had placed together the boots and the jeans, denim coat, the big belt, the very look of his face. He was a country boy, but not from Louisiana or even Texas.

You're smiling.

Cass looked up, into the large face of Collis Mudd.

Oh, I was just thinking of . . . Colorado.

Of Colorado?

No. I mean, Trevor. He's from Colorado, I think.

He waited but she didn't say anything more.

Miss Tipton, about the note, the last thing in it: "Whereof and Thereof." It sounds like a quote. Do you know what it means?

I don't know.

She was only half listening. She was still remembering. He had told her once, at least once, where he was from.

Wyoming, she said to Collis Mudd. He's from Cheyenne, Wyoming.

Trevor was lying on his back along a hiking trail at Poudre Park. He could hear the rush of the river, not far away. There was rabbit brush and thimbleberry, sage and thin grasses around him. Above was the sky, the tops of pine, the ridges of rocky land limning that sky. He smoked and listened to the wind and water, detached himself from the emotions of the day, from seeing his godparents. He was calm enough now to think of them: Gus and Frida. To think of his mother in Glenrock. Of Ross and his grandfather, Thor and of his father, Trig Kallengaard. And Darcie. Darcie Featherstone, whom he had loved, though she belonged to his brother.

He thought of them in the manner he had for many years, as distant things. Human relics. He thought of them as if they were dead. Of course, it was only an illusion, a mind trick, because they weren't dead. Not his godparents or his brother or mother. And in many ways, his father and Darcie—and now Thor—all still lived within him, still piloted his actions and beliefs in ways he did not fully comprehend..

Trevor rolled to one side and then sat up. He let the sun warm his back as he looked at the river. He continued to smoke, saw that his new boots were now dusty, scuffed. Above the river, he could hear the occasional car along the highway, voices and footsteps of hikers on the trail. And he heard it now, footsteps, footsteps coming closer, behind him, and when he turned his head he was not surprised to see her.

She circled around and stood in front of him, her face lit by sunlight.

I should be very cross with you, Mr. Trevor Kallengaard. You left me waiting this morning.

Trevor stubbed out his cigarette and placed the butt alongside the other three he had smoked. He looked again at Bisma Patel. She wore a loose shirt, shorts with many pockets, hiking boots with thick grey socks rolled above them. Her legs brown, slender, her knees dimpled. She was not wearing his jacket. Despite himself, Trevor felt a certain satisfaction in seeing her.

I'm not reliable.

Nor are you a gentleman. You're only a carpenter from Florida.

Trevor shrugged.

Sorry, she said to him.

What?

Tell me you're sorry.

Trevor eyed her, resisted, but could think of nothing better to say.

Okay. Sorry.

Bisma. Say my name with it.

Sorry, Bisma.

It didn't hurt him to say it and it made her smile. She sat down next to him.

It looks like you made it out here just the same.

No thanks to you. I told you I wasn't afraid to hitch a ride. She ran her fingers through her hair. It's not as though I'm stalking you. I like hiking here and saw your truck at the trailhead.

Okay.

So, I hiked along, up and down, smelled tobacco and knew it was you in the grass here. Should have known you couldn't smoke and walk at the same time.

She smiled to herself then looked at his hair.

Where is your hat?

Trevor pretended to look for it.

Didn't you take it?

She lifted her head and regarded him with her eyes, dismissing his point, his joke.

I knew I'd see you again. Have you ever felt that, that you're certain of seeing someone again, like you share some kind of fate? . . . Yesterday at the laundry you looked so alone and out-of-place. She shaded her eyes and made sure he was looking at her. Are you following me? You looked like someone I wanted to know, cowboy or not.

I'm only a carpenter from Fort Lauderdale, as you said.

But when he said that he felt it was untrue. Already there was a great distance from what he used to be and what he planned to become, now that he had returned.

I know that it sounds nutters, she said, but yesterday I could see you in my mind, on a horse, you know, riding . . .

Trevor laughed, saw that she was embarrassed.

Don't make fun of me, she said. Please don't do that.

I'm sorry.

Then Trevor thought of his brother. Ross was a horseman. He cut the calvers from the herd, he could break a horse. Ross rode rodeo, the small circuit in places like Gillette and Miles City, Spearfish and Williston. His brother was the cowboy, not Trevor.

Don't destroy my illusions—not even with the truth. I'm very fond of my illusions.

Okay.

Thank you, she said.

He could tell that she was done talking. And then she laid back in the dry dirt and grass. She closed her eyes against the sun. The shadow of the hillside was now deep in the river bottom. There was only the sound of birds and insects and water. The wind in trees. Trevor studied her and thought she looked like a woman who wanted to be kissed.

I'm hungry, she said and opened her eyes to look at him.

He gave her a ride back into town. She pointed him to a strip mall west of downtown where there was a Middle Eastern cafe. She invited him to eat with her and Trevor—surprising himself—accepted.

So, how old are you?

They sat at a table, food on their plates.

Trevor wiped his mouth and asked how old she was, certain that she would demand to know his age first. But she did not.

Twenty-four.

And you're almost done with grad school?

My plan is to drop out—I told you that, didn't I? My visa is good for another year and I have some money. I was thinking of going to California.

Trevor ate more from the plastic plate, the food heavy with lemon and parsley.

Would you like to go with me? Bisma asked. To California?

I'm going to Cheyenne. Tomorrow.

Really? I've been to Laramie and Cody. Jackson Hole. Yellowstone. But, yes, I could go to Cheyenne. I'll bring the lovely jacket.

Trevor eyed her, tried to determine if she was joking.

I'm just going to see some old places, he told her.

That's okay. I've never been. There's nothing here for me—no family or boyfriend, school or employment.

Cheyenne's just up the road.

Is it? But I've never been. London, Paris, New York, Mumbai—but Cheyenne? Never.

I don't think there's anything to gain by it.

That's up to me to say, don't you think? You wouldn't offer and then leave me stranded again. You're not heartless, are you?

Trevor didn't bother to point out that he had offered nothing. That he had not stranded her anywhere. He reminded himself that he wanted no one with him, yet also admitted to himself that he was pleased—to some degree—with her company. She was a curious person. She was a distraction, anyway. A distraction from his own thoughts.

Maybe, he said.

Maybe you'll take me or maybe you're heartless?

Just maybe.

He dropped her off on Myrtle Street, where she had a room in a two-story house.

So, noon tomorrow? she said, standing by his open truck window. And you'll really be here?

Morning. Eight.

She nodded and did not argue. But she placed her hand on the door, her brown fingers curling over the rim.

You never told me how old you are.

Trevor shrugged.

I'm forty-one.

She looked away for a moment.

You don't look it.

Does it matter?

No. I like to know these things. Details.

I'll see you in the morning.

She did not let go of the door. She gave him a long, almost expressionless stare.

I promise, he said.

Cass stood at the sink washing her dinner dishes because there were not enough to bother with the machine. There was a glass of white wine on the counter beside her. She looked out the window into the back yard, the low light of evening shading the areca palms, the big mango tree. She looked at the royal palm that jutted up above the tiled roofline of the house behind hers. She liked the view, had always liked it and thought Trevor had too.

Collis Mudd said that he would be in Everglades City tomorrow, that she could call him tonight or tomorrow night if she made the decision to hire him. He had asked her to think of things that would define Trevor and to provide at least one current photograph. He had asked again about money and Cass had said she had the funds to pay him and he had laughed. No, he said, I mean Mr. Kallengaard's access to money, your money. So she asked if she should change her accounts, put them only in her name and he said not to. The best way to find him was through the money.

She went through the motions of soaping her dinner plate, rinsing it, placing it in the drain board. She reached for the silverware and thought about what would define Trevor . . . He was quiet and not generous with emotions. He had a subtle, deadpan sense of humor that some people mistook for ignorance or arrogance. He could be too blunt. He was happy to be alone. Aloof. Insular. He smoked but did not drink. He was secretive, unhappy . . . But he had seemed happy with her. They had fun, at times, they made love and had intimacy . . . Trevor read a lot, didn't watch much television, no sports. He liked novels, particularly Russian writers: Dostoyevsky, Tolstoy. Turgenev. He had a few philosophy books but didn't read much non-fiction. She liked to read as well, but not so much those books. They rarely went to the movies . . . She didn't know if any of this would help Collis Mudd.

Cass rinsed a fork. A spoon. Knife. Set them in the rack's cup and looked at them there and she felt very alone. She looked out the window again and felt an urge to call her mother, to drive down to Bal Harbour and talk to Mava. She always thought of her mother as Mava—had taught herself to do it, long ago.

This was all Trevor's fault, she told herself. This loneliness. This displaced need to see Mava. The need to hire someone like Collis Mudd. Trevor was monopolizing her thoughts, her life, and she didn't have to let him. She did not have to find him and could just let it go. In the note, he said that it was for the best. Maybe she should believe him. There was a lot she did not know, never knew about him. Maybe he could be some kind of criminal. Or an idiot. He was a passive-aggressive idiot and she should just wash her hands of him.

Looking out the window at the darkening world, she felt the tears begin to well in her eyes and she did not like it. She wanted no self-pity. She did not want to cry. Cass reached quickly for the stemmed glass that held the wine. Too quickly. The glass fell to the floor, spilling the wine, splintering the glass. Glass in uneven pieces across the white tiles, shards beneath the stove.

Cass bent down to pick up the larger pieces but as she did so she could feel her heart in her chest.

Goddamn you, Trevor, she said, out loud and she stood up, reached for her phone to call Collis Mudd.

She'd clean up afterwards.

THREE

Harriman Road

He drove around the corner and saw her standing beneath the trees, waiting for him. Her hair was brushed and ponytailed. She wore loose pants, a purple shirt, hiking boots and the jacket.

Trevor had considered that she would not be there, that she would have second thoughts and decide, correctly, that it wasn't smart to travel with someone she had only shared a few moments with. Someone she had shared a jacket with because she had stolen it . . . Maybe she was only going to return the coat and wish him well. But then he saw the suitcase. Large and scuffed, it sat on the sidewalk like a loyal dog.

He pulled the truck to the curb, under the spread of maple trees, and she met his eyes. Her eyes were lidded. Her face sleepy. Trevor got out to lift the suitcase and found that it wasn't as heavy as it looked.

Inside the truck, seated next to each other, she told him she wasn't a morning person.

Don't expect anything cheery.

I won't, he said. But . . .

Yes?

She stared at him with her catlike eyes.

It's only for a day or two, this trip. You'll have to take the bus back to Fort Collins.

She dismissed him with a look and a shake of her head then closed her eyes.

Trevor put the truck in gear and they headed off for Cheyenne, Wyoming.

They drove against incoming traffic, people headed for work in Fort Collins. The sun shone on the western foothills, bald land in shades of tan and red and copper. He drove Highway 14 until Laport, then took 287 North. Trevor passed the exit for I-25, the easy route to Cheyenne.

Bisma Patel, quiet and looking out the window, noticed.

Not taking the Motorway?

The Interstate? No.

287 was a big, clean highway. Trevor remembered it as only a two lane, dangerous in winter, but a straight shot to Laramie. He had used it—his family had—because it connected to a smaller road that led to the high plains around Cheyenne. Trevor had driven it many times, that small gravel road, including the night with Darcie and his father.

I've been this way, Bisma said. It goes to Laramie, to that park with the rocks. Those strange rocks. It has an almost Hindi name . . .

Vedauwoo.

That's it.

In the Medicine Bow.

Will we go through them?

No. We'll turn on Harriman Road.

Harriman? I don't know that.

It's small.

Small? Is it paved?

Didn't used to be.

She fell silent and watched out the side window. The eastern embankments made round, lulling shadows on the asphalt. Her eyes drooped. When Trevor looked again she had fallen asleep.

He drove past The Forks at Livermore Road, saw the old roadhouse still there. Timeless and paint-faded, there were a few cars in its lot. He could not help but to think of it.

It had been his college graduation party, at Gus and Frida's house because it was close to the university, to Fort Collins. Everyone had been drinking, eating, giving Trevor small gifts of money because he was the first Kallengaard to attend and graduate from college. His mother was there, his father, some family friends, a few classmates who had showed up—for the food, mainly—but had then returned to town

and the bars. And Darcie was there. She had come down from Douglas, from the ranch,
even though his brother and grandfather said they couldn't make it. They had to stay
on the ranch for the late calvers. For the cattle. And his father drank too much, as he
had for years by then, and though Trevor drank also he anticipated leaving the party,
his party, that night alone with Darcie. Darcie was Ross' girl. She and his brother were
to be married, or so people said, though within the family it was a standing joke. But
Trevor, Trevor thought that he would marry Darcie, that she would prefer him, even if
she was currently attached to Ross.

Darcie had left her vehicle at the house in Cheyenne, where his father and
mother lived. Where his father owned a café. But when he and Darcie made to leave,
his father—Trig—insisted on coming with them. Trevor did not understand why. All
night his father kept saying how he wished he had gone to school, to college, that he
had wanted to study biology, study ornithology, but Thor would not allow it—all of
this the first time Trevor had ever heard of it. No, Trig—the only son of Thor and Lina,
Lina his grandmother who had been dead for quite some time—Trig would be a
rancher. His father kept saying how proud he was of Trevor but all Trevor could think
of was why his father had to ruin it, ruin his night with Darcie. No one intervened,
stopped his father from asking, demanding to come along back to Cheyenne with
Trevor and Darcie and so finally he gave in: Fine. All right. It didn't matter. So his
father came along.

The three of them left after ten, darkness glued into the pines along the canyon
road. Trevor would take the back route—Harriman Road—not just because he had
been drinking, but because that was how they did things as a ranching family, take the
gravel roads, the slow roads, the places where there were fewer people. Trevor now
hoped the longer route would allow his father to fall asleep, to crawl into the back
under the camper top, where the old blankets and ballast bags of sand were, where he
could pass out and leave Trevor alone with Darcie. But for now his father rode up front,
smoking his Marlboros, Darcie between them.

Trevor lit a cigarette and rolled down the window. He looked over at Bisma
to see if it would wake her but she sat with her mouth open, her head gently lolling

with the movement of the truck. He considered that he shouldn't take Harriman, shouldn't make himself think about it. But he had already planned to take this route and think of that night, had planned it since the day he left Cass in Florida . . . though not with a passenger in tow. But Trevor hoped her presence would mitigate, would help him with, the memory. Anyway, if he was going to stay on the ranchland, live in what Trevor saw as his rightful place in the world, then there was no avoiding what could never be changed.

Trig had wanted whiskey. Trevor had stopped at The Forks to buy Darcie some beer and now his father wanted some whiskey. Trevor was embarrassed, resented it, but he went inside and took a half-pint of Old Crow off the shelf and a twelve pack of Olympia from the cooler. The woman at the counter carded him and when he showed her his drivers license she said, Come on now, in disbelief. He had always looked too young and he resented that too. He resented a lot of things. But she sold him the beer and whiskey and he went back outside and saw only Darcie in the truck's cab. She was smoking her Lucky Strikes and peered up at him through the windshield. Trevor gave her a questioning look and she thumbed to the back of the truck. And there was his father inside the camper, curled like a dog with a blanket over him, his head on a bag of sand.

Trevor smiled and got in beside Darcie. He looked at her closely, her bare neck and thighs, the red cowboy boots she always wore. He checked on his father again and saw that he was passed out, then as Trevor leaned over to set the box of beer on the floor, he put his hand on Darcie's neck, her clavicle, then reached down to knead her right breast. He kissed her. She let him kiss her and feel her but she did not kiss back and Trevor thought it was because they were in the parking lot or because she thought his father might still be conscious. He withdrew his hand and his head and started the truck, pulled out of the lot as Darcie opened a beer. On the highway she offered him the beer and he took two quick gulps before handing it back. She did not slide over, did not talk.

They had slept together many times by then, outdoors and in motel rooms, at his apartment, at the ranch and in Cheyenne, and he had no doubt she would sleep with him again, that she would respond to whatever wishes he had, especially in the darkness and isolation along Harriman Road.

Trevor drove silent, smoking, looking at the sign for Virginia Dale and Red Canyon Road, a road he did not recall. He wanted to turn on CR 37, which was Harriman, but saw no sign for it. He wondered if the name had been changed. But then he saw, around the bend, Red Rock Butte and he knew where he was and where the turn would be. So he slowed, pulled toward the shoulder and threw his cigarette out the window. Keeping his eye on traffic the Butte, he slowed further and made the sharp right onto a road of red dirt.

The land was empty now, as he drove away from the highway, just hills holding buffalo grass, sage and prickly pear. The dirt road was rough in places, a washboard that made the truck shiver. There were no houses that he could see, yet a few cars came towards him, big, newer SUVs. He watched them go by as the road curved around the big sandstone butte—a prominent and distinct landmark. He wondered how he could have forgotten Red Rock Butte, but he had.

Darcie was on her second beer by the time they wound around Red Rock Butte—the butte like a huge black stump against a moonless sky. Trevor tried to catch her eye in the green glow of the dash, wanted his eyes to convey his desire for her and he drove slow to gain more time. After rounding the butte he asked for a beer and he touched her hand when she did so. He saw her smile but it was not the smile he knew or had expected.

He had never really had to ask for sex with Darcie, to initiate it beyond small glances or touches. She always knew, it seemed, or she was the one to initiate. But he placed his beer between his legs and put that hand on her thigh—felt her leg jump a little from the cold—and then he gripped her thigh and tried to tug her across the bench seat. He wanted her next to him. On him. But Darcie did not move over and he withdrew the hand. He drove another mile and then she came to him, slid next to him, put her arm on him, kissed him on the ear and she said, I have to talk to you . . .

Would you mind putting up your window?

Trevor turned to see Bisma awake, but he had not understood her request.

The window . . . There's dust everywhere. Please? Close it?

He looked: red-orange road dust had filtered into the cab. A fine layer sat on the dash and vents, in the creases of his knuckles. She coughed now and he rolled the window up. They were silent for a while.

What's this? she then said.

Red Rock Butte had fallen behind and the red road had turned to white gravel and there were houses. The road curved upward and Trevor saw big, exurb houses where there had never been homes before; new homes with ranch rail fences, paved drives, cedar shake roofing. Green watered lawns. Distant snow fences marked the development's property line along a western slope.

The red dust gone, Trevor unrolled the window and lit a cigarette. He did not look at Bisma. A Range Rover came, went past them on the white gravel, rocks pinging, white dust billowing. She coughed but Trevor didn't look at her, kept the window open, smoked.

Past the houses the road grew rougher, less traveled. Here were weedy ditches, stands of hackberry and boxelder and the empty hills of wild grass. The gravel road followed the contours of the land, Trevor watching it all carefully, minutely, and then Bisma asked him if he'd ever been married.

Married?

I only wondered, considering your age. I assume there was someone, or is someone. So, are you married?

He thought of Cass—a nettle of guilt working within him; a nettle of longing as he wondered what Cass might be doing, thinking, or if she saw his leaving as a positive. Maybe by now she welcomed his absence, her freedom from him. He thought of how he had never called her back.

No, he answered. There's no one but me.

She gave a purposeful sigh. One of disbelief or disappointment, Trevor couldn't tell.

Well I almost married. I met him in New York but he was from Belgium. Went so far as to introduce him to my father and my uncle when they came over to visit. They thought—to my surprise—that he was just fine. Quite the match. Which, I believe, is what soured me on him, the man from Belgium. Couldn't get away fast enough, though he was good in bed.

The land leveled out, the road running straight and empty. They passed an old house on a rutted road beneath old trees. Trevor remembered the house, had never know anyone to live in it yet it was still there, long lasting and vacant.

You realize you never told me why you left.

Why I did what?

Why you moved away, went to Florida and gave up being a cowboy or whatever.

Trevor didn't look at her or answer.

I like to know motivations, the whys and whatnots, the desires. I like to understand human nature, human character.

Really? he said and drove and she appeared to give up the line of questioning. They traveled in silence, in the gravel and dust.

I get the feeling that you ran away, Bisma said.

Trevor did not react, let the silence return to the cab of the truck and made his mind think of only what he wanted it to think of.

Baby Brother, Darcie said knowing that Trevor hated the term but also loved it, coming from her. We've had some fun but it's over, she said and his stomach knotted up. She was so close to him now, up on her knees in the seat. They didn't use seat belts. What? he said. Why? Ross, she said, Ross and I are going to get married. No one believes that, he told her. The fact that she and Ross were supposedly engaged had never stopped Trevor, stopped her. Not even when Ross came back from Rapid City, after giving up on baseball, even then she and Trevor had continued with their trysts. Anyway, Trevor would marry her. He had just finished college. He would find a job, a career. She would come with him.

You said that you never came back, right? So, I'm thinking you hated this place or something happened.

Trevor did not listen.

You can't blame me for asking. I'm curious. You're quite the puzzle.

No, Darcie told him, it's more than that. And she leaned away from him, took her hands away, she took her can of beer and tossed it out the open window into the roadside brush and the black of night. Her pack of Lucky Strikes followed the beer: out the window. What? he asked. What more?

So you won't tell me? It will, you know, only make me more curiouser and curiouser.

I'm going to be a mommy, Darcie said. I have Ross' baby inside me. I can't see you anymore. He's going to marry me and I'm going to be a mommy and he's going to be a daddy. With that, Trevor stopped driving. He let the truck roll to a halt in the gravel on the flat land. A baby, he said and she nodded. And Ross knows? He doesn't know yet. I just decided tonight to keep the baby, to marry him, to have a family. But Trevor was thinking: Why is it his brother's baby? He had slept with her just last week at the Cache Hotel in Fort Collins, he had been with her two weeks ago in Cheyenne at the Plains Hotel—she had come down from Douglas just to see him, just to get the room and be with him and get him to do everything he wanted, everything she wanted him to do. They had never used protection. He had always assumed she was on birth control. She was the one who knew all about it, about sex, about fucking, not him. Everything.

I won't give in. Eventually I'll crack you open like an egg and see what's inside. You'll tell me everything.

Trevor turned to her then, his face bare of any emotion.

What?

An egg—I'll open you up like an egg. Crack.

No. That won't happen.

Oh? A challenge? We'll see then, won't we.

She smiled. It was a beautiful smile and behind her out the window the sun was bare and bright and the sky all blue save for a calligraphy of clouds in the distance. And ahead of them were the lines of the Russian olive trees, the line of trees and brush that hid the gully, the tops of two pines rising just above the gulley—all of which Trevor had been looking for.

So he asked why, why Ross' baby. I think it's mine, he said. She didn't look at him but looked back through the small window into the bed where his father was, asleep, curled beneath the blanket. When she did look at him her face was slack, her body slack. It's his, she said. I know it is. And Trevor felt something in his own stomach—anger, depression, a turmoil he didn't exactly recognize. Listen, Trevor. I decided to keep it. Ross'll marry me. He's the daddy. I'm telling you now. You have to promise. Promise not to tell. It was just kicks, you and me. Now it's over. You have to promise. And Trevor knew what it was—that Ross had always left her behind, whether it was to go ride rodeo, or play baseball, or attend cattle shows, but now he was done with baseball and she wanted him to stay done, to stay home. But Trevor could not accept that. He was her lover, more so than Ross. He was the father. He would marry Darcie, not his brother. She looked at him closely and said again for him to promise but he never did.

He began to drive again. He screwed his eyes to see her in the cab light, next to him, saw her face begin to melt, become liquid as he tried to stifle his tears but couldn't. He let out hard sobs. Trevor had never cried in front of her, did not think he was capable of it, didn't understand why he was crying and it aggravated him further. It was kicks, she said again. I don't love you, she said and then Trevor hit her.

He reached across and rapped her skull with his knuckles, quick, violent, the truck lurching to the right. He corrected the wheels and looked at her. He raised his hand again and saw her jerk back in fear, her head knocking against the window, her own hands now going up like birds to protect herself though Trevor did not hit her this time. He looked through the windshield at the blunt darkness, the blunt landscape and

wondered how it could be, how she could love his brother, not choose him. And then the
unrest that had gathered in his stomach boiled into his blood and Trevor punched the
gas pedal, keeping his foot pressed as the old truck lurched with power towards the
line of Russian olives.

They were the only his vehicle on the road, in the wide and unremarkable landscape. Trevor looked ahead at the trees where the cut in the land, formed by Spotwood Creek, sat invisible from the road. Where the twin pines grew at the bottom. He tried to listen for the trill of the creek, a splash of water but all he heard was the truck on gravel, the wind, a red-winged blackbird in the brush. And Bisma Patel.

We shall see. A lot could happen in Cheyenne.

Trevor sat up straight, gripping the wheel as they approached the silver-green trees.

What's the matter?

If he'd taken the Interstate they'd be in Cheyenne by now. He could be thinking of breakfast, of getting a room. Thinking of Cheyenne things. But, no, really, would that afford him anything different? He had wanted this route, had wanted to be forced to think about it.

You really need to work on your communication skills.

Trevor looked over at her and he stopped the truck. He sat still, the sun beating on the hood of the Silverado.

I'm sorry, he said to her but added nothing more. He got out of the truck and stood by the open door. He lit a cigarette.

Bisma got out. She came around and stood next to him. She looked where he looked: the simple line of trees and empty sky. Empty road.

What is it? He didn't answer. He smoked. Well, what?

Trevor then pointed ahead where there was still no evidence how the road snaked downward into more trees, down to the shaded gully of the creek. He thought about what Bisma had said, earlier, about an egg.

It's nothing, he said. I haven't been here in a long time.

She made a soft sound of disappointment or disgust. She returned to the truck, leaving her door open. Trevor, done with the cigarette, got back in as well. They shut the wings of the doors and he drove forward into the trees.

Collis Mudd was in Everglades City. There was a rental truck backed up to unit 106 at Barron Storage. The hired men were loading the items—the ex-wife's personal property—into the truck. Things were going well enough. Collis Mudd couldn't quite understand why the ex-husband had done it, other than out of retribution. Spite. Out of emotion. The ex-husband didn't get the children, he didn't get his wife back, so he went into the house during the day and took the objects she both cherished and needed for the household to function. He didn't sell them or destroy them, only hid them . . . Here was a man who no doubt made more money in a month than Collis made in a year and he took those things and brought them to this backwater, all out of blind vengeance. Punishment. Maybe, Collis thought, the man was even punishing himself. He must have known he'd be a suspect, eventually be caught. Still, it was better than how some men sought vengeance.

The reasons why mattered little now. The things would go back to the house in Palm Beach. The ex-husband would settle out of court—if charges were even pressed. Collis himself had already, mentally, moved on. His mind already on Cassandra Tipton and Trevor Kallengaard.

He thought of calling her but decided to wait until he got back to his office in Hialeah. Collis already knew that Trevor Kallengaard had called her from a pay phone in Sterling, Colorado. He also knew that Kallengaard had used a credit card at Pard's Western Wear in Fort Collins, Colorado. And if the man was from Cheyenne, Wyoming, Collis surmised that that was probably where he was headed. Still, it was best not to assume too much, best to start where you had solid evidence.

He would tell Cassandra Tipton all of this, when he called her.

Collis Mudd had to admit—compared to things he had worked on, had seen, knew about—that Kallengaard had shown at least a modicum of integrity. Some honesty. He knew that Cassandra Tipton would not see it that way. But the man at the very least left a note. Made a phone call. More importantly, he had taken nothing that wasn't his. He had even left money in the bank that was, probably, partially his . . . Kallengaard was a man who just wanted to disappear. A man who wanted a new life—and no doubt he knew exactly where he was going and what he would do there.

But that kind of speculation was not his business. Cassandra Tipton was. She had hired him and if she wanted Kallengaard tracked down then that's what he would do. Still, he thought it would end in disappointment. Because even though she was a very pretty woman, a sweet person, Collis didn't think Trevor Kallengaard would be coming back to her.

Trevor followed the road into the line of trees, hearing the wind in the leaves then the low murmur of Spotwood Creek as the trail began to curve downward. Down into the checkered shadows where it was windless, dark, the heat now damp, the road in switchbacks. He saw two doves pecking in the dirt, both of them taking flight as the tires, crunching gravel, neared. He peered further into the scribbled shadows, Bisma also silent and looking.

Darcie yelled his name as they rammed past the trees and into the first drop and curve of the road. He knew the switchbacks were there, knew of the creek and trees and descent, but all of that was momentarily forgotten: the lay of Harriman Road, Darcie, his father. There was only the surge of poisonous anger within him and there was the speed of the truck to express it. The truck flew over the rim, gravel spraying, hitting the first branches of the trees, a sleet of leaves. Yet the truck—airborne over that first curve—landed back on its wheels, its nose digging the hard earth and that's

what brought Trevor back into the world, made him try to find the brakes with his foot,
to control the wheel with his hands, but the truck had too much velocity. It tumbled
forward, downward, through the next switchback towards the bed of the creek where
the big, double-trunked pine grew.

She called his name again during the weightless flight, in the whistling and
snapping, the truck making a half-turn as it stripped leaves and branches and then the
sudden loss of motion as it hit the base of the twin pines at the bottom of the draw.
Trevor lost his grip on the wheel and was thrown sideways and down into the lower
hulk of the cab as glass rained down.

Then, almost as quickly, everything settled into silence. Only the run of shallow
water.

Trevor saw the creek below and the trunks of the pines. He looked for the
scars, the gashes of missing bark and wood, but they were not there. Time had
healed them or perhaps they had grown higher up, somehow. But he did not see
them. He felt calm, was surprised that he could remember it all with only a
weariness. Though he knew, he knew the harm that had been done here, at the
bottom of the creek. It was a knowledge that had never left him for one minute.

Trevor's ears rang. His head, his vision, all senses were muffled, confused. Yet he
could also hear the water, could sense every detail, everything paradoxically sharp yet
unclear. He called out for Darcie but she was not in the cab of the truck. He didn't think
of his father, only of Darcie and himself. His knees hurt, ached worse than the rest of
his body, as he clambered out the open door of the truck—Darcie's door. Everything
was dark, silent but for water, the trees crowded him. But he made his legs work, made
himself stand, his eyes see the truck as a whole, see that it was wrapped around the
base of the double pine, folded, sat at an angle with the whole camper top dislodged
and split, a husk among the trees. The pain in his knees was electric and he walked
bent over, gripping the smaller trees with his hands to help steady himself. There was a
large hump on the ground, a hump darker than the darkness, there among the leaves
and dried mud near the creek. A body like the dead seal he had seen along Cannon

Beach in Oregon when his father, his mother, had taken them there as a child. Though it was not a seal, Trevor would not admit to himself what it was. He was looking for Darcie.

He thought he would vomit. The pain was in his stomach now as he hunch-walked among the trees, among the wreckage, across the bed of the creek and a short ways up the embankment. Darcie. There she was. She had been thrown across and into the barbed wire fence that kept cattle out of the creek bed. Her clothes were ripped, her skin was ripped, her face. He took her head in his hands and she was not awake. Then, even in the darkness, he could see the blood. He could see the slim metal post coming out of her torso.

He fell backwards, down the embankment and into Spotwood Creek. Stood up but was hunched again. He crossed the water and did not look back, did not look at the hump, the dead seal, in the leaves and dried mud. He went past the pickup and to the road and had to crawl its steep pitch, crawl up the two switchbacks and out of the draw, out of the trees where the sky was full of stars.

Trevor drove upwards, taking the sharp curves out of the trees and shade, back into the open country. Everything quiet except the wind and the truck and the ping of gravel. Bisma asked if she could play some music. She had her phone but could not connect it to his radio, as Trevor's truck was an older model.

She turned the radio itself on, searched for stations, and was able to pull in the college station from Laramie.

When we get to Cheyenne, she said above the music, which side of the bed do you want?

He pretended not to hear her. The radio played songs that were foreign to him. Trevor didn't mind the music or the presence of Bisma beside him, he wasn't sure if she had proved to be the distraction he had expected her to be—a help or hindrance while driving Harriman Road. He only looked ahead to see if the switch house was still there along the railroad tracks, where Colorado became Wyoming.

He had no true sense of how long he walked the gravel road, the road white and luminescent beneath the sky. There were no headlights, no houses, no lights of town. Then finally there was the light pole and the train tracks, Lombardy poplars near the tracks, and the switch house.. Trevor did not know how often trains passed or if the switch house was manned or if there would be a telephone. And when he got to the house—a squat, utilitarian structure with small windows, a pitched roof—he tried the knob of the door and was surprised when it opened. He stepped into a narrow hall and then to a square room with two desks and metal filing cabinets and a coffee pot and a telephone and then a man entered the room and that's when Trevor collapsed.

You're turning out to be a difficult traveling partner, she said.

Trevor thought he could see Harriman up ahead. There were trees, a water tank, corrugated shed roofs shimmering with sunlight. He sped up a little.

That's Harriman up ahead, he told Bisma and she turned off the radio. Cheyenne isn't far from here.

He was in the hospital in Cheyenne for three days. It was there he was told that his father was dead. That Darcie was dead. But he already knew that. There was no mention of a pregnancy and he did not ask. Trevor talked to the Larimer County Deputy Sheriff, admitting that he had been drinking, speeding, that it was all his fault. He did not talk otherwise. His mother came once, distraught, maybe sedated. She was unable to say anything either. Trevor had a hard time even looking at her. Ross—his brother—did not come. Uncle Gus and Aunt Frida saw him the most but he wouldn't talk to them. His grandfather, Thor, came on the third day, held his hat in his hand and stood over Trevor. They did not talk. And it was Gus who checked him out and took him home to the house in Cheyenne, who told him his father would be buried on the ranch, that Darcie would be buried there too. That Darcie's people—from Scottsbluff—had been notified but they did not want her, were not coming to the funeral.

Trevor stayed in Cheyenne and did not attend any services or burials.

He spent days in bed. His mother was seeing a pastor for grief counseling and she wanted Trevor to see him also but he did not. He took painkillers that made him

sleepy and dreamy but when his uncle saw how many Trevor swallowed, he took them
and administered them one at a time. Then one night his brother came down from
Douglas, from the ranch. Ross still in his work jeans and boots and cowboy hat. He
closed the door behind him and stood next to Trevor who was awake and aware of his
brother's presence. They had not spoken since the accident. In his brother's hands were
the painkillers—the whole bottle. He set them down on the bed near Trevor's hands.

Go ahead, he said to Trevor.

Before dawn, Trevor got out of bed and dressed himself: jeans, shirt, socks and
boots. He took the envelope of graduation money that had been put in his dresser. He
left the bottle of painkillers on the bed. On the way out of the silent house, from the
coat rack laden with jackets, he picked out his father's old denim coat, put it on and
went out the door.

He walked downtown to the Greyhound Terminal and bought a ticket to Kansas
City, which was the first bus coming. And while waiting for the bus for Kansas City he
put his hands into the pockets of his father's jacket and inside the left one was a pack
of cigarettes. Matches. He lighted one while waiting. Smoked one of his father's
cigarettes.

In Kansas City he decided to get a ticket for Houston. But before the bus
reached Houston—in Huntsville, Texas—he got off and started walking. He smoked
another cigarette while walking east, out of town. Just outside of Huntsville a man
offered him a ride. And two rides later he was in New Orleans.

The Lombardy poplars were there. The railroad tracks were there. The
switch house was gone. There were two aluminum sheds. Some poles stacked
nearby. A white work truck was parked near the water tank.

This is Harriman, he told Bisma.

This is a town?

A railroad stop. Used to be, anyway.

He looked over at her, the ends of her black hair floating along the open
window, her polished eyes, white teeth, the way his father's jacket hung on her
frame.

They crossed the tracks and drove into the high plains of Wyoming.

FOUR

Cheyenne

He asked for only one room at the Plains Hotel. Bisma said nothing as Trevor paid in cash. They took their own bags and walked across the wide lobby, below the empty mezzanine, across the inlaid mosaic of Chief Little Shield at the center of the floor. Trevor had his duffle slung over his shoulder and he took the suitcase from Bisma as they neared the marble stairway. At one time the Plains had been one of the most luxurious hotels in the west. Now it was not.

Only one room? she said.

There are two beds.

From the mezzanine level they looked down at the empty lobby, at Chief Little Shield, at the Victorian Rose Café and the Wigwam Lounge. The mezzanine itself was but a collection of tables and chairs and dust. Trevor knew the hotel well and was pleased to see that it hadn't changed, that it still had a certain moribund splendor.

He opened the door to room 209. Inside he set their luggage down on the musty carpet. It was a large room with wooden furniture and brick framed windows. There was a feeling of stillness and disuse to it.

Look at this place, Bisma said, turning in a circle. It's so . . . well, not exactly poxy but something. It does have electricity. Running water.

Trevor could tell that, despite the criticism, she was pleased.

While Bisma showered, Trevor sat at the round table by the window and smoked. Aware of the smoke, he went to the window and opened it a crack and stood there. Outside he saw the dark Gleason's Building, the Union Pacific Yard and the hump of Highway 85 where it went over the yard. It was familiar and also unreal to be back in Cheyenne, to be downtown and at the Plains. And he felt a sudden pull in his stomach, a longing unexpected and uncertain. He realized that he missed Cheyenne, its trees and buildings and the stark land beyond it, a city plain and direct, unrefined by certain standards. It was home, as much of a home as Douglas and the ranch. And he thought of his brother, of high school and friends from high school. He thought of Thor and of his mother and of his father until the reverie was too much and he made himself not think of it, made himself concentrate on his cigarette and the Plains Hotel ashtray and of the sound of the shower running in the bathroom.

He put the cigarette out, watched the smoke trail out the window into the dry air. He turned and saw her suitcase there on the banded rack by the bed. His jacket was slung casually on top. His grey Stetson was on the bed table. There was a phone on the desk next to the closet and Trevor thought of Cass. And he thought how he could just take the jacket and his hat and his unpacked duffle and walk out the door. He could go to his truck. Drive to Douglas. Or, he realized, make the long drive back to Cass.

The water had stopped. Trevor turned and saw her there in the now-open door. She wore only a towel and she was looking at him and he felt guilty as if she knew what he was contemplating.

I'll just be a minute more, she said and went back into the bathroom.

Trevor went to the bed and stretched out on top of the quilted spread. He left his boots on and closed his eyes. Bisma began to sing and he listened to her sing and tried not to think of her only in a towel.

Bisma Patel liked the feel of the towel on her skin. The fabric was so rough and worn that its threads felt almost like beads. And she had finally gotten a reaction out of him, gave him a little jolt, wearing only the towel. As she worked her long blue-black hair in front of the mirror, brushing it out and down and back, Bisma sang a little song and wondered what else she could do. She saw no reason to get dressed if the towel felt good.

In the mirror she laughed at herself, to herself. She knew how foolish she could be—a childish trait, one that she could not abide in others but that she sometimes fostered in herself. Like at the Laundromat in Fort Collins, when he told her he wasn't a cowboy—that's what sealed her initial attraction to him. It's what made it humorous. Most men would have said yes. Would have gladly been a cowboy—what man doesn't want to be seen as a cowboy? Especially if she wanted him to be one. She knew very well what most men wanted. One could both flirt and make fun of them, could make them grin like boys or fume like old men. Their desires and motivations were easily understood.

Men, in her opinion, were short-term thinkers. Yet, she trusted them more than women. They didn't have the slyness, that often underhanded sense of competition, that women had. Women—in general—were often too smart for their own good. That's how they ended up letting men run everything, because it was so easy to do so. Men were so open about what they wanted to do—so obvious—that's why she trusted them more in the long run.

And this man, the one she had made take her on a trip to Wyoming? This man was a cowboy because she wanted him to be one. She liked Trevor Kallengaard in that illusory way as much as she liked him for his physical structure. And there was some mystery to him, some stoic fragility she had yet to discover the cause of. But when that mystery—the enigma of Trevor Kallengaard, if there even was an enigma—when that had been cracked then it would be over. She understood this as well as she understood men: When she figured him out she would be done with him.

Still dressed only in the hotel towel, Bisma stepped out into the room. She was a little disappointed to see him on the bed, his eyes closed, his boots on. She smelled the lingering smoke of a cigarette, saw the ashtray on the table. She saw the parted curtains and the opened window. She went and closed both. She looked at him again, his position unchanged. She stayed by the window and took in the large, old room with its mismatched furniture. Almost a tawdry room. Like the hotel itself—something so time-warped and otherworldly, with its dun-colored bricks and musty atmosphere, that it was almost beautiful. Almost. And she loved it. The city itself—what little she had seen of it—was exotic in its plainness, in its strange, drab quality. Her compatriots would like this, this American West: the old hotel, the dusty town in the middle of nowhere, a man in his boots on the bed, a single dead cigarette in the ashtray. All that was missing was a deck of cards and a bottle of whiskey. Maybe a dagger, a gun and holster. It was like a lovely movie scene.

And here she was, within that scene.

Bisma went to Trevor. She sat on the bed, hiking the towel up toward her hips, keeping it wrapped along her breasts. Again she had that sensation, that awareness, of her own skin, of her nudity beneath the cheap fabric. She placed her hand gently under Trevor's shirt, felt his flat belly, the lean-ness of him. He did not move.

You're not asleep, she said.

She liked men thin and hard. Caucasian. Slow-witted. She now liked Americans over Brits, over Europeans in general, especially since the man from Belgium who had wanted to marry her. Her father had never been happy with her choice in men, happy about anything she did. No, she thought, that was unfair to her father. In many ways she was like him—adventurous, strong-willed, not afraid. She was sure her father had lovers. English. White women. Her mother had returned to Mumbai after all, and Bisma was sure that her father's affairs was the reason.

But her father would not care to see her now, in bed with this man. Even if that man was asleep. Even if he was maybe more a Swede than a cowboy.

Bisma lifted Trevor's shirt, un-tucking it to see the stomach she had touched, his skin pale, milky-white in contrast to his brown arms and neck, his face. She touched the small hairs around his navel but he still did not move. Not even the lids of his eyes.

Oh come on.

She kissed his stomach. Let her wet tongue stay there and he tasted of salt and dust and smelled of the land they had just come through. He unfolded his arms but his eyes remained closed. Encouraged, she smiled at him anyway. She pulled the towel higher—unabashed—and then straddled him. Looked into his handsome face

What shall we do, now that we're in Cheyenne?

He opened his eyes then, giving no clue if he had been asleep or not. The towel was loose, slipping, but he was calm. He made no effort to engage her or touch her.

Get something to eat, he answered.

Oh, you're hungry.

You said you wanted to wash up. Get some food.

She gave a low laugh. She could feel him now, the swelling of him, and she reached for his hat on the table. The towel slipped down but she saw no register of reaction in him, other than what she could feel between her legs.

I have your hat. She placed the Stetson on her own head, cocking it upward, trying to at least elicit a smile. Mister Trevor Kallengaard.

His face did not change. His arms did not lift and his hands did not reach for her. Only his eyes betrayed a restricted emotion.

No, he said. Please don't. And he reached up, his elbow brushing her right breast, to take the hat from her head.

She dropped her smile. She felt embarrassed, a little angry. Rejection. She told herself not to feel it, but she did. She rolled off him, put her bare feet on the old carpet, gathered the yellowed towel but did not cover herself. She wasn't going to feel shame.

He sat up and slid his legs off the bed.

Did I do something wrong? she said, more accusatory of him than of herself.

He didn't answer but stood. He put the Stetson on his head and went to the table for his cigarettes.

No, he said and said nothing more and lit a cigarette.

That's how he is, she told herself. More of a nut, perhaps, than an egg to crack. She had misjudged him—the thickness of him. There were layers to peel back.

I'd better dress then, so we can eat.

It's getting towards noon.

Yes, she said and looked into his eyes. She still felt some anger but tried for neutrality in her expression, in her voice. I'm famished—and we just missed breakfast, didn't we?

They didn't talk as they walked out of the Plains Hotel. Turning the corner, the wind hit them, blowing grit from the street and Trevor had to put a hand to his hat. She wore his jacket and pulled it tight around her.

He took her a few blocks from the hotel, to Albany's. It was a place he knew, popular during cattle conventions, during Pioneer Days and Saturday nights. At least it used to be. And it was still there, new red paint over the bricks but the same overlarge sign out front. It pleased him to see it.

Holding the narrow front door for her, Trevor was conscious of the awkwardness between them since the incident on the bed. But there was nothing to be done about it. They could only eat. He was hungry.

Inside Albany's, little had changed—everything colored in maroon and white, plush and soft, the carpeting worn with traffic patterns, the high-backed booths and handmade signs posted around the cash register. But it was warm and it smelled good—at least to Trevor. The hostess gave Bisma a second look before pointing out the specials on the chalkboard and then seating them at a booth in the smoking section in back. Trevor hung his hat on a hook along the aisle. Bisma handed him the jacket and, after holding it for a moment, he hung that also.

The restaurant was busy enough, noisy. It seemed like a long time before she spoke.

You're not gay, are you?

Her face was screened by the large paper menu.

No, he said.

She set the menu down and looked at him.

You don't have an untreatable disease? VD? HIV positive?

Trevor looked around at the tables and people near them. No one appeared to be listening. When he looked back a small smile played about her lips.

Erectile dysfunction? . . . No. I know that wasn't the case.

It's just how it's going to be, Trevor said. He studied the menu.

No one can say how it will be . . . Forty some years old, are you?

Trevor ignored her.

Were you were worried you'd get me up the duff? Up the spout? You know, pregnant? . . . I do have condoms. Carry them for such occasions. Party favors almost.

He didn't answer and she didn't say anything more. He took the ashtray from along the wall and then lit a cigarette. She waved the menu at him as they waited for the waitress to come. Trevor felt compelled to say something, to try for equanimity.

I'm going to have a steak—you like beef?

Beef? She laughed.

Trevor found that he was glad to hear it, thought that her laugh repaired something between them.

What? he asked.

That would be quite bad, if I were Hindu.

You're a Muslim? Or do I say Islamic?

Either or, but I'm neither either. My parents are Hindu, though my mother now claims to be Sufi—to get at my father. Their true religion is money. Business. I believe in God but practice nothing . . . Who wants to practice when you can just be?

Okay, he said.

And you?

Me.

Are you a good Christian?

No. Neither good nor Christian, really. I don't believe.

Not at all? Not even as forgotten or forsaken?

The waitress came, took their drink orders. Trevor was ready to order his meal but Bisma had not decided. The waitress said she'd give them a few minutes.

So, you're an atheist. A nihilist? . . . You've got a Nietzsche thing going?

We're just little lambs on our way to the slaughterhouse.

She leaned back into the booth and gave him a look of delight. Her eyes incandescent in their blackness. Who said that? Not you.

Schopenhauer, I think.

Trevor felt slightly embarrassed. Though his mother was Lutheran, his father had never been religious and his grandfather was a stout nonbeliever. Trevor had been ambivalent and assumed Ross had been too, if his brother had even troubled himself with such thinking. But Trevor was not contemptuous of religion, as Thor had been. He was not angry. He disliked the often labyrinthine dogma of it as it tried to explain, or make exceptions for, the harsh reality of life.

So you see no order to anything? There's nothing divine? No judgment or karma or larger purpose?

Trevor shrugged.

But there's order in nature, in physics, no? There's even order in disorder—there's chaos *theory*. And beauty. Don't you see beauty? Mystery?

Sure, he said. At times.

And that's not God?

She was smiling. He could see her enjoyment in the discussion. Trevor felt he had already said more than he wanted. Theological arguments, philosophical ones, were long behind him. Maybe even before leaving New Orleans with Cass.

If you want it to be, he said. I still hope you like beef.

I don't eat red meat. Fish. Chicken sometimes. But there are things I won't put inside me.

Trevor nodded, thought how Cass had never been big on meat.

Just like I won't drink hard alcohol. Beer, wine—okay. But no whiskey or gin and such. My father loves his gin . . . Marijuana, mushrooms: okay. But no pills. Nothing made in a lab.

Tobacco? He felt he had to ask.

She made a face.

Trevor put out his cigarette.

The waitress returned. Trevor ordered prime rib. Bisma a salad and baked potato.

And when the food came, his meat was sliced thick and pink. There was bread and steak fries and slaw, so much food that he balked at it initially. But when he started eating, he could not stop. He dug in without conscious, using lots of horseradish. Just like the old days, he told himself, though he knew it was not.

Collis Mudd had called and told her what he knew—about the location of the phone call, about Fort Collins, Colorado. He wanted to know if she would sign a contract. So, Cass had invited him to her house because he was driving down from

Palm Beach—he was giving a deposition up there, he'd said—and Fort Lauderdale was on his way.

And now he was on his way.

So, Cass showered and changed into a little less casual clothes. She put up her hair and applied a little makeup, wanting to look presentable and not forlorn. Afterwards she looked at herself in the mirror. She was an attractive woman. She kept herself up well—well enough. She wasn't crazy. Why? she asked when she looked at herself. Why had Trevor left her? But she also wondered why would he come back.

She straightened up the living room. Dusted the coffee table after removing the magazines and clutter. In the kitchen she placed things in cabinets and the dishwasher. She hadn't quite realized how slovenly the house had become—so that was at least one good thing about the detective was stopping in, a sliver of a silver lining no matter the ultimate outcome of it all. In back, she opened the blinds to let in the light, but saw the humps of mangoes that had fallen into the uncut grass and closed them again.

Cass went to the front of the house where there was the small Florida room that served as the entryway. All the room's shades were drawn. She flipped the overhead light and the way it shined upon the Mexican tile, on the shelves and the books in those shelves, on the odds and ends of her and Trevor's life, it made her feel terrible.

Was he thinking of her? Was he still in Colorado or had he gone to Wyoming? Or was he heading elsewhere, further away? Would she ever find him and understand why—why had he done it, executed an escape plan like he did? . . . Then Cass caught herself. Reminded herself that such thinking was unhealthy. That this was Trevor's doing, not hers. Collis Mudd was coming with a contract and Collis Mudd would find Trevor Kallengaard and she would see him again and she would slap his face and then ask him why.

Cass left the light in the Florida room on, then went to start the coffee before the detective showed up.

Trevor and Bisma walked the streets of downtown after the meal, along Sixteenth and then up Capitol Avenue under the sidewalk trees, the golden dome of the State Capitol shiny in the afternoon sun. The wind was constant, but at their backs now, and Trevor was able to keep his hat on. Bisma had the jacket tied to her waist by its sleeves.

At the Capitol itself, Bisma said she wanted to go inside. So up the steps they went and through the big door.

The interior was hushed and empty. There were marble floors and paneled wood walls, polished banisters on the grand staircase. It felt bureaucratic, museum-like. The center of the lobby looked all the way up to the dome. It was a place Trevor recalled from class field trips and occasionally business. There were a few voices from offices with frosted glass doors. There were no other visitors but them: Trevor and Bisma.

On either side of the room, behind a string of low chains, were a stuffed elk and a buffalo. They went to the elk with its five point antlers and its plastic tongue poised in mid-bugle. Bisma reached out over the chains and touched the taxidermied coat, despite a sign that forbid it. Then they walked across the marble—Trevor's boot-steps echoing in the chamber—to the buffalo.

The buffalo—the American bison—was massive. Black and brown, its brutish head horned and bearded and glass-eyed. Trevor saw how old it was, the fur worn, fresh stitching visible along its flank. The bison had been in the lobby for decades—longer than the elk—and he had always liked it. He had loved bison as a child, continued to admire them as he got older. Standing in front of the ancient, dead animal, he tried to conjure that feeling, that rise of simple excitement over an animal . . . Perhaps it was all a matter of imagination, he thought. But Trevor had considered raising buffalo. He had entertained the idea as a business, even as he neared graduation from CSU. He knew of the Buffalo Commons concept—an idea to return most of the Great Plains to its original habitat and to return the buffalo to its traditional herds and herding patterns—and he knew of wealthy people who kept herds on their land. There were also bison used for blood sport, for butchering and consumption. Trevor was not sure if, in good conscious, he could raise an animal for slaughter. Not any more.

Bisma had wandered over to the lobby information booth, where a lone clerk worked behind a veil of clear glass. There was a large guest book on a stand and she stopped to look at it.

Do you want to sign it?

Her voice carried across the empty room and up to the dome. Trevor saw the female clerk look up sharply.

No, he said, softly. Go ahead if you want to.

But this is your hometown, she said.

Trevor left the bison and walked to her.

No. Douglas is my hometown.

But this is your home state.

Trevor saw her smile. She picked up the pen and wrote in the book while he was thinking of Douglas. And then he thought of the Kallengaard Ranch itself. He wanted to live there again—settle there—but only in the canyon. That was where Thor had built the original homestead cabin. And that's where he would build his own house—in that low land with its sandstone walls, where Pearl Creek ran all year long . . . But if he were to try raising buffalo, then he would need the Bedtick land just south of the canyon. He did not know if Thor had left any of the ranch to him and, if so, how much or what part, but he would have the canyon no matter. The Bedtick property was only a wish.

When they left the Capitol, Trevor led them north, towards his old neighborhood. They stayed in the sun as they walked. Streets now of modest homes and yards, established trees. He had no problem guiding the way. As he closed in on Rollins and Twenty-Third, he recalled who lived—or used to live—in what houses, which ones he had been inside of and small memories of his high school years.

Bisma chatted, asking some questions which he listened to and sometimes answered. Internally, Trevor was alert, alive, monitoring what memories he wanted and which he wanted to keep purposely forgotten.

They were on Sixth now and he stopped. This was his street. This was his house that they stood in front of. It was a single story red brick house with a detached garage. It looked smaller. It was trimmed in black now, not white. The front door looked new. The hedge on the right side—where Trevor's room was—had been taken out. There was a fence instead. The maple tree out front was still there, grown huge and leafy. The Red Hawthorn was gone.

And what's this? she asked.

I used to live here.

Do you want to knock? See if they'll let you in.

Trevor didn't answer. Seeing the house again, the one he had walked out of almost twenty-five years ago, the one he had disappeared from, brought the ghosts. He remembered his friends, his brother. His father and mother. High school. He recalled playing basketball in the driveway with Bill and Kevin. With Larry and Monte. He remembered playing touch football in this very street. Staying up studying for classes in his room. He remembered his brother, Ross, before he became an enemy and then left Cheyenne to return to the ranch and live with Thor. Before Darcie. But the ghost he most clearly saw was that of his father, saw him behind the walls of the house that had been home. His father the café owner. His father the son of a ranchman. His father the alcoholic. His father . . . But he did not want to see it, to remember it.

You'd be interested, I'd think, in seeing the inside.

No. I'm ready to go back.

And so they walked back towards downtown and the hotel.

Cass heard the car pull into the drive and she got up to look. She saw the same old Mercedes sedan that had been in Opa Locka. She saw Collis Mudd emerge from the car, slow and deliberate. Again he wore dark slacks and a white shirt. A black tie. He held a black briefcase. Cass didn't open the door but waited for him to approach and knock first.

Hello, Miss Tipton.

Come in, Collis.

He filled the frame of the door and she stepped back to let him enter.

Thanks for saving me an extra trip, he said.

Or a trip to your office. Would you like some coffee?

Sure. That sounds good.

She left him standing in the living room with the wood floors that Trevor had refinished. In the kitchen Cass poured two cups. There were two saucers. Two spoons. All of which she had gotten out before Collis Mudd's arrival.

Sugar? Milk? she called out.

No thank you.

She returned to the living room with the black coffee and saw that he was still standing in the same spot.

Please, sit down.

Thanks. This is a nice house. Nice part of town.

It used to be run down, but it's changed. Thank you.

He sat on the sofa and placed the briefcase next to him. She set the cups and their saucers down on the table there. Cass sat on the sofa also, the case between them.

So, you understand about Mr. Kallengaard, where he's been?

Yes. I'm surprised. I mean, all of a sudden we know where he is.

Where he was.

Yes. That's right.

He's not exactly hiding, Collis Mudd told her and then he took a sip of coffee. Not that he needs to hide. He's using his name, using the card for some things.

Western wear . . . That's a little strange for him.

He's not stupid—excuse me for saying that—but I'm thinking, Miss Tipton . . .

Cass, please.

Cass. I'm thinking maybe he doesn't mind if you know where he's gone off to. Or, maybe he doesn't think you'd bother to find him.

Okay, she said and took a breath.

Now, if you want to proceed, we can wait. We can see if he calls again or uses the card again or what-have-you. I can only track the use of his card if you allow it. I did it once, dishonestly you should know, but I doubt I'd fool them again. So that'll be on you. I'll need his social security number and some other information . . . But, to me, honestly, it's wasted time. He hasn't gone too far since he called you and he's originally from Cheyenne . . . You see what I'm saying, Miss Kallengaard?

Tipton.

Of course. Sorry. I had his name in my head.

It's okay.

I apologize. But what I'm saying is that I can go out there. It's up to you, seeing as it's your money, but it's the quickest way and pretty much how I do things. I'm hands-on. Work by myself. Try to get the quickest results. I have the time right now—nothing else pressing. Mr. Kallengaard may even still be in Fort Collins.

He waited a moment. Drank from the cup of coffee again. She held her cup in both hands but didn't comment.

Though, before we go to the trouble and expense, Cass, you need to tell me what you really want to do. I get a sense of some reluctance. That is, do you really want to find him? Do you want him to come back? Collis Mudd set his cup down neatly upon the saucer. You've had a little more time to get over the shock, mull it over, and I want to be sure—want you to be sure—it's what you want . . . Do you just want him to know you're looking for him and see how he reacts? Or, do you really want him to return to you? Can you see the difference, Miss Tipton?

Cass, she said.

Yes. Cass.

She felt he was being a little condescending. Unhelpful with the formality of names, the confusing of names. But, she realized, she liked hearing her name, liked putting out things in twos instead of ones, even if it was only the detective.

Cass?

Yes, yes, she said and looked at him.

I'm also trying to convey that there's cost involved. I have to get a plane ticket—short notice—to Denver. I'd have to rent a car. There's lodging—nothing special—food and other expenses. I'd need an account, basically, and my fee on top of that. I'm sorry to bring all of this up, but . . .

Of course. Of course.

Miss . . . Cass . . . Do you want more time?

No. The money, the costs, that's okay . . . I was just thinking about what you said, that maybe he doesn't care.

I can hold off. But I'm available now and something else might come in. I work fast but I'm kind of old-fashioned in my style. A lot of legwork.

It's okay. Let's go ahead with it. Maybe he wants me to find him. Maybe, she set her cup down next to his, maybe he doesn't even realize it, that he wants me to find him. That he needs me to do it.

You never know, Collis Mudd said.

After going over the contract and signing, Collis Mudd looked slightly uncomfortable to her. He avoided her eyes. Maybe he was only distracted—she remembered that he'd said he was getting divorced. But then he did look at her, as if he could hear her thoughts.

I've got to get going, he said. I'm having dinner with my son. My oldest, Todd, not James, who you met. Thank you for the coffee.

Collis.

Yes?

No. Your name. The name Collis . . . I knew a man in New Orleans who had that name. He'd been a boxer. But his last name wasn't the same.

My people are from Atlanta. I moved away when I was young but we still have family there.

Really? I lived there. My mother did anyway, in Buckhead. You?

Cabbage Town, Collis told her.

Oh, Cabbage Town. Your name, it's just unusual, a little like Trevor's. His last name at least.

He stood and took the briefcase in his left hand. She noticed he wore no wedding ring. They shook. He had soft fingers.

It was very nice to see you again, Miss Tipton.

In the room, Bisma took out a small spiral notebook and sat on the second bed, the one by the wall. She started to write. Trevor watched her and she did not look up at him. He showered. Changed into new jeans and other clothes. When he came out of the bathroom, she was still engrossed with writing words.

He went to the round table by the window, slid the ashtray closer to him and then lit a cigarette. He was conscious of her presence, of her pen on paper. Outside the hotel sunlight stretched down the streets, offering up long shadows. Again he looked at the highway and the rail yard, at the big Interstate signage for Denver, Laramie and Pine Bluff. He though about the act of leaving.

He knew that his leaving—and he was thinking of both Cass and of his mother—had been a callous deed. Cowardly in many ways. Walking out without a word, to forget and be forgotten, and not seek forgiveness, well, what could one say? That it was simply a character flaw? An act of aggression? . . . Yet, to Trevor, it was a strength. Or a necessity, maybe. Sometimes he thought that being able to leave, to disappear, was his only control in the world. To be able to dispense with the old and start anew, to abandon people and place—knowing that he had the ability to do this—was a way to make sure nothing could harm him. Or at least pretend so . . . It wasn't as though he was unaware of the harm, the hurt, but right or wrong, ultimately, leaving was the weapon or defense he possessed. Life always held the potential for something bad, even horrific, and a person needed something to defend themselves. It was, to him, not a matter of escape as much as to never be caught in the first place.

Looking out the window at the winnowing light, Trevor decided that he did not want to linger in Cheyenne. That he had already seen enough.

Are you bored yet? he asked with his back to her.

With you or the trip?

Does it matter?

She didn't answer and he turned to see her. She had stopped writing but her neck was still bent to the notebook, her long hair falling over her face. But she was looking upwards at him, her eyes sharp from behind the strands.

Not bored, she said.

I'm going to Douglas tomorrow. I can run you back to Fort Collins.

Is that what you'd like—she closed her notebook—to run me back?

Trevor didn't answer. He finished his cigarette.

Yes? No? Maybe? she said. Or is it my decision to make? Bisma gave him a look that he could not interpret, then got off the bed and returned her pen and notebook to the suitcase. My decision is that I need a short nap.

Trevor didn't comment as she removed her shoes and socks, her shirt and jeans. She stood in her underwear showing all that olive brown skin that he could not help but to look at. He realized that she wanted him to look, to prove something or to show him that he couldn't help it. Then she went back to the bed, drew the covers, got in and pulled them over her. She turned her face to the wall.

He sat at the round table while she slept, or feigned sleep. He smoked another cigarette, certain she would raise her head and say something, but she did not. He put out the cigarette and decided that she was, indeed, asleep. He went to the desk in the room and took out the hotel stationary. He wrote only a note saying that he would be downstairs, at the Wigwam Lounge or the café. As he wrote the note, a small stone of guilt formed within him and he briefly touched the phone that was also on the desk. In his head he recited his—Cass'—phone number. He didn't call it. He only put on his boots and left the hat and jacket and his duffle of belongings.

Trevor bought a carton of cigarettes from the woman in the gift shop and took them outside to the truck, which was parked in the street. He put the carton in the glove compartment after taking out a pack. Then he leaned on the Silverado, in the shade cast by the Plains Hotel. He looked up at the black Gleason Building and then at the sky between the two buildings—a narrow slot of blue, clouds high and wind-riven.

He considered walking to his high school, where—for all he knew—his brother's home run record still stood. He could visit the old café that had belonged to the family, his father's business after his father had left the ranch and gotten away from Thor, but Trevor didn't move away from the truck. He listened to traffic and the wind, then walked around the corner of the hotel, to the street entrance of the Wigwam Lounge.

The lounge was dark, maroon in color. There were heavy red window curtains and heavy red carpet and red painted walls, neon beer signs already lit in the sunless interior. Soft yellow lighting. A Marty Robbins song played on the jukebox, low, only adding to the quietude, the sense of padded silence from the outside world. Trevor listened to the song, which was familiar to him, just as he was familiar with the Wigwam Lounge and its faded lushness. He made his way past the tables—empty—and took the last stool on the right hand side of the bar. There was a couple on the other end, the bartender talking to them.

Trevor waited. He lit a cigarette and listened to Marty Robbins, who was his father's favorite. He looked at the framed photos on the wall behind the bar: bull riders and rodeo stars, fishermen and hunters, obscure dignitaries and celebrities. Jerry Mack—the lounge's owner—was in most of the photographs. Trevor had known Jerry Mack to some degree, had liked him well enough, and guessed he was still alive. Jerry Mack was from Tensleep—the Big Horns—as Trevor recalled. Ross knew him, but their father knew Jerry Mack best of all. Trig Kallengaard had been a regular at the Wigwam.

Another couple came inside from the street, joined the others at the opposite end. The barman served the new comers before he bothered with Trevor. Trevor pulled the black ashtray closer. He knew how to be patient. When the barman came over, Trevor ordered a ginger ale. The man gave him a can of Canada Dry and a glass of ice then rejoined the cluster of people down the bar.

Trevor drank ginger ale and smoked and listened to more Marty Robbins songs. He thought of the Wigwam—much like the hotel itself, much like Cheyenne itself—as a place hanging on by its own stubbornness, by a Westerner's sense of loyalty, habit and adverseness to change. Things could survive that way, he told himself and tried to believe it, because he was going to survive that way when he got to the ranch, to the canyon and Pearl Creek. He looked up at the lights above him which were small bulbs encased in shot glasses. Then he looked at the wall, to the right of the framed photos, where the shift-bartender's name was engraved with looping letters into a wooden sign: Lane Waters.

Trevor knew Lane Waters.

He finished his cigarette, caught the barman's eye and waved so that he came over. Trevor held out a five for the Canada Dry, the barman taking it and ringing it up and giving the change. Trevor handed him a dollar tip and the barman gave him a look.

Do I know you?

I went to high school with you, Trevor said.

You did?

East. You lived on Dunway.

The barman's eyes opened with recognition. He gave a shark's grin.

Shit. Kallengaard.

That's right.

Trevor Kallengaard.

Trevor couldn't help but to smile. He didn't want to but he did and he shook Lane Waters' extended hand. Lane looked at the customers down the bar but they were talking amongst themselves.

Well, hell . . . How goes it?

I'm visiting.

You staying with Ross?

Lane Waters had lived in the same neighborhood. He had always been more of a friend of his brother's than Trevor's.

I haven't seen him in a long time. I haven't been up to Douglas.

He's still on the ranch—guess you'd know that—but Ross comes in now and then. Used to, anyway. Lane Waters lost his smile for the moment, then brought it back. Anyway, Trevor, where the hell have you been?

I've been gone.

Lane Waters looked upwards at the shot glass lights.

Yeah, yeah. You went away. Ross told me that, long time ago. I remember . . . Where you staying?

In town. For now.

Okay. You doing good?

The others were watching now. Tentatively eavesdropping while the jukebox played Patsy Cline.

Fine, Trevor told him. The town looks about the same.

Lane Waters rolled his eyes.

Doing better. Frontier Days is coming up—we'll be busy with that. City's changed, really, pushing hard for tourist dollars these days. You'd be surprised.

Trevor shrugged. He took a moment to study the bartender's face: the hairline and hair color, the skin, the beginning of jowls. Trevor suspected Lane had been in the bar business for a long time.

Hold on, Lane said and went over to where a woman stood at the service bar. It was the same woman who worked the gift shop and now she looked over at Trevor. She tried to hold his eyes but Trevor looked away. She left and Lane Waters returned.

You want a shot? Wild Turkey—on me.

Trevor shook his head no.

What have you been doing with yourself?

Trevor felt an edge of gossip in the question.

Carpentry. Out east. This is my first trip back.

Yeah? Married? Kids?

No.

Me neither. Divorced though. Twice.

Trevor nodded.

But you're just visiting?

For now. Plan to go up to Douglas.

Lane reached down below the bar, opened a silver cooler and brought out a banquet bottle of Coors. He twisted the top, took a drink, kept the beer along the sleeve below the bar top.

Ross's living on the ranch, like I said, but his old man—his granddad, yours I mean—he's gone. Died a few years ago . . . You knew that or have you really been like, *gone* gone?

Someone told me, Trevor said.

Well, there was that and then some back taxes and cattle prices bottomed out. Ross had to sell the herd. He won't lease the land—you'd think it'd kill him just to have someone else's cows on it . . . I heard from some cattlemen up in Converse that he's thinking of sinking some wells.

Oil?

Gas, or fracking most likely now, but he was saying that years ago, when the old man was out of it. But you got to have Sinclair or someone out of Gillette do that these days. Lane Waters quit talking then. The jukebox had been silent but one of the men walked over and started it again. Trevor saw Lane holding his lips tight, thinking, trying to decide what should or shouldn't be said. But Ross is doing okay.

He never married?

Was married to Thor. Married to the old man.

Trevor didn't smile.

That's what the others always said. Just a joke.

Lane Waters took a quick drink of beer, asked the other customers if they were okay. Fine, one of them said. Merle Haggard was singing now and Lane dumped Trevor's ashtray for him. Trevor lit another.

Well, when you see Ross tell him to give me a holler. Lane cocked his head then and looked at Trevor from a new angle. Does he know you're coming up?

Trevor smoked, shook his head no.

Lane put his hands on the bar.

I don't know, about going up there out of the blue. A lot of water under his bridge. I don't see him but I hear about him.

I'm his brother.

Lane looked at him.

Yeah, he said. Exactly.

Then Lane Waters wasn't looking at him any longer. His head turned. The group down the bar, their heads turned. A long rectangular of light had spilled in from the lobby entrance, sharp upon the maroon carpet, like a cutout. A young and beautiful woman entered and it was Bisma.

Her hair, sleek and long, was lit by the light from the lobby and shone blue-black. Her age and features, the ocher of her skin, were obvious in comparison to the others in the lounge . She wore a simple yellow sundress, exotic for the Wigwam Lounge.

Bisma blinked and looked about, her big eyes adjusting to the maroon world. When her vision locked in upon Trevor, she smiled. Everyone watched as she came and sat down next to him at the bar.

Lane Waters missed none of it as Bisma leaned into the padding of the bar's edge, as she rubbed her bare brown arms as if chilled. She asked him for a beer.

What flavor?

A Smithwicks, I should think.

Sorry?

No? . . . A Stella? Or something local.

He brought up a bottle of Rainier. Made a show of wiping the moisture from it, of getting a glass and setting it before her.

On me, Lane said, for a friend of Trevor's.

She looked at Trevor, curious about the use of his name, then said thank you.

I slept too long, she said to Trevor. I didn't know where I was when I woke and you weren't there . . . Bisma then looked at Lane Waters, who had not moved away from them. She turned back to Trevor . . . You simply were gone.

Are you from Australia? Lane Waters asked.

Bisma didn't answer.

This is Lane, Trevor said. Lane, Bisma. She shook his hand lightly. Lane's from Cheyenne.

I'm a friend of Ross', Lane said.

Ross?

Trev's brother. Bisma now showed some interest in Lane Waters, which pleased him.

Trev ? He never told me he had a brother.

Lane sat sideways on the cooler. He put a cocktail straw in his mouth and chewed on it.

You two are staying here, at the Plains? You're going up to Douglas and he didn't tell you about Ross?

Lane was smiling.

I'd like to know about this brother, she said and looked at both of them.

He's Ross Trigvie Kallengaard. I'm Trevor Thor Kallengaard.

Baseball, Lane said.

He was good at baseball, Trevor went on. Good at a lot of sports.

Home run king of East High. On Base king, too.

So, Bisma said, he became a famous baseball player?

Sure, Lane Waters said and laughed a little.

Trevor eyed the barman, then looked down, saw his cigarette in the tray. Burnt. A pencil of ash. Trevor felt uneasy, a niggle of caution within as Bisma turned towards him.

You have other brothers? A sister?

No.

And the one brother, the older brother, this Ross, he lives in this Douglas town?

No.

No?

Not exactly.

Bisma looked frustrated.

He lives on the family ranch, Lane Waters offered.

Trevor didn't say anything more. He placed his cigarettes and his lighter in his pocket. The couples at the other end asked for drinks and Lane held up a hand to them. We need some dinner, he said.

I'm done at eight, Lane said, when the old man comes in, Jerry. I'm living out on Happy Jack Road. Number's in the book. Give me a call, I'll take you two around.

Okay, Trevor said but knew that he would not. He stood up.

Good to see you again, Trev. And nice to meet you . . . I'm sorry.

Bisma, she said--she had not finished her beer but she stood--Bisma Kallengaard.

They began walking towards the door.

Lane asked Trevor something but Trevor only said goodbye and they left the Wigwam Lounge through the lobby door.

They stood in the lobby, atop the mosaic of Chief Little Shield.

Now he thinks I lied to him, Trevor said. He'll think I have a wife.

Or a daughter, she told him.

He picked up his son in Miami, at Florida International University, where Todd was taking classes. His son's car was being fixed and Collis was glad to spend some time with him, whatever the circumstance. Todd rarely asked him for help anymore, for advice. True, he asked for money now and then and was pleasant company when together, but that was about it.

So he took him for dinner—Cuban—and he told Todd about a case he was starting that would require him to go to Colorado. But it wasn't until on the way to the house, in Opa-Locka, that he asked about the case.

When are you going to Denver?

Tomorrow. I want to get a jump on it.

Tomorrow?

I've got to track someone down. Maybe if you didn't have summer classes, you could come with me, Collis said though he knew that he wouldn't bring his son along.

Todd shrugged. He was tall. Athletic. Good-natured—good-natured enough not to comment on the *maybe*. They drove along a canal in the darkening light, the outdoors damp with humidity and recent rains. There were more thunderheads out west, above the Glades.

I've got work to do, too, he said. He had a job at Publix, a supermarket. My car's ready tomorrow. Mom can take me to get it, I guess.

I guess, Collis said.

They came into Opa-Locka from the west, all of it familiar if no longer routine to Collis, and he pulled up in front of the house. He turned to his son before Todd could open the car's door.

So, everyone's good?

I told you, Todd said. We're okay.

Your mom?

Yeah . . . Come in, Dad. If you're going you can say goodbye. Everybody's home I bet.

I'll only be gone maybe a week. I was going to come in. I just thought you and I, if there was anything . . .

His son smiled, his face broad, the eyebrows starting to get bushy. He was a fine kid. A young man that Collis was proud of.

I'm good. Busy, you know, like you.

Still smiling.

Inside the house the central air was running, colder than Collis liked it. He and his son went into the living room where James sat on the couch playing some game on a laptop. James only looked up for a moment to meet Collis' eyes.

I'll find Mom, Todd said and went down the hall.

Collis sat next to his younger son and felt the old feeling of exile creep into him, that imposed alienation from his own family. Imposed by his wife or himself, was the question. Technically, he was free to come and go from the house, sometimes even summoned to the house—like the day Cassandra Tipton came to meet him—but not free to stay the night. And whenever Liv and all the children were together, he was especially conscious of what used to be. Of how things had changed. Of that alienation.

Can you turn that off? Collis asked about the computer.

Hold on, James said and did not look at him.

Hold on?

I'm in a battle.

Collis placed his hand on James' head and the boy rocked his neck to get out from it, looking at the screen. So Collis let go. He stood up and went down the hall.

He could hear Liv and Todd talking in what used to be his bedroom—his and Liv's. Todd had his own room. Lakeesha had her own. James and Keena still shared a room, though he knew Keena usually slept with Liv. Collis stopped at Lakeesha's closed door, knocked once, then entered just as she was saying, Come in.

Dad. She smiled. She was at her desk, at her computer. And to what do we owe the honor?

I'm going out of town for a while, for a client. Not too long, but can't be sure about that. So, thought I'd say hello.

She stood up then and gave Collis a hug. An embrace that made him feel good. She was tall like her brother, though still only sixteen. Both Lakeesha and Liv insisted that she wasn't seeing any boy, but Collis was unsure.

You're working this summer?

Same place, she said. Haven't quit yet.

They talked for a while. Small things. He saw his daughter's eyes jump twice, focusing briefly on something behind him. Collis turned and saw Liv standing in the doorway. She didn't smile or say his name though he said hers.

Lakeesha, she said, would you excuse us and let your daddy and me talk here. Would you look in on Keena, just for a while please.

They weren't questions.

Collis Mudd's elder daughter shut down her computer and said nothing. She walked past Collis and then Liv and out into the hall.

When Collis and Liv talked—in the house—it was always in someone else's room. Never in the room they had shared. Sometimes it was in the kitchen. Usually it was on the front stoop. They had been separated for almost two years now because Livian Mudd had had an affair, when Collis was still on the police force. Collis had discovered the man in their bedroom. Collis was going to hit the man with a baseball bat, but Livian stopped him. It was true that Collis himself had had an affair prior to Livian's, but they had reconciled. No, it was the way in which she stopped him from beating the man in his bedroom that did not allow him to remain married to her.

Collis had tried to forgive her—even had said so on a number of occasions— but in his heart, he wasn't so sure. He had left. They legally separated. Liv ultimately filed for divorce, right after Collis retired early from the force and set up his private investigating service.

Liv stepped into the room and closed the door behind her.

How have you been, Collis.

Fine.

He was waiting to see what this was about.

I've got the kids in camp in two weeks—Keena and James. Theater camp.

I thought James was doing Ocean camp?

Marine Science, she corrected him. No, I set them both up for children's theater. If you want to drive James out to Haulover Beach every day—if you can be around for that—then fine, I'll switch him to marine science.

Okay, he said.

But if you're going to be in Colorado, then I don't see how you can do it.

Collis was on one side of the room, Liv was on the other.

I don't think it'll take long, Liv. I'm not going away because . . .

I know. It's your job.

Yes, Livian. It's my job. It's how I make money.

She closed her eyes and left them closed. He studied her face then. Her body language. He liked the way she looked but not the way she stood.

Is she pretty? she asked and opened her eyes.

Who?

The woman you're working for. You're always working for women. Latinas.

They're clients . . . What kind of question is that?

A none-of-my-business question, I guess.

Collis said nothing.

Are you taking your gun?

He put his hand on the back of Lakeesha's chair and tried not to become angry.

I doubt it. There's nothing dangerous about the situation.

She gave him a judgmental look. Sometimes Collis could not understand her—she wanted the divorce but she also interrogated him. She still wanted something from him beyond alimony and shared duties. Maybe Collis still wanted something from her, too.

I guess I shouldn't mention anything about guns either, Liv said.

It was dark when he headed home and the thunderheads had moved in. It was one of those big summer rains, tropical, hard and heavy, that obliterated the sky and flooded streets. His windshield wipers were almost useless against the volume of falling water. His car roof a continual hollow hammer.

He was soaked just walking from car to house. The house was an office in a neighborhood with other homes turned into offices. Small time, white collar businesses mainly. Collis was renting. He would have left a light on if he'd known he'd be coming back this late and in a rain.

Inside he removed his shoes. Turned on a light and checked the office phone to see if there were any calls. None. He made his way past the desk and filing cabinet. The rain still fell, he listened to it on the roof tiles. He took his wet shirt off while passing the little kitchen, then the little bathroom, the room he used for storage, going to the room where he slept. He dropped the shirt into the hamper. On his back was the circular scar where he had been shot by a small caliber pistol. In his armpit was the larger, irregular exit hole.

He turned on the closet light and pushed aside the wrinkled clothes that hung there. He reached for the suitcase that was there and set it behind him, off to the side. Then he reached for the top shelf and pulled down a smaller case. He took the case to the bed and rolled the combination to open it and took out the 9mm Glock. He checked the chamber—empty. The clip also empty, though there was ammo in the closet as well. He'd have to clean it, he told himself, but he placed it back in its case.

Then, thinking of the night, of the house and kids, Collis Mudd reached over to touch the scar under his arm, the place where Livian had shot him.

After breakfast they checked out and went to the truck and placed their luggage in the back. The wind was low and cool and he remembered that it was always windy in Cheyenne, even more so in Douglas and the ranch.

He drove Warren to Federal to 219—Old Yellowstone Road. The distant, humped mountains water-colored with morning light. Bisma sat close to him—he had not asked her about returning to Fort Collins. Last night they had slept in their separate beds. In the morning she was up when he was up, packed her bag and ate with him and that seemed to be that. For the time being, she was staying with him.

You're not going to take the small roads all the way, are you?

Just for a while, until it plays out. Then it'll be Interstate.

Good. I'd like to get to—wherever it is—before tomorrow.

They passed Four Mile Road and Riding Club Road. In what used to be well north of town, Trevor saw the new developments: Roundup Heights, Grey Fox Estates, Wind Dancer Ranches. Gated communities sprawled out into the empty land with curved streets and light poles, watered lawns and planted trees. And then, out by Green Door Road, were places still under construction: land scrubbed of vegetation, meted into parcels of dust. And Trevor realized that Cheyenne had not escaped the world after all.

Trevor lit a cigarette, wanting to smoke before they reached the Interstate. He momentarily thought of Florida: the humidity and green, the importance of shade and of the trees that made that shade. He thought of the ceaseless flowers, the fruits, the insects, the Atlantic Ocean. Then he tried to stop. He looked over at Bisma, the stranger next to him. She had her window open, her hair schooling with the wind. And then there was a sign for Douglas—76 miles—a sign for Casper, and then there was the Interstate and he tossed the cigarette, sped up as he and Bisma closed windows, and they were on their way, Florida forgotten.

FIVE

Douglas

He came up from the south along Miller Draw, where the town of Douglas sat with its low-slung houses and brown-bricked buildings, its green trees incongruous against the otherwise desolate landscape. Douglas a small place, though not that small by Wyoming standards. In his mind, Trevor still knew its streets, its railroad tracks, downtown, Park Hill and the North Platte; its graveyards. He knew the things that lay outside of town as well, the ridges, coulees, creeks, sumps, the back roads and fenced lands, the patchworks that made up family ranches. The Medicine Bow and Thunder Basin. . . . Of course, things were different as well—after Fort Collins and Cheyenne, Trevor expected it—because as they drove in he saw the new subdivisions, a Pizza Hut and Taco Bell and Starbucks, the intractable expansion outward that all American settlements have, and have had. But when he drove down Richards and saw the Plains Trading Post—hotel, restaurant and gift shop—with its uneven bricks and totem pole porch-posts and the sign for the Powder River Bus Depot, he had to smile. And then on Sixth the Texaco station, the Key Bank of Douglas, the liquor store still a liquor store under a new name, and then Center Street—downtown—all the brown buildings as mundane and utilitarian as he remembered them, their flat pebbled roofs, only a few more than one story, the streets open and newly paved yet still a little suspect. There was a surprising amount of people and parked cars downtown, citizens out on the sidewalks, standing or moseying along in their boots and hats, jeans and cowboy shirts. Douglas an active western town in the bright morning sunlight.

What is that?

Bisma was pointing out his window as they passed the town square. She was pointing at the statue—seven feet of concrete and gray paint depicting a jackrabbit with four point antlers.

A jackalope, Trevor said, in Jackalope Square. Part antelope, part rabbit. They invented it here, in Douglas.

She turned her head, her body, to look at the statue as they passed.

Mythic, she said.

He took them past the heart of town, where there were fewer people in the streets though still plenty of parked cars.

Is this a real cow town?

It used to be, he told her. Cattle, then coal, then oil. It was a uranium town for a long time.

Uranium? So it has a glowing reputation?

Trevor ignored her.

Douglas does all right.

Perhaps. But it is so plain—other than the Jackalope.

Trevor saw something from the corner of his eye, looked down a side street, and then pointed it out to Bisma.

Someone's lost their ponies, he said.

Two yearlings—barebacked—were crossing the pavement. They looked like palominos to Trevor, with white manes and coats the color of goldenrod.

Oh. It's a two-horse town.

Trevor turned on Walnut Street, passing two boys with lariats in their hands. They were heading in the direction of the horses. He watched them in the rearview as the boys crossed the street.

He parked in the angled spaces under the trees in front of the Hotel LaBonte. The hotel was made of dark brick and sat far back from the sidewalk. It had three stories and narrow, untrue windows with brushed-metal frames. To the left, attached, was the LaBonte Café, and to the right was the windowless LaBonte Bar & Lounge. In the middle, recessed and with dark purple hawthorns against the somber brown brick, was the hotel's entrance with tall double doors.

We're staying here?

Yes, he said.

They got out of the truck, stood and stretched in the shade beneath the leaves. Travis got their luggage from the back and they headed up the walk.

My, the places you take me.

As they walked he saw her slip her hand into the pocket of his father's jacket and withdraw a hair tie. She stopped then to gather her hair and create a disordered ponytail. Trevor said nothing but he did not like her carrying things in the pockets. He didn't know why, exactly, just as he did not know why she was even with him. Why had allowed her to come, to stay with him, why she was present at this very moment? Not just that, but what was her own reasoning, exactly? . . . He did not know what she saw in him, what she wanted. There was little future in their companionship, cohabitation—their coincidence—or however one defined it. He did not think it would go on much longer.

They entered the double doors into a lobby of dark wood and little light. Drapes were pulled and the high ceiling trapped the heat, even though it was not even ten in the morning. A hushed lobby of black oak and mirrors, tiles, empty tables and sitting chairs along the sides, all semi-dilapidated, a single, fat fly searching for sunlight. It was a place of questionable quality but it was a place as Trevor remembered it.

The registration desk was further back, bookended by two narrow staircases. An old man behind the counter watched them approach and nodded when Trevor arrived, though his attention was with Bisma.

The hotel clerk had rooms ready but took a long time to do simple paperwork, take Trevor's cash up front and hand them a key. Bisma was amused but Trevor found a certain impatience rising within him, until he saw the room key which was an actual key made of brass with an oversized green handle. It was the same keys the hotel had used over twenty years ago, when Trevor had stayed at the LaBonte with Darcie.

Are you here for Jackalope Days? the man asked.

It's Jackalope Days, Trevor said aloud and not as a question. Which explained to him why there were so many parked cars and people downtown.

What is it, Bisma asked, a fiesta?

This got a coarse laugh out of the clerk.

There's a parade and music on the square. A circus in town. The rodeo was yesterday.

Without being asked, the man produced a paper map of Douglas. He used a pen to show the parade route and to circle the grounds along the North Platte where the circus was set up. Bisma appeared delighted and took the map. The old man was pleased.

They ascended the slender staircase on the left, its boards creaking, the steps restricted at the turn. They walked the empty hall of the third floor looking at the numbers.

The room itself looked out on the street. Trevor opened the curtains and saw his truck in the shade. He lit a cigarette and opened the window—there was no screen. There was no air conditioning. There was an old-fashioned metal radiator along the wall by the bathroom door.

Bisma lifted her suitcase onto the bed, opened it and began to put her things in the drawers of the wooden dresser. In the closet she hung a few items—the yellow dress, his father's jacket. Trevor recalled Cass doing the same with her things at hotels in Key West or Tampa or in Cedar Key.

Staying a while? he asked and then regretted saying it.

I'm tired of searching for things in the case. She didn't look at him. My clothes need some air. It's so dusty. She smelled herself, her arm. Dusty, dirty, horsey. This old hotel is like that. Everything. She held up her soft pouch of toiletries, her hairbrush. She had left a few folded clothes on the bed which she swept up in her free arm. I'll be in the loo, she said. She went to the bathroom and closed the door after her.

Trevor stayed by the window, smoking, looking at the street and the trees in the wind. Then he put the cigarette out and took off his hat, hung it on the chair and he tried to recall the last time he had been to the LaBonte, if he and Darcie had been in this very room.

He had been living at the ranch for the summer, doing chores, helping with the business of cattle—a family business, even if his father had tried to escape it by moving to Cheyenne. By buying a café. By drinking . . . That summer was when Ross was gone, off in Rapid City playing baseball and not taking Darcie with him. All in all, Trevor had been awed by Darcie: her fearlessness, her certainty that she could do as she pleased without consequence. He couldn't fathom her appetite. She would call him into town, to the LaBonte, sometimes the Plains, where she would inevitably be sitting at a table with a cigarette and a glass of whiskey waiting for him. Or on the ranch itself, where she lived in Ross' room, when Trevor was out doing chores by himself in the Bedtick or along Pearl Creek, in the canyon or even in the thickets of White Spring Sump, she would come find him and they would make love. But never at the house. Darcie was able to keep it secret, make Trevor keep it secret, their duplicity.

Darcie's overt sexuality, her physical needs and offerings, seemed so deep within her that Trevor saw it as a strength more than a flaw. Or he saw it as evidence of his own worth . . . But he had been so inexperienced, so lonely inside, that he didn't really understand it. Maybe he mistook that duplicity for love, the sex for proof of that love. Trevor was still unsure.

Some of it was competition—having sex with Darcie was competing with Ross. It was defeating Ross, even if it was a clandestine defeat. Ross the bully. His tormentor through childhood . . . And Thor—sex with Darcie defied Thor's cold code of manhood, the rough stoicism where negative emotions were valued and more likely to be expressed than their opposite, like joy . . . Joy—if it existed at all in their household—came only in hard work, maybe in whiskey and card games. If it came in sex, it was not talked about . . . Darcie was joy for Trevor. Darcie was intimacy, manhood, revenge, animal pleasure and love. In that life, there had been school and a few friends, family and cattle, and there was Darcie. There was a future, back then, but for him it too included Darcie . . . Yet now, back in Douglas, Trevor wondered how much of it—that vision of a future that included Darcie—how much of its overriding principle was based only on revenge, not love.

Bisma stood in the bathroom doorway and watched him while she brushed out her hair. Her face scrubbed, dressed in clean clothes, she felt much better. But

Trevor was pacing, thinking, unaware that she was watching, that she listened to his boots march on the wooden floor.

Is your brother as silent as you?

She didn't think he would answer her, or even quit pacing. She had observed him long enough now to believe that he was troubled, that he could shut himself down into himself like something collapsible, like an old spyglass. But he did stop suddenly and looked at her as if he had forgotten her presence.

No, he answered. My brother talked a lot—well, maybe not a lot—but he always had something to say.

Really?

She watched as he began to pace again, more slowly now, more deliberate or self-consciously.

Ross always had more friends, followers. He was popular and pretty much said what was on his mind. Not much of a filter . . . At least he used to be like that.

Bisma thought about it, was curious, and wanted Trevor to keep talking.

That would be bad, I'd think.

Trevor stopped and looked at her.

Bad?

I mean about no filter . . . I know I talk a lot, but it isn't what's always on my mind.

There was some humor in his eyes.

You don't believe me? She offered him a smile from the doorway. I'm always thinking, always making mental notes, analyzing this and that. That's how I work.

Stories?

Yes. Stories. Poems. I suppose that sounds barmy to you, but yes. I've published.

Where?

She felt a little defensive.

Small magazines. Literary ones. The Mississippi Review. Cut Bank. Others. Less than a handful, really.

Bisma was pleased that he had stopped pacing, that he had taken—finally— an interest in her. At one time she had liked talking about her writing, though not any longer. She didn't think it was a lack of confidence, but now talking somehow cheapened it, the writing. It made it not real. And also—in school, in the last workshop where everyone read her fiction—it had been miserable. Laughable. No one liked it, no one understood what she was doing, trying to do with that story. The professor had laughed. And, after all, it was only talk. They sat in a circle and talked. Talked and talked.

Who reads these reviews? Trevor asked.

Agents sometimes, depending on the review. They're small . . . No one, I suppose. No one looks at them except those who are published in them . . . I'm being bad about this. Of course people read them, just not a lot, but they count for something, somewhere. Down the road, perhaps.

Is that why you're here with me? he asked. For something to write about?

Bisma was surprised by his question. She took a moment to look at her brush, to run it through her hair where there was no resistance. She went to the bed and sat on it, set the brush on the nightstand there.

I could accuse you of self-aggrandizement, thinking I'm only here to write about you.

But she felt uncomfortable. She no longer liked his questions; did not want to talk about her writing. It was something she couldn't joke about. Her writing was something better, more important than herself. At least it used to be. And, no doubt, it was the driving principle that brought her here, to this town, this room, with him. But it was not so simple, not in the way he was thinking. She didn't even fully understand why. But writing . . . They had laughed at her, at school. There was ridicule. And this confused her and made her want to quit, quit both school and writing. And if she didn't have something better, if she no longer had the very thing that was more important than herself, what would she do?

I don't mean me, Trevor said. I'm asking about you.

I'm not here to find a subject. Really. Maybe subject matter, but it's not quite that either. He kept looking at her, waiting, listening. I just needed to change things.

A new venue. Lose some control or gain some. I can't answer it. I suppose I wanted to become lost for a while.

You're here with me because you want to be lost?

She picked the brush back up and played with it in her hands. She ran her fingers over the bristles then looked at the fingers. She looked across the room at his face, his unshaven face. His tight face and thin lips and strong jaw. There was something about that face, enough to it, that she had attached herself to it. Something about him as a man, some enigmatic gravity that had drawn her and continued to draw her. It was not purely a physical attraction, but she did want him to kiss her, to put his arms around her. Care for her. Like her writing, she wanted something more for herself than just herself. Maybe, she thought, thinking of Trevor, that it was the opposite. What she wanted was the opposite of being lost. But she could not bring herself to tell him that.

Yes, I suppose it is.

Lost?

Yes.

Collis Mudd stood outside Terminal Two at Denver International, waiting for the shuttle to take him to his rental car. While waiting, he unzipped his single bag and felt for the hard case in there. He had already checked it once before—to make sure it had not been confiscated or stolen by luggage handlers—so it was just a matter of reassurance. He had been questioned about the gun in the case, had had to show two forms of identification as well as his concealed weapon permit. He was used to extra scrutiny, depending on what part of the country he was in, or what part of a city. Small towns, too.

He thought about calling home, possibly talking to Todd—or Lakeesha—but he'd already texted them to let them know he'd landed. Normally, he did not text. There were many advances in communication that Collis had not cared to master.

He also thought of calling Cassandra Tipton, but decided he'd wait until he got to Fort Collins for that. Better to keep such calls, especially the early calls to your clients, at a minimum. Better to wait until you have information. No useless calls, he reminded himself.

They gave him a purple car. It was a midsized Dodge and it was, no denying it, purple. Collis felt a little cramped inside but he wanted to keep his costs low for Cassandra Tipton. He might have to spend more down the road, depending on what happened or how long this took. He did not get a GPS—had rarely used one—but did have a map and with that he navigated the boulevard to the E-470 and eventually onto Interstate 25 North.

Heading away from the city, he settled into the small confines of the Dodge. He cracked two windows and turned the air conditioning off. He left the radio off and listened only to the rush of dry Colorado air and traffic. He looked at the brown foothills to his left and the still-white peaks of the large mountains behind those foothills—which he had mistaken for clouds at first. He had never been to this part of the West. He'd been to southern California a few times, to Las Vegas and Phoenix, Seattle, Portland. Albuquerque once—where he'd found a teenage girl at the morgue . . . Most of his travels had been in the South and up along the Eastern Seaboard. But not the Midwest and not this West.

Collis thought that he should bring his family out this way. Todd at least, show him there was more to the world than Miami Beach, which was where his son was spending a lot of his time. Out with his friends to the clubs or, well, who knew where. Collis didn't now the details—Todd had said he didn't have enough money to get into any real trouble. But Collis knew that lack of money didn't always correlate to lack of trouble. People—especially young people—wanted things and they wanted them now. They wanted cars, apartments, clothing, electronics, special meals and special drinks—a lifestyle—that Collis never would have thought of having. He didn't think his own kids were that way, but then again, what did he really know?

So, to find out, bring Todd out this way. Camp and fish. Hike. Why not? Maybe James, too. But that wouldn't be fair to Lakeesha or Keena. Maybe he could afford to take them all—except Liv, of course. He could handle the four of them. Sure he could. They were good kids and, really, kids in general were good. People would turn out okay, on average, no matter what *he* thought about them.

He saw a billboard advertising Tom Terry's Buffalo Ranch—thought about that for a while—then a sign for Fort Collins.

Coming off the Interstate, he rolled down the windows of the rental as he headed into town. After a strip of franchise establishments, he took in the pines and wood-sided houses, the dark green grass, the dry air and rise of hills. He liked it. He liked not sweating in June . . . Collis turned down College, saw the Best Western across from the campus and pulled into its lot. He looked at himself in the rearview mirror before getting out.

In the small lobby, the male clerk eyed Collis carefully then asked if he needed help.

I have a reservation, Collis Mudd said.

The clerk inspected him again while bringing his name up on the computer and he asked for the verification number as well as identification when Collis produced his credit card.

Key card in pocket, he went to the car for his lone suitcase and then to Room 106 on the first floor. He set his suitcase on the bed. He took the Fort Collins and Vicinity phone book out of a drawer of the dresser, sat on the bed next to his suitcase, and leafed his way to the "K's" and saw that there were no Kallengaards listed. He'd already done this via computer, but it didn't hurt to double-check; sometimes the simplest ideas worked out. He had hoped for a relative. Maybe an ex-wife, though Cassandra Tipton said he'd never been married. And, true, the man had been very young when he lived here. But people could do a lot of things by the age of twenty or less, people make a lot of mistakes. And for a woman who had lived with the man for twelve years or so, there seemed to be quite a bit Miss Tipton didn't know about Kallengaard.

The next step would be to talk to the clerk. Show him a photo. But Collis figured, when and if he got the right clerk, the one who checked Trevor Kallengaard in or out, that clerk would not recall or would not want to say anything. Just by the way this clerk had checked him in, Collis could tell that the man wouldn't be helpful. He'd go to that western wear store and ask.

Collis was certain that Kallengaard wasn't in Fort Collins anymore, that Cheyenne would be the place to look. Still, there were things to attempt here. You started where you started—the last place you knew the man to be—and you try not to waste any moves. The man had driven only eighty miles after that phone call, so he'd made a deliberate stop in this town. Most likely at this very motel, as it was the only one within walking distance of the clothing store. Why stop at that particular store when there were others out along the highway, which was also where most of the hotels were?

Collis Mudd used the bathroom. Washed his face. Cleaned up a bit after the flight and drive, the change in time and landscapes. Then he sat on the bed again and took out his phone. He called Cassandra Tipton. She answered right away.

Miss Tipton.

Collis. Mr. Mudd—how are you?

I'm fine. I'm in Fort Collins. At the motel.

Oh.

No news yet. I just wanted you to know that I'm here and that I've started looking.

Yes. I appreciate it. You haven't . . .

I'm thinking he's not around here, but I've got to check. Try to get a bead on his motives, what he's thinking, if I can.

Good.

There was a moment of silence.

You okay, Miss Tipton?

Cass.

Cass, he said.

Yes. I'm okay. I took the day off work.

I'm thinking he's probably in Wyoming, since you said he was from there. In Cheyenne. He's gone home—as it is—for some reason.

I didn't really give you much to go on.

Well, if you think of anything else, let me know . . . You told me that he smokes but doesn't drink?

He's never drank but, yes, he smokes.

And he's never been in AA or any program like that?

No. Not that I know of and I have known him a long time. No.

Okay. It just helps me think who he is, some idea of who the man is . . . There can't be too many Kallengaards in Wyoming—there's not too many people in the whole state—so I'll see.

Collis Mudd had done a search for the name already, for Cheyenne, but it had turned up nothing, which surprised him.

Okay, she said. And you'll let me know?

You bet, Collis said and he thought of the day she had come to the house, of her smiling without knowing she was smiling. I'll stay in touch as much as you want. You've got my number, so you can call me.

I'd like that.

And check the credit card activity.

I will.

This may not take too long. A few days. A week. If I can't find him within a week, we'll talk it over, see how or if you want to proceed. Okay?

Yes.

Be optimistic, he told her and thought of her. I could see him coming back, you know, to someone like you.

Oh, she said and Collis wondered if he'd said the wrong thing. Mentally, he reprimanded himself. That's nice of you, Collis. Okay.

Right. Goodbye, Miss Tipton.

Collis Mudd stretched out on the motel bed. He tried to think only of Trevor Kallengaard.

Are we going to the ranch? Today, perhaps?

Trevor shook his head. He stood near the window. Bisma was on one of the beds.

You expect me to just sit here and wait around while you have all the fun?

Going to a ranch will be fun?

Of course. Just the sound of it: To the ranch . . . It has so much possibility. Earthy implications.

Trevor almost smiled at her, for her. He had no plans to go out on the land today and was satisfied just to be in Douglas. He did want to drive out to Glenrock— alone—and find his mother. He did not know what she would do when she saw him. Did not know what he might do seeing her again.

We'll go tomorrow, but I have to do something else first. In the morning by myself.

What? How long?

By myself. A few hours.

She gave him a long look, slyness in her eyes. Her mood had appeared downcast a while ago, but now there was a recrudescence of the extrovert.

Go on. Keep your little mystery tomorrow morning. But we will go to the ranch.

That's what I'm thinking.

And we go out today.

Out?

On the town. I want to see the parade. The circus. No doubt there'll be music. Jackalopes and all that.

She stood up quickly and came to him. He thought she would take his hands, touch him in some way, but she stopped short. Still, her nearness and gaze made him uncomfortable.

Okay, he said. But no circus.

Fine. Clowns are pissers. Bloody chained animals, too.

Outside the hotel, they could hear the notes of an organ, comical music emanating from the grounds down along the North Platte. They walked together towards downtown, in their shirtsleeves, Trevor in his hat.

It was very crowded on Center Street. Lots of young children sitting along the curbs, the young parents of those children, teens coming and going, older women and their men with their denim and boots and hats. Trevor and Bisma made their way just across from Jackalope Square, stood in the well-behaved crowd with only a partial view of the street.

The parade came with little fanfare—slow and simple, a man on a loudspeaker commenting from the square as the homemade floats went by, as tractors and other machines, done-up with colorful bunting, passed by, then crepe-covered wagons with little children, cowboys and cowgirls, dogs with bright bandanas trotting right along with all the rest. Horses. Shriner clowns. Streamers. It became noisy. Bisma said something to him but he could not hear it over the tractors and wagons and the announcer's bullhorn voice. He could only see the light in her eyes and so nodded his head, held his hat for a moment when the wind came and then, as he put his hand back down she grasped it. Clasped it. She didn't look at him but watched the parade and held his hand.

They ate a late lunch at a café that used to be a bank. They had sandwiches and then coffee and pie. Out the window, where the post-parade crowd milled, the sun shifted in a cloudless sky. After lunch they walked the streets for a while and then, at the square that held the concrete jackalope, they saw that a band was setting up. They saw that grey tents had been erected where beer and wine was being sold. There was orange plastic fencing to direct pedestrians. There were portable toilets. Someone was stringing lights.

A party, Bisma said.

Looks like it.

Come on then.

She again took his hand and pulled him towards the square where a crowd was beginning to form. But Trevor held his ground and told her he had no interest in festivities.

Oh, come along, Bisma said. You can't ignore it. A fiesta is important. It's ritual and plays a role for a healthy society.

Trevor shook his head.

This is your town and you're being a dreadful host.

The band started up in the square and Bisma looked back at Trevor and she put out her hand. She smiled and held her hand until he took it and they crossed the street to the square.

Cass told herself that she did not want to even think of Mava let alone talk to Mava, and certainly not go see her. Yet the idea of it, the urge to do it, would not leave her alone. It was a primal urge, she told herself, half-seriously, to see one's mother, even though her intellect told her it would only be detrimental. Mava would only add to the injury if Cass confided in her about Trevor. Once again she'd point out that Cass was only reaping what she had sown.

It would be the same slicing disapproval like when Cass dropped out of Auburn and went to stay in Mexico—way down south at Puerto Escondido—with three boys who wanted only to surf. Or like when she moved to New Orleans and moved in with Marcus—*shacked up with a black boy*, as her mother said. Even when she came to Fort Lauderdale after Marcus' death with another man in tow, Mava pointed out that Cass was still unmarried, still lacked a career. Yes, to tell Mava that Trevor had left would only serve to prove Mava's point, to further cement her disappointment in her only child. Yes, the last thing Cass needed was a yearning for her mother.

Yet there, inexplicably, it was.

She'd rather turn to the detective. Release all her worries and fears and heartbreak to Collis Mudd. He was, after all, the one out in Colorado, the one looking for Trevor Kallengaard. But even that was no doubt misguided. She didn't really know the man and was paying him. His concern was not out of comradeship or generosity of spirit, it was only a business transaction . . . She did not want to confide in Tina or the neighbors or Trevor's co-workers, like Miguel who had called twice. And certainly she didn't want to confide in Mava.

Did she?

Cass went into the kitchen to make tea. She put water in the kettle and put the kettle over the stove's blue-gas flame. And while she waited she felt the sudden presence of Marcus. No, she told herself, it was a sudden memory of Marcus. She did not believe in *presences*. Yet it wasn't an exact memory of him, just a sudden feeling of him, who he was, how much he had meant to her, how much she had loved him. She sometimes still wondered, if Marcus had not been killed, what her life would be like. There would be no Trevor. No Fort Lauderdale. No desire to see her estranged mother. She and Marcus would still be in New Orleans—or somewhere else, maybe—and they would be happy together. Satisfied.

She could never go back to New Orleans, just as she couldn't stay after the death. Marcus' dying, the way he had died, was what enabled Cass to settle for Fort Lauderdale and, she thinks now, settle for Trevor. She was no longer the girl who ran off to Mexico or who could get by in New Orleans.

Marcus. She thought of Marcus. Her lover. Friend. Confidant. Marcus was a musician, a handsome and charitable person. Funny. Smart . . . Marcus had been out late and Cass wasn't worried. He was often out late. But then, he did not come home. And it was Chad King who brought her the news. Marcus had been busking in the Quarter and, while riding his bike home past Frenchman, someone ran him over. Chad King said the police told him that Marcus had been run over twice. No money was found on him. His guitar was broken along with the bike, along with his body. No witnesses, no evidence beyond the obvious, nothing to go on and no one was ever caught. Just one more black man killed in the city.

The kettle sang and startled Cass. She removed it from the flame and turned the burner off.

Trevor could tell it was a local band, maybe not from Douglas but not likely from Casper either. The amps were too loud, the covers of country songs almost amateurish. But the crowd enjoyed it. People danced in Jackalope Square.

Bisma stood next to him, watching, listening, as the sun made its way towards the Laramie Mountains. Trevor was conscious of Bisma moving her head, then her arms and hips, conscious of when she turned to him.

I don't dance, he said before she could ask or further imply.

Buy me a pint then.

A can. Out here they drink from cans.

Purchase a can, then.

They joined a line at the beer tent. The line moved swiftly and soon they were near the tables with the galvanized tubs of ice holding Coors Lights and Rainiers.

What do you want, he asked and told her he was only buying one.

I have to drink alone?

Trevor looked around. There must have been a hundred people in the square. Doesn't look alone to me.

You've come all this way, you're back home and in the middle of a fiesta—with a very pretty woman, I should add—during Jackalope Days, I'll also add—and you won't have a single beer? . . . You said you weren't an alcoholic, or did I just imagine that?

Trevor wanted to tell Bisma that his father had been one, but he said nothing.

Trevor Kallengaard, she said, her face no longer holding an ironic or mocking expression, have a beer. Please. Life is not that difficult.

He didn't answer and she didn't look at him as they approached the table where Bisma stepped in front of him and ordered two Rainiers. She took them from the attendant and paid and carried both out of the tent and to the edge of the crowd where she held out a cold can to him.

The sun was low and someone had turned on the string of lights.

I insist, she said, still holding the beer outward. There's nothing dangerous about it.

She allowed the depth of her eyes to fall into his own. Something new was expressed within them—her eyes—a sincerity, a vulnerability, enough so that Trevor put out his hand and took the beer.

Trevor had not tasted a beer in some twenty years, but he popped the can open and took a tentative sip. It tasted of metal, of an almost-almond flavor, of grain, he supposed. Carbonation and foam. A taste he remembered, the very smell of it. Yet, it was not the taste of horror or shame, of death. If anything, it was the flavor of nostalgia, a cold beer on a warm Wyoming night ... And how could he explain this? Where was the self-discipline? The danger? Where was the punishment he so deserved? How could he ever explain it to Cass, who had almost begged him to have a beer or glass of wine with her? And now, back here, with a woman he barely knew ...

Come on, Bisma said matter-of-factly. Drink up. Don't be ridiculous.

By the time the sun had reached the Laramies, Trevor had finished a second beer. Bisma danced in place, giving him sidelong glances as the ragged country tunes began to smooth out in her ear. Such maudlin and saccharine songs, she thought, but they fit the time and place, the here and now. She asked him if he knew them and he told her the names of the songs. And by Trevor's third beer the mountains were but shadow, like a line of ripped construction paper lit from behind by alpenglow.

Bisma was very pleased that she had come to Wyoming.

The band came back from break and said it would be their final set. They started with a slow song, plenty of steel guitar, a song she found so ridiculous yet pleasing she tried once more to get him to dance. And he did. He took her in his arms and they entered the small clump of humanity in front of the stage, on the square, under the little lights, and they danced. He smelled of smoke and beer and reticence. Yet he danced and seemed to know the song.

Who is this singer? she asked, her lips close to his ear.

Marty Robbins, he told her.

Cass had given in and called her mother. Now she found herself driving down A1A at night, with the Atlantic on her left and the lit honeycomb of condominiums of Hallandale on her right. She crossed the county line into Golden Beach, where she slowed down because she remembered that the town was notorious for speeding tickets. And after that it was Sunny Isles, then Haulover, then over the little inlet drawbridge and into the enclave of Bal Harbour.

She tried to retain her objectivity, rationalizing to herself the need to see Mava, while at the same time not quite believing that she was actually doing it . The Bal Harbour road was clean and curving, overindulgent sprinklers already running in the median making its Augustine grass glisten. Palms all trimmed of any dead material.

I will not freak out, she told herself but noted her own terminology. *Freak out?* Those were words she used back in college, in Mexico, and she wondered if she was regressing, just because she was going to see Mava.

Cass had not explained to her mother the reason for this sudden visit, but knew Mava would extrapolate that something was wrong. And she thought of turning around, even as she drove to the condo tower's security gate and gave her name and who she was visiting—Mava Leeman in number 16--and parked where they allowed her to park, in a visitor's space for not more than two hours.

Cass entered the large, airy lobby and she pushed the button to bring an elevator down and then she rode the elevator up, up, up. Alone in the elevator, she could only think what a cliché it was, what a cliché her mother was: multiple marriages, multiplying wealth from those marriages, Cass the single child born out-of-wedlock before Mava came to understand the power of her own beauty. All of that: Mava Tipton out of Johnson City, Tennessee—where Cass had been born, then Mrs. Mava Loudermilk of Knoxville, Mrs. Concannon of Atlanta, until finally—or currently, Cass supposed—Mrs. Leeman. Now the "Widow Leeman", of Bal Harbour.

Cass exited the elevator with a sense of dread.

Her mother opened the door and invited Cass inside. They stood apart for a while, not really speaking, just a few words and Cass tried to think of the last time she had seen Mava. Maybe five years ago around Christmas, no, two years ago in Fort Lauderdale, she and Trevor had run into Mava on Las Olas. That was the last time. And they had talked on the phone maybe once this year, around Easter.

I'm sorry it's so late, Cass said.

You sound worried.

Cass only nodded and she looked again at her mother's face, its surgical tautness, the painted brows. Mava looked fastidious and imperious, yet also brittle.

I wanted to tell you, see you . . .

Something happened?

Behind Mava, across the great room of the condo, the glass walls revealed only the balcony and the endless dark ocean. An unlit sky.

Yes. It's Trevor . He . . . He's gone.

Gone? As in passed away or . . .

No, Mava—Cass had called her mother Mava ever since leaving Auburn University—he's not dead. He's gone away. To be blunt, he's left me.

I'm sorry, she said, her voice like paper. And you've heard from him?

He called once, days ago. He left a note but it was a shock . . . It's still a shock.

So he's disappeared . . . Did he take your money?—to be blunt.

No, he did not take my money. Our money.

Well, there's that then.

Yes, there's that.

Her mother looked offended without looking offended—an acquired trick Cass knew well enough.

I don't know why I came here, Cass said calmly. I just wanted to talk to you. And she couldn't explain further, hoped that her mother would do the talking.

You're hurt. Confused. Unhappy.

Yes. I am. All of that. And I want to find him.

Is that what you wanted to talk to me about? You don't know where he is?

No, he . . . Yeah, I suppose.

Cassandra, you do or you don't?

What?

You do or you don't want to talk to me about it? Or you want me to help you find him? Is that it? Or do you want me to tell you it will all be okay and that you'll meet someone else, as you always seem to do?

Her mother stood stiffly. Her mother like a spider at home in her web.

I'm not sure what you mean.

Cassandra, he'll come back if there's an incentive for him to come back. Or you'll find another man. It's simple. Mava loosened her stance. There was something conspiratorial in her voice. You always get through these things.

These things? What things?

These crises. Your choices in life. But you've managed along through your mistakes.

At first Cass thought that it was sympathy Mava offered. Then she understood that it was criticism. A dig.

Look, Cass said, I thought maybe I could talk to you. I guess I thought I needed something from you, some consolation. My mistake.

There's no need for hostility. If you need financial . . .

I'm not being hostile, Cass said. I was wrong. Her voice began to rise. I don't need a thing from you, Mava. If anything, it was good I came by to remind myself of that.

Her mother did not flinch. She did not reply. There was only a slight play of amusement, or disgust, around her lips.

It's okay, Mother. Mom. Mommy. It's all right. Now we both know.

And Cass turned around and let herself out and rode the elevator back down to the lobby.

She drove carefully and purposefully back to Broward County and to Fort Lauderdale. She was done with Mava. And now that she was done with her, Cass could no longer blame the woman for being a cliché, for moving from man to man and place to place and putting herself first. She couldn't blame Mava for her own insecurities or for the death of Marcus or for her own move to Florida or Trevor.

There is only me and I am alone and there is no one to blame for it. There is no one to judge me or take anything from me or to expect anything from me.

It was sad and good at the same time. She could do anything, really. Anything she wanted. And that meant, when Collis Mudd found Trevor Kallengaard, she could sure as hell fly out to Wyoming.

Yes, she could do that.

They walked back in the dark and as they neared the hotel, Bisma spied the colored lights of the lounge and she wanted to go in. Trevor let her lead him along the darkling path to the lights and the entrance of the LaBonte Lounge.

Inside it was half-full of patrons, there was amber light, noise, smoke, a jukebox playing country music. The wood-paneled, windowless room trapped everything within it.

Trevor and Bisma took stools along the bar and ordered bottles of Rainier. Trevor felt fine, not drunk, not euphoric or despondent, just fine. They sat and drank, Bisma peeling the red and white beer label with her long nails, her face bright, eyes happy.

How about a vodka, she said.

No.

Yes. Cold cold vodka.

You told me you didn't drink hard liquor.

One night is okay. It's clean, clear, made from potatoes and all that.

The woman bartender, who was attendant without seeming so, brought out a bottle from a freezer. Absolut. She poured two clean thumbfulls into scratched shot glasses.

Trevor didn't touch his but Bisma picked hers up quickly and washed it down her throat.

Santé', she said and waited for him.

Skoal.

Trevor drank the vodka, feeling a rush in his head. He lit a cigarette quickly.

Let me have one, she said.

A cigarette?

Yes.

You don't smoke.

And you don't drink.

Trevor looked at his beer, the empty shot glass in front of him, and she smiled.

It's a vile and filthy habit, but it's not as though I've never had one.

She did not reach for the pack, which sat on the counter by his elbow. She waited for him to shake it out and hand it to her. She waited for him to light it.

He watched her draw the smoke in, saw her expel it a little roughly, a small cough, but under control. She did it one more time, the smoke exhaling from her nose and throat and rising up to comingle with the haze that already hung along the low ceiling of the lounge. Then she held the cigarette aloft and studied it.

Yes, vile and filthy, like snogging and rogering. Bisma smiled. All so very filthy.

It was late when they returned to the room. There was only a single light on, in the corner, giving the plaster was a sorrel color. Trevor was sweating at the base of his neck, his temples, the pits of his shirt were wet. He placed his hat on the dresser and went to the window and opened it, allowing a dry breeze to enter the warm room. He turned and saw Bisma, who still stood by the door, who had removed her shoes and socks. She was looking at him.

I'm hungry.

The café is closed by now.

No. Not that.

She walked to him and took his hand, placed her other hand on his neck, brushing the damp hair at the back. Then she let go and undid the top buttons of his shirt, ran a hand inside along his collarbone. Trevor didn't stop her. Instead, he kissed her. He kissed her again and felt as though he could not get enough of her lips.

They stood by the window, pressed together in the sallow light of the room. She ran her hands along his back and buttocks. In her mouth he could taste the beer, the cigarette, a saltiness. Her skin smelled like walnuts. Then she was undoing his belt, his fly, Trevor now hard against the pressure of her palm and without wholly separating they made their way to the bed, removing clothes before they lay upon it.

Trevor could not detach himself from the physical pleasure. They were on top of the bed, on the beaded spread with Bisma beneath him, the smooth plumpness of her, the smolder of her skin, hard breaths, the rhythmic grunting and unencumbered movement, the night air of Douglas coming through the window.

He woke hours before morning light. His head numb and stomach uneasy. Bisma was aligned with him in the bed, leg and arm, breast against his rib. He slid out from the covers and stood for a moment in the dark, then made his way to the bathroom.

Closing the door behind him, he turned on the too-bright light. Urinated and washed his hands. Washed his face. Catching his visage in the mirror, Trevor held it and felt a guilt rise inside him. Trevor thought of Bisma and tried to trace where the guilt came from . . . and he thought of Cass.

Why feel guilty about Cass? he wondered. Hadn't he left her, with no plans to see her again? Yet, the sense of betrayal was within him. He told himself that he would not allow it. Betrayal, guilt, regret. It was only a momentary, residual emotion. And, even if it wasn't, it was too late to do anything about it.

SIX

The Ranch

In the LaBonte café, Trevor ate breakfast alone at the counter. The sun had not been up for long.. He lingered there, smoking a cigarette and reading the Douglas Budget, delaying the walk to the truck and the drive to Glenrock.

Bisma had only briefly acknowledged him when he woke her to say he was leaving the room. She only said okay and did not ask to go, as he thought she might. As, he realized, on some level, he wished she might. She only burrowed under the covers. The window had been left open and, though he had closed it first thing, the room was still cold. So he'd taken his hat and wallet and cigarettes and gone to the café.

Cigarette out, he made himself rise from the stool at the counter, leave a tip, pay at the register, and go outside into the dissipating coolness. Another blank, brown day. His Silverado under the trees. He drove Brownfield Road, heading towards the river where he saw that the travelling circus packing up. They had mural-painted trucks and busses, their rides now moribund, folded and disassembled, looking like great insects on trailers. The grass along the river was flattened in the shapes of their tents. Then he crossed the North Platte—water slow and shallow—and saw that the city of Douglas now continued across its banks.

He left Douglas, taking I-25 towards Casper.

And from the highway he saw Table Mountain—a plateau—somber and russet-colored against the early sky. He slowed and brought his window down a few inches, the air like cornstarch as it rushed in, lit another cigarette and looked out at the kneaded, treeless landscape, the grasses beginning to turn brown already. And Trevor knew what lay beyond the highway, he knew where LaBonte Creek flowed, where Bedtick Creek and Wagonhound, Buckshot ran; he knew Cold Spring Road and Spring Canyon Road, the Chalk Buttes and Laramie Mountains, and that, further in, was Pearl Creek. The Pearl, which ran through the Kallengaard property, eventually tumbled downward, having cut its way through soil and sandstone to carve the canyon, and to create the natural bridge there. Wi-Sake was the bridge's Lakota name, if Trevor remembered correctly, and it had been called Sawyer's Bridge at one time. Thor had always referred to it, simply, as the rock. Or his rock. Nothing more than that.

But the canyon, the bridge, the alluvial land along the Pearl, was what Trevor wanted for himself. It was where his grandfather had first built a structure, the homestead cabin. Trevor reminded himself that that parcel of land was why he was here. Nothing else accounted for his presence. Though right now, he needed to drive to Glenrock to see his mother.

Glenrock had a Wal-Mart and a Hardees and more of the same. It appeared the town was now an appendage of Casper, and Trevor imagined that Casper was maybe a city he didn't want to see. He took Drumin through downtown, to where he knew the county hospital was, then passed it, found himself out among newly paved roads where there was a nursing school. Assuming it would be nearby and be the only one, he looked for the nursing home. And he saw a sign for Glenrock Care Center.

It was a newer brick building, single story, with wings. Its large parking lot was divided by grass medians where young planted trees threw small, hopeless shadows on the dry grass below them. Trevor parked in the lot and got out. Behind him, a lawn mower started up and he turned to see someone cutting the grass, though it looked more like he was only mowing dust.

Trevor removed his hat and held it in his left hand as he entered the building.

Inside was a short hall that opened into a wide day room then a reception desk straight ahead, where two women dressed in white sat. Walls were egg white, the floor tiles bright white with grey grouting. He was conscious of the click of his boots as he walked to the desk. A group of residents were playing cards in the day room.

He held his hat against himself and stood a foot from the counter. One of the women behind the counter sat with her back to him, entering information into a computer. The woman in front looked up and asked if she could help him.

Yes, he said. I'm here to see Mrs. Kallengaard, please. Anna Kallengaard.

Anna? She looked at him for a while, then looked at a chart or list that he couldn't see. May I ask who you are?

He cleared his throat, shifted the hat in his fingers.

I'm her son, he said.

She looked at him anew, closer. The other woman didn't turn around but he could tell she was listening.

I'm sorry, but you're not her son. I know who Anna's son is.

I'm Trevor, he told her. Trevor Kallengaard.

No, the woman told him and did not smile. It's . . .

Ross, he said.

The woman sat back in her chair and the other one now turned to regard him.

But I'm Trevor. Her other son.

The nurse, or administrator, looked at him blankly, then turned again to the unseen list or chart, some fount of information on her desk. The other woman stood up and went to a file cabinet while Trevor took out his wallet and produced his Florida drivers license. The first woman took that, then swiveled in her chair to look at the other woman who held a file. They had a small conference of whispers. The second woman took his license and came to the counter to address him.

You want to visit with Mrs. Kallengaard?

My mother, yes.

This woman was short, round, she had curly hair, glasses. She came out from the station and stood next to Trevor. She handed his license back to him and he put it in his wallet.

Anna is in her room—she has her own room. She finished breakfast and has an appointment with the beautician in an hour. You can follow me.

Trevor cleared his throat again and said, Thank you. He held the hat away from him as he followed her past the commons and down a wing with doors to individual rooms. There were people in the rooms, many with oxygen, some in wheelchairs. Only a few were in the hall and they did not look at him. The woman stopped at a closed door—number 122—which she didn't open.

Mr. Kallengaard, the woman said, do you know about your mother's affliction?

She has Alzheimer's . . .

She won't recognize you.

Trevor only gave the slightest of nods.

The woman knocked lightly and then opened the door without waiting for a reply. She stepped in and Trevor followed. The room was small, dark save for the flash of a television and the squint of sunlight against closed blinds. The nurse switched on a wall light. There was an old woman in the room, rigid in a chair, her attention on the television—a game show.

Anna, you have a visitor. The nurse switched on a table lamp near the window. Anna, it's Trevor Kallengaard.

The old woman in the chair looked up at the nurse but not at Trevor.

Oh. Thank you, she said.

The woman—the nurse—turned to him and reminded him that she had a hair appointment and that he should stop at the desk on his way out. Trevor nodded and saw the woman hesitate.

When you see Ross, she said almost intimately, tell him Helen says hello. Tell him to stop in.

Trevor didn't answer her but met her eyes, then stepped aside so that she could leave. She did not close the door behind her.

Trevor turned off the television and took two steps toward the old woman's chair. He placed his hat on the table where the lamp was and remained standing. He looked at her. He had not recognized her or her voice but knew, at the same time, that it was her. He looked around the room, taking in the small closet, the bathroom, the single bed with its white covers pulled crisply around the mattress, the hump of pillow. There was a dresser with a mirror, a brush on the dresser top and a hairband with blue and yellow flowers—Scandinavian. There was a single painting of a garden on one wall, a wooden crucifix with a wooden Jesus, face averted and downcast, above the bed. He looked back and the woman was looking at him.

He looked back at the woman who was his mother, a woman thin and boney, face sallow, wrinkled. She wore a light blue blouse and navy skirt. No jewelry, not even a wedding band. Her eyes were very blue. And it took him a moment to place the features with how he remembered her. To account for the mark of time and hardship. Her thin lips twitched slightly and she looked straight at him and Trevor's heart beat heavily in his chest. He had to clasp his hands together to keep them still.

Mother, it's Trevor.

She shifted in her chair and smiled. Her eyes did not appear vacant but they did not register anything particular either.

I'm Anna.

She put out her hand.

He looked at the hand, veined and weathered, spotted, spidery, and he took it. Held it. Felt a tremble but realized it was his hand, so he held it harder and then squatted down in front of his mother. She let him hold her hand.

Mother . . . He did not know what to say . . . It's Trevor. Your son. I've come back to see you.

She appeared confused then and pulled her hand, which he let go. She made to stand, placing her hands firmly on the chair's arms so that she could rise. Trevor stood and stepped back. She made it up and smoothed her skirt and walked to the dresser. Trevor watched her.

I don't get many visitors. She picked up the hairband. Do you like this?

Yes. I like it.

She set it back down next to the brush.

Mother . . . Does Ross come to see you? Gus and Frida? Do you know them?

He watched to see if the names could light her blue eyes.

No. No one comes to see me. The nurses. Mr. Hammer comes.

She smiled and looked at the bed so that Trevor looked at it too.

The ranch. The Kallengaard Ranch—Ross lives there. I've come back to see it, to build on house, a cabin, in the canyon. Pearl Creek. The bridge . . . I'll live there, not that far from you .

The words meant nothing, yet Trevor wanted to tell her more. He wanted to confess, to explain his years away from her, to ask her for forgiveness—forgive his absence, forgive his killing of her husband. He wanted to tell her that he loved her but could not bring himself to say it.

It's been so long, I'd like to tell you about everything if you want to hear it.

But she turned her back on him and opened the top drawer of the dresser, took something out. She kept it clasped in her hand and came over to him and allowed him to see what she held: two wood screws, both black, one larger than the other. She pointed to the smaller screw.

I don't know if this is a number six or a number three. But this other one is a number eight. You can't have a number eight. You need a number six.

She stared at her cupped hand holding the wood screws.

Trevor nodded and closed her hand with his own. He led her back to the chair, where she sat down. He let go of her hand and she placed both of them in her lap, still grasping the wood screws. He leaned down and kissed her on the forehead, then lightly on the lips though she did not acknowledge it. He straightened himself and took his hat from the table. He turned off the table lamp and turned the television back on. He said goodbye and left the wall light on, only looking back once at his mother in the chair before closing the door.

He walked back along the wing of the nursing home, his boots on the polished white tiles. Everything in his vision appeared stark and fine-edged and of little importance. He glanced at the two nurses at the desk and they looked at him but he didn't go to them. He went out the front doors and put on his hat. He could hear the mower still going with its plume of dust. He went to his truck and got in the cab, closing the door tightly, opening the window and fumbling for a cigarette which he didn't light. He got the window back up then pushed at his eyes with the balls of his fist before bending his head and weeping.

Collis Mudd rose early. Had breakfast. Came back to the motel and asked the clerk in the lobby—a young man, not the one who had checked him in—about Kallengaard. Collis used the full name but did not show him Trevor's photo—he didn't want to turn it into a *wanted man* situation. Instead he simply told the clerk they were friends but he'd shown up later than expected and asked the clerk if Trevor had left any information as to his plans. The clerk found Trevor Kallengaard's name among registrations but only said he was no longer a guest.

You can't call him? the clerk asked.

No. He doesn't carry a cell phone.

That's weird.

Collis nodded.

Back in the room he made a few notes in his case log. He took out the photograph of Kallengaard and held it by the big window of the room. The window looked out at the university across the street and at the mountains rising above it. Collis had chosen this motel because it was the only one close to where they last placed Kallengaard—at the western wear store. And Kallengaard had chosen this motel because? Because it's across the street from the university.

Cassandra Tipton didn't know if he'd gone to college, but even if he worked a trade in Fort Lauderdale, it didn't mean he hadn't. And if he had gone to this one, to Colorado State, they would have a record of a Trevor Kallengaard. And they would have some kind of home address.

Okay, Mr. Kallengaard, Collis said to the photograph. Let's see how you did in school.

Bisma was still in bed when he returned to the room. He stood over her, his hat on, his boots, and he looked at her before reaching down and pulling back the covers, revealing her nude body. He touched her then with his right hand—the skin of her hip, her back, the flesh of her breast. She opened her eyes, rolled over, confused.

I supposed you think I'm lazy.

She didn't ask him to remove his hand and he kneeled down beside the bed.

What's the matter, cowboy?

She smiled but he didn't return it. Then she gripped his arm and pulled him closer.

What is it?

He moved on top of her, his clothed body on her unclothed one, his hat falling to the floor as he kissed her lips, her neck, her breasts. Then he moved to her ribs and naval and down, smothering himself in her, Bisma with her hands on his head.

She sat up enough to pull him up, his face back to hers and then it was not long before she opened the fly of his jeans, his shorts and then he was on her roughly, almost frantic in his quickness.

Trevor, she said.

They were next to each other on the bed. He felt very tired. Damp with sweat, his neck drying, her skin hot where they touched. Bisma sighed, she hummed deep in her throat then stopped. He saw her close her eyes.

That was very nice, she said. And last night as well.

I'll be right back.

He got up and headed for the bathroom.

Start a shower for me, will you? she called.

With the door closed tight, he unbuttoned his shirt to cool down. He washed his face and looked at himself in the mirror, contemplating his actions. Sex. Lovemaking. The sudden need for it after returning from Glenrock . . . He did not understand himself . . . Trevor thought of Cass again, thinking he should call her, that he wanted to hear her voice, that he wanted what was familiar and what had belonged to him. But he did not trust this urge and told himself it was a weakness, a momentary wish, and that it would disappear.

It was best that his mother did not remember him, Trevor assured himself. He almost envied that—to remember nothing for long, each day new and empty . . . No, that was an ignorant, self-pitying idea. He wished such a disease on no one . . . All that was really left of the Kallengaards, now, was his brother and himself. A brother, Trevor was sure, who would not be pleased to see him. But Trevor didn't care if they saw each other. Ross would have the majority of the land and he would have his small piece. Trevor was going to see the property today, with Bisma. Ross wouldn't even know they were there.

Bisma rapped once on the door and then opened it. He was standing by the sink, his shirt unbuttoned. She stepped into the little room, naked, and sat on the toilet. Urinated. She wondered if such informality, this invasion of his space, bothered him. She hoped it did—it was amusing in a way.

Are we going to the ranch?

The canyon.

What canyon? I thought . . .

It's on the ranch.

Let's shower and eat first. Do you want to shower with me or without?

He didn't answer and she looked at him, could tell that he had closed up again, that he was somewhere within himself. But she expected as much and would not let it concern her or change her disposition. The day would go forward.

It will be a good day, she told him.

They rode together in the truck down Old Yellowstone Road past the park and fairgrounds and over the North Platte. Trevor turned onto Sunflower Road, narrow and roughly paved, with the wrinkled humps of the Chalk Buttes visible to the south.

Will we see your brother?

I don't plan on it.

Trevor knew they would pass the ranch house. There was a longer route, from the Bedtick property, that avoided the house, but he'd have to ford Buckshot Creek, drive over open tableland, before meeting the road to the canyon. Anyway, he wanted to see the house, drive the familiar route, see the sheds and pastures, the piney hill behind where the graves of his people were. Then he could go off road, visit the sump and follow the Pearl's narrow floodplain to the rise, before connecting with the dirt trail that curled down into the canyon.

Does this brother—Ross—have a position? A job? Or is he an unemployed cowboy as well?

I'm not sure . . . Trevor recalled what Lane Waters had said about no cattle. He looked over to see Bisma, her head turned as she watched the treeless countryside out the window. Wind rasped against the pickup's cabin, through his half-open window, and he had a sudden sense of pity or misplaced sorrow for her, Bisma Patel, that he couldn't place the reason for . . . I suppose he works for himself, Trevor told her, as a rancher. He used to be a rancher but really, I don't know. It's been a long time.

Why?

Why what?

Why has it been so long? Why don't you know about your own brother?

I can't answer that.

She nodded, then said, You don't want to answer.

He turned on Cold Spring Road, the faded asphalt of it weaving between high pasture and wire fencing. There were no other vehicles in sight.

He looked for the Oregon Trail marker he knew to be along Cold Spring. There were places on the Kallengaard land where the ruts of pioneer wagon wheels were still visible, though his grandfather, Thor, had been unimpressed, saying that ruts were only ruts. Trevor spied the rose-colored granite head of the marker above the grasses and pointed it out to Bisma. She smiled. He smiled also, because he knew they were passing family property now.

Two more miles down and he saw the nameless gravel road that came to a T with Cold Spring, a drive that rose to a bunch in the land, a buckle of earth that hid the house from the main road.

Up there, that leads to the ranch.

Bisma looked forward as he slowed and turned onto the gravel.

More rocks, she said.

But the gravel petered out, leaving a road of dry red earth with many washboards. The shuddering truck threw up plumes of florid dust, dust that came in the windows and gathered on the dash.

It's like Mars.

Trevor shrugged as she put her window up against the filtered soil. He kept the truck in the center of the lane, a few stray rocks pinging against the undercarriage. The fence along the road was in disrepair, poles at angles, wire sagging, tumbleweeds gathered in low spots. Old boots were stuck on some poles, soles skyward. Old boots were usually a message board to save someone a long drive to the house: if the toe pointed in—someone was home; pointed out—they were also. But there were too many boots here, as if they were reminders to fix the fence, or there only as markers for confusion.

Up ahead Table Mountain came into closer view, its flat plateau cut cleanly against the sky. Below it was the rumpled land, the long, almost invisible indentation of Pearl Creek, and somewhere the small mark of a house and its outbuildings.

Is this the ranch?

We've been driving past it for the last few miles.

How big is it?

It's under three thousand acres, most of it dryland grass.

Trevor tried to remember, he knew Thor had to keep his holdings small enough for him and his father, then he and Ross, to work it. Thor wouldn't hire any hands on a permanent basis. It had become more difficult after Trevor had started college, and after his father, Trig, had moved to Cheyenne. He knew that Thor, under the Homestead Act, had homesteaded four hundred and sixty acres as a young man, that Thor had come down from the silver mines of Butte, Montana, maybe as a teen. Trevor had seen the homestead deed, signed by President Harding.

Most of the property is here, connected, but there's another parcel on the other side of that mountain.

What mountain?

Trevor pointed to Table.

That's not a mountain, it's a mesa.

We call it a mountain.

She rolled her eyes.

It does sound like a lot of land, she said, even when you don't have the proper geographical names for it.

It's not that big—just a family ranch. The land doesn't give you much, especially by August.

Give much what?

Sustenance. For cattle. For crops . . . People.

Specifically?

Lack of water, mainly. Low spots are okay for haying, but not if there's a snowless winter or a dry spring. We never irrigated like they do now—my grandfather was a dry rancher. He'd pay for hay in a bad year. This was some of the last free land for homesteaders and there was a reason for it. Not many who tried stuck it out.

Ah, but your grandfather did.

Yes, he did.

And you didn't.

He felt her eyes on him but didn't look, said nothing.

Trevor could see the stand of cottonwoods now, the hill of Jack Pines that his grandfather had planted. He knew that the road would curve, revealing the house and barn and shed. He knew Little Lope Wash—which curled behind the house, probably already dry by now—would come into view, dividing First Pasture from the hill. And the road did curve and the physical world held true to his memories of it: the house and outbuildings, the hill and wash and trees.

Trevor studied it very closely from the distance, then as they drew closer, he didn't look at it anymore.

Bisma looked at the house, then at him.

Is that it?

He nodded but only watched the road. She honored his silence and turned again to look at the house and tried to place him there, as if the image would reveal something about him to her. But she wondered if she really wanted to know more about him, considering that more knowledge could ruin what she already felt, what she already assumed she knew of his character. The affair between them was something that felt fragile, clandestine—though she wasn't certain why—and unshaped. Any further discovery—or final discovery—about him could be its undoing. A loss of friction or more friction between them would end it, perhaps badly or, more likely, with a puff of nothingness. And Bisma was not ready for it to end, she would hold back because she was enjoying herself. The relationship could meander, as far as she was concerned.

She looked again at the house: from the dirt road there was a gravel drive that splayed downward to a low table of land with a yard of burnt grass and weeds and spots of bare earth. The house was old and yellowed, a worn coat of brown paint. Single story. Roof low. Its front facing the south with one big window to catch the sun. Bisma took note of all of this. There were two gnarled trees in the yard that looked like apple, but she saw no blossoms or apples in the branches. There were tall trees behind the house and then a hill with pines. There was abandoned machinery and trash near an old shed, and what looked like a barn nearby. There was a single brown pickup parked in the gravel near the front door.

It was not what she had imagined.

She had pictured a larger home, something made of logs and glass among the hills—like those she had seen in Colorado. But this was a derelict home with a poverty of form and character. She could not imagine Trevor living there, ever.

And as the dirt road curved and the truck curved with it, more of the house was exposed, more weather-damaged siding, great gobs of weeds growing around a broken wagon and a motorcycle on its side. Here was a clear view of a large metal shed, a smaller wooden shed, the barn with its wood thin as paper and a broken-fenced corral. A rusted livestock tank. Then after that was only open pasture, a streambed with a copse of leafy trees, the rise of land to a hill of skinny pines. Dirt and more dirt and dust, dust, dust.

She gave another look at the house and at the dark brown pickup—a truck beaten down like the house, colored like the land, worn and used without the beatified beauty she often saw in old things. It was only an ugly truck with a shovel sticking straight up—like a hard metal flag—from one of the holes in the bed's sideboard.

She turned to Trevor to see his reaction, but he was still not looking—at least she could not catch him even stealing a glance. He sped up, the road descending a little towards a narrow wooden bridge and a wash before it rose again into more brown emptiness. And she gave a last look behind them, craning her neck to see out the dusty back window, placing a hand on Trevor's shoulder to do so, and this time she saw a man, or thought she saw one, a large man facing in their direction, but then just as quickly her view was cut off by the stand of cottonwoods. She was uncertain about the image, thinking it was perhaps only her imagination at play. Then, after the bridge and the dry wash, Trevor turned off onto a rutted path—west, she knew, because it faced the pale and distant mountains—a path until it became only a slender trail of tire marks. Then it was nothing, only open country of clumping grass, sagebrush and diminutive prickly pear.

Bisma did not know if she should mention her vision. If she had indeed seen his brother. She promised herself, then she would ask him nothing, would not break his silence. She thought that she too could be silent—so would leave it alone. All was well enough as it was.

But as they passed through the monotonous scenery, with the truck jouncing and the dust filtering in and out, collecting and drifting and being replaced with more dust, she found it difficult to remain silent. Not in this barren land.

Who was your grandmother? You act as if you had no one but your grandfather. Your brother.

She was from Sweden.

Did you know her?

No. My grandfather went back, to Jutland, for a wife, and brought her back here, after he owned the homestead.

Just like that? He went back for a wife?

Yes. Like that. Ingrid. She died long before I was born, not long after my father was born. I was told it was tuberculosis. No one said much about her.

He never remarried.

My grandfather? No.

And your mother's parents?

My mother was from Chicago. Swedish, mostly, as far as I know. She was an influenza orphan and came out west as a teen.

Trevor wasn't looking at her, he kept the truck pointed on a path, in a direction, that made no sense to her. Bisma told herself to shut up, that that was enough questioning. She asked herself why she should care about his mother or father or any relation, yet she did. Her curiosity would not let her alone and she decided to ask one more thing.

And your mother and father—they've both passed on, I take it?

Yes, Trevor said. They're all dead now.

Trevor was aware of her silence, of her boredom. There's something up here you might like, he told her and watched as her head came up, her eyes lit upon the repetitive landscape.

They began to descend along a rough slope where rocks were exposed. Then there was a bluff—bare on top—where lemon-green willows grew in a semicircle along its base.

This is the homestead?

No. Not this. It's a sump. It has water, though it's not much good. Alkaline.

He slowed the truck, then stopped along the vegetation. Bisma lowered her window. There was no dust here. Scrub junipers grew on the bluff's face, there were dragonflies and redwing blackbirds. It was hot and it smelled like eggs.

Like the canyon, it was a spot Trevor had come to when he was a boy. Thor had kept a lot of the brush clear so that cattle could reach the water. It was later, when Trevor was in college, that he told his grandfather that clearing the vegetation every year had ruined the water, that the willows and reeds cleansed it, which was why the cattle would not drink it. But Thor said it was not true, even the next year when it was blatantly obvious, he said it was not true.

Trevor could see that the sump had not been cleared in many years.

I don't see any water. Bisma was disappointed in this place, as she had been with the house, with the monotony of hill and rock and sky. She didn't hold out much hope for the homestead. But the bluff is nice, she conceded, for Trevor's sake.

They left the sump, the land rising to open country hemmed in the distance by Table Mountain and the Medicine Bow. There was no road or path or trail. No fence line.

Are we lost?

Trevor was smoking.

I don't know—are you?

I mean out here. Do you know where we are.

Yes.

Bullocks. You don't know what you're doing.

They connected with a dirt road, a road narrow and rutted with vegetation in its center. A barbed wire fence ran raggedly alongside it.

It's up here.

Is it?

The homestead. Where I'm going to live.

She looked ahead but could see no difference in the land, no mark of distinction as to why it had been chosen, why Trevor would value it beyond anything else in sight.

The sump had more character, she told him.

Trevor said nothing as they came to a deviation in the land, a small ravine that soon widened, the road following it, then the road descending. The land swallowed the road with a twist, then another, a sudden steep curvature and Bisma held fast to the open window as the truck went downward into the earth's furrow, a hillside of scrub on one side and a long drop to the ravine on the other.

This is better . . . Not that it's like the Poudre, but it's a surprise.

The truck followed the switchbacks, almost circling downward, until they were on a wide hollow of bottomland that stretched a hundred yards or more, all of it contained within water-carved walls of sandstone—walls striated orange and rose and brown.

The canyon floor was flat and green-grassed, many large cottonwoods grew there, the tall grass spattered with their shade. Trevor parked beneath the trees, whose branches and leaves moved with the wind. There was a stream cutting along the far side, water shallow and clean, running strong along a pebbled bottom. Then Bisma's eyes took it in, saw that the water flowed through a stone almost the size of a city building. Trees and sage grew along its summit, but the stone's inside was an arch, a large tunnel of limestone—tall and wide—mottled grey and cream and sooty black. Many fleet-winged swallows flew and dove and nested on the rock's underside, above the rippled creek that ran straight through.

Trevor saw her look, saw her wonder and was pleased.

That's the rock, he said.

It's an arch.

A natural bridge, he told her. It goes from one side to the other.

He turned off the ignition, opened the door. They both came out of the truck and stood in the wind. There was the smell of the trees and grass, of water. The cottonwoods, seeding, let loose wads of fluff with each burst of wind so that it looked like snow.

People along the Oregon Trail stopped here, once it was found.

What's it named?

Nothing, Trevor told her. My grandfather referred to it as the rock.

It's a natural bridge, not a rock.

He only saw a rock, I guess. He wasn't sentimental about anything.

But he homesteaded here.

Because of the water and it provided protection for cattle. Plenty of grass, plenty to drink.

So, not because it was beautiful?

I doubt it. He didn't see things as pretty, just as functional. As owned or not owned.

She looked at him and then at the bridge with the creek running through its center—an eye of stone and water and birds. She turned and took in the cottonwoods, their snow of seeds, the grass and sage and stunted cedars, juniper, the tall smooth walls that looked hand-painted, that narrowed to almost a crevice where the water was held up, backed up into a pool. It was almost surreal. An unexpected dream. When she turned back to him he was walking away from her, towards the creek and bridge.

She watched him, recognizing the sober posture and stride. He went to the creek's edge, where a gravel bar angled out into its shallow running. She thought maybe he would walk into the water, but he turned along the bank, trailed it to where willows grew along the left base of the natural bridge. Trevor was small against the backdrop and he entered the rock's shadow where swallows flitting and jumped in sunlight and shade, eating unseen insects. She saw him touch his palm to the limestone.

Eventually he came back into the sunlight and away from the water and rock. He walked up to a low mound of patched earth and began to kick at the dusty soil with his boots.

Her presence no longer distracted him. Trevor was lost inside himself, sorting images and emotions, assembling memories in files, opening some, hiding others. He dug his boot heel into the mounded soil looking for signs of the cabin that had stood here. There had been a cistern, a hay trough, water trough. All were present, in some decayed form or another, the last time he had been in the canyon: the one-room cabin a group of dry-rot logs and rusted tin; the cistern half full of dirt, its mud-brick walls caved in; troughs rusted and rendered into flaking chips and rims. All here, even if in pieces, when Trevor had left this place years ago. But now there was no sign of it except the mound he was scrounging in with his boot.

He continued to dig, using heel and toe of his right boot, the wind catching florets of dust. Then his heel caught something and he crouched and dug with his hands. He dug further and pulled a narrow ragged board from the earth. Black and thin, the board had a knothole in its middle. The board was no longer than his forearm, or much wider, but it had been part of the cabin. The cabin had been propped up when he was a boy, its fallen roof replaced by tin, its door gone, and only used to store extra hay in the winter. Then it wasn't used at all. Trevor was the only one who seemed to care about it. He had visited it and the canyon often, played here, hid here as a teen. He and Darcie had made love here . . . He dug further, the red soil beneath his nails and there was more wood, slivers of brown metal, brown nails. Artifacts of Kallengaard history—forgotten, dispensed with.

But this was where he would start anew. Or, perhaps, restart from twenty years ago and live a life he should have lived. Stay until there would be no further history. He would have no offspring, his brother also none. There would be nothing to leave to anyone after they were gone, he and Ross. No more Kallengaards. And, Trevor thought, maybe it was just as well.

He took up the old board, stood, held it out in front of him and looked through the knothole. Like a lens, he studied the world through the limitations of the board's eye. He looked at the trees and then the water, looked at the eye of the Rock through the eye of the board, then he turned to take in more of the canyon and was surprised to see her. Bisma. She stood yards away, perfectly captured within the worn wood's scope.

He brought the board down, placed it upon the mound.

This is where the cabin was. The homestead.

She stood with her arms crossed, the wind blowing her hair. She said nothing.

He paced off some twenty steps diagonally away from the cabin site, walking into some brush—thistle and chokecherry--and kicked the ground, moving roots and stones. He saw rounded river stones, brown and white, chunks of brick, mud-colored and brittle.

There was a cistern here. A root cellar at one time.

He walked further, found a stump of sheet metal in the ground, flakes of rusted metal like fish scales.

A tub here. A hayrack.

He wasn't looking at her when he said these things, but he was addressing her.

What about winter, Bisma asked, called to him. He looked up, surprised she had spoken. Doesn't it get cold? Very cold? You wouldn't have much sun in a place like this, I'd think.

Winter, he said and met her eyes. Snow doesn't drift too much down here, water all year round—there's a pool of it where the canyon boxes together, you can break the ice.

Oh, that sounds wonderful.

He smiled but, to Trevor, it did sound wonderful. Appealing. Not so much the aspect of winter but the idea of isolation, the physicality of rock walls, of a world hidden from above, the stream and the cottonwoods and the great bridge of stone—a place for him and him alone. And if it meant breaking ice for water or to chop and stack cord after cord of firewood, to live without electricity and plumbing, without television, phones, computers, without daily human interaction, then so be it. It was—he had told himself—what he wanted. The sky itself would be but a strip above him, limited and contained like everything else.

Cocoon or coffin, he thought, it was what he wanted.

Trevor looked again at Bisma Patel—the young woman from Fort Collins, from London—who stood beneath the cottonwoods. He didn't know her place in his own private equation; no, he knew that, really, she had no place in it.

You look very self-satisfied, she said and came towards him. It's quite beautiful. But there's nothing here—no road or buildings. No people. She was next to him now, she put her hands on him.

He looked at her.

You're smiling again. You really should do that more often.

She moved herself into his arms and they held each other.

Are you feeling randy? I am, she said.

But then there was a sound. An insistent engine—diesel, by the resonance of it—in low gear. A machine coming down the steep switchbacks into the canyon. And a dark brown pickup came into view, its windshield catching the sun, then going black with shade as it reached the trees. A shovel sticking up from the side of the bed.

Who...

It's my brother.

They let go of each other.

He got out of the truck and stood there. Trevor recognized him by his shape alone: Ross with his hulking shoulders and oblong head, the bowed legs. And then Trevor could see the girth of his belly. He looked large and slovenly, wearing jeans and ill-fitting t-shirt, a straw cowboy hat with thin grey hair spilling out of it. Ross looked back at him and said nothing.

Then Ross went to the rear of the truck, pulled the shovel from its slot. He held it in both hands and came towards them—a deliberate lope with the wood handle angled across his chest.

Bisma took several steps backward but Trevor stayed put, quiet, hands to his side.

Ross, Trevor said, loud enough, but there was no answer. He turned to look at Bisma, told her that it was okay. When he turned back he heard a thin whistle, saw the flash of flat steel as the shovel caught him full in the face.

Trevor collapsed. He felt more dazed—surprised to be on the ground—than any pain. He was aware that his hat had flown off somewhere. He rolled onto his back, catching a glimpse of Bisma's face while doing so. He could not hear her but her mouth was open. Then his vision tunneled with only a black penumbra in its periphery.

The brother raised the shovel again, held it aloft, but took two steps backwards. He stared down at Trevor in the dirt. Then he stabbed the metal shovelhead into the soil and left it there, removed his hat and took a swipe at the sweat on his forehead.

Bisma went to Trevor, kneeled and put a hand on his head. His eyes were open but they did not seem to register her presence. She looked up at the man who had hit him.

My god—he's your brother!

I know who he is.

Trevor's brother put his hat back on, looked down at her, at both of them on the ground.

You think I don't have an uncle, too? That I don't have friends in Cheyenne and my phone doesn't work? I know why you're here .

He was talking to Trevor but Bisma didn't think Trevor could hear him.

You'd better get off my land. Go back to wherever you've been hiding.

He pulled the shovel out of the dirt and Bisma tightened her grip on Trevor, thinking that she would drag him if needed. But the brother only returned to the truck, putting the shovel back where he had taken it. Before getting into the cab, he picked up a bottle—small, square, brown—and took a drink, screwed the cap back on then tossed it on the seat. He leaned inside, this time bringing out a long-barreled pistol. Bisma watched him shove the gun into the front of his pants, the white bone handle tight against belly. He didn't get into the truck but went to the front and leaned against the hood, crossed his arms, the butt of the gun obvious. He watched and waited.

Trevor could only hear a ringing, like cicadas in the live oaks in Fort Lauderdale. He could feel the wind when it gusted, felt the sting on his cheek. He understood what had happened, and though there was no other pain, yet, he knew there would be. He then felt Bisma's hand beneath his neck, and he tilted his head enough to see the cottonwoods. Then Bisma's face came into view.

We have to go. You've got to get up.

Her words were hollow sounding, almost lost in the wind.

He's still here. I can drive but you'll have to tell me where to go.

Bisma looked back at the brother by the truck: Ross Kallengaard leaning and watching, neither smile nor frown on his face; observing them as if they were birds or cattle. Trevor's face—she now saw—was purplish on the right side, a deep blue just below the eye which was swelling.

Can you get up? I can't carry you. I can't.

He understood that she was scared. He felt her hands try to lift him and he tried to aid them, but he was not ready to stand yet. Then she was behind him, her arms under his pits. She pulled. He tried to help her again, felt himself sitting up— seeing a dizzy world. He could not focus on much. Bisma pulled harder and he found he could get to his feet, though his legs were uncertain of their orders. The side of his face felt tumescent, overgrown. He was aware of a sharp pain in his right eye and a rising ache in his head.

Can you walk?

He said nothing but lifted his foot, took a step then another. Bisma stayed at his side, supported him. His head, his vision, were still unclear, but they walked together to the cottonwoods.

Bisma tried to steer them clear of the brother, but they passed within a few yards of him.

When he gets his wits, you tell him to leave and not come back, Ross told her. He looked directly at her now. If I see him again, it'll be worse.

You could have killed him—she spat the words, could not contain them.

Ross straightened himself against the truck

He's the killer, not me. You better watch the company you keep.

Bisma led Trevor to his truck, could not bring herself to even look at the brother again. She feared him and only wanted to get away, back to town and among people, among streets and buildings and highways. But when they reached the truck, Trevor drew away from her.

No, he said.

He detached himself from her, walked on his own away from the truck and towards the creek. Trevor not even looking at his brother, just a slow, drunk-looking amble towards the water. Bisma did not know what he was doing but she did not call to him. She did not want to leave the truck.

She followed him with her eyes, did not look to see what the other man was doing, was afraid to. Trevor, she saw, was going for his hat, bending down and retrieving it from the gravel spit. She did not know how or why he even bothered, but he slowly placed it on his head and turned, came back to her on unsteady legs, not once looking or acknowledging the brother.

You'll have to tell me how to get back, she said when he was beside her.

I'll do it.

You can't.

No. I'll drive. I want him to see me drive out of here.

And he opened the door—leaning on it as he did so—and sat behind the wheel. The keys were still in the ignition.

Bisma did not argue. She went in the passenger side and sat next to him.

Trevor concentrated on the keys for a moment, then touched them and turned them, starting the engine. He put the truck in reverse, curling the wheels with some effort before stopping and changing gears and moving forward.

They left the cover of trees, went up the switchbacks, the canyon now invisible, the sound of Pearl Creek, of the birds and wind gone. They rose up to open land, rolling pastures of dry grass, sage, rocks and dust. Away in the empty land.

You should see a doctor, she said again.

They were in Douglas, back in the narrow room of the LaBonte. Trevor had been able to drive the whole way, silent and concentrating, had made it up the stairs, but collapsed into the bed. He had refused to go to the ER, as Bisma had wished, and now she was afraid he would fall asleep. She had read somewhere that someone with a concussion should not go to sleep.

I should call the police and charge the bloody bastard with assault.

He looked at her and, again, didn't talk to her. He closed his eyes.

She sat on the edge of the bed. The right side of his face was purple with red welts inlaid upon his cheek. Below the eye it was black, swollen. She had gotten ice from the machine down the hall and now had some wedged into a damp hotel washcloth. She placed this gently to his eye, his face, saw him grimace.

I'm going to call someone.

It's just sore.

She was glad he wasn't asleep, that he had finally spoken.

It's more than that. He almost killed you.

He didn't.

Are you mad? He hit you with a bloody shovel! He had a pistol—did you see that? A man like that would kill you.

No.

She took the ice and cloth away from his face and pressed it hard into Trevor's palm. He could use it if he so wanted.

She got off the bed and paced the room. The curtains were drawn. Outside it was quiet, Douglas silent behind the panes of glass.

You need something. Prescription medicine. Ibuprofen —the word ibuprofen sounded comical to her, inappropriate—or some vodka at the very least. You need to do something about your eye.

Later.

We should go back to Cheyenne. Fort Collins. We need to get out of here.

I'm not going back.

Bisma stopped pacing and looked at him. His left eye was open, the right only a slit surrounded by pink, a welling black bulb beneath it.

Look, I'm going to go out and get some pain reliever, some Advil. Maybe some vodka. Okay? . . . She waited and looked at him and did not leave . . . Trevor, we could go to California, you and I. That's where I wanted to go this summer, to San Francisco, or somewhere. Some place along the coast, Bolinas, I don't know—it's supposed to be beautiful.

He turned his face to her, gave a slight shake of his head.

She turned from him and went to the closet, took out his jacket. She didn't put the jacket on, only folded it and held it in her arm as she went out the hotel room door, closing it sharply behind her.

Outside, under the windblown trees, she stopped. There were the parked cars. Trevor's truck. The street was empty. No pedestrians on the sidewalk. The sun, angled from the west, was stringent, strange. The sky looked so thin . . . She recalled that there was a drug store on the main street—where the parade had been. R-D Pharmacy and Books; remembering it because it had books in its windows. She herself did not like pills. Did not like putting unknown pellets into her body— whether for pain or congestion or to protect her ovum. But he needed something.

Then again, perhaps Trevor didn't. Perhaps he liked pain. Maybe he was all about pain.

She walked only a few steps, holding the jacket in her arm, and stopped at the truck. She looked at it then touched it—its metal warm and layered with dust. When she withdrew her hand the imprint was there. She looked at it for quite a while, thinking, before she went back up to the room.

She found him crouched in bed, knees up, his back against the headboard. He had lit a cigarette and was using the water cup she had given him as an ashtray. The washcloth of ice sat alongside him on the bed spread, a damp ring around it.

Bisma placed the jacket on a chair and stood before him.

Trevor. This has been fun. Very interesting to a point. But that man, your brother, he did have a gun. He threatened me also, you know. Perhaps this is bad timing, but . . .

He looked up at her. Smoked. Kept his good eye steady. Bisma wanted to say it right, to state it simply and have him understand, but more importantly, have herself understand.

I think this is where I get off the train. I should go back to Fort Collins--she began to speak rapidly now--I'm sorry. Very sorry. But this is too much for me. I wanted to keep it going, for me, for us, but I'm not good with this, being in the middle of nowhere, the firearms . . .

She turned her head. She didn't want to look at his purple face, his handsome face so discolored and bloated in the bed where they had made love. She felt guilty for leaving him when he was injured and a side of her wanted to recant what she had just said and then she heard him tell her that it was okay.

It's all right. I can take you back tonight, if you want.

Bisma looked at him again.

No. I can take a bus. There must be one to Cheyenne and from there I can get to Colorado. Someone will come get me.

Okay.

Okay?

We'll do that then, get you on a bus.

She went to the corner table, where the light was on, and sat in the wooden chair, the jacket draped on the chair opposite.

I can drive you, if you want. Or you can take the bus—the Powder River bus goes to Cheyenne, in the morning. I'll buy your ticket.

She ran her hands through her long hair, felt the grit and dust and dryness in it. She looked at the worn carpeting, then looked up as he dropped his cigarette with a hiss into the water glass.

Bisma? he said.

What?

Did you want me to say something different?

Such as?

Such as, don't go?

She stood up, looked at his cold, painful face. Then she saw his boots by the door—the leather now scuffed, dirty, stained with soil and creek water.

I don't expect anything, she said. Not from you.

She went to her suitcase and opened it, took out the notebook and pen. She went into the bathroom and closed the door.

I'll find out what time the bus leaves, he called.

She sat on the stool and opened the notebook—her journal—took pen in hand but wrote nothing. She put her hands on her eyes.

Okay, she called back, through the closed door.

After that she tried to be very quiet, as if she had already left.

Cass . . . Miss Tipton . . .

Cass had answered the phone after falling asleep on the couch and dreaming of Trevor. Some inane dream about a wedding party and a card game, but Trevor had been there, and when she first answered the phone she thought it was him.

Yes. Collis . . . I'm sorry.

I'm still in Colorado but I'm leaving tomorrow. I checked out Colorado State, the university here, and found that Mr. Kallengaard went to school there. He graduated the same year you said he turned up in New Orleans. They gave me his home address and number from that time, in Cheyenne.

Cass felt a quickening within her but she tried to suppress it.

Did you speak to him?

No, no. Nothing like that. The number didn't lead anywhere, but I'll try the address. Tomorrow.

There was some disappointment, but Cass also sensed a shift, a change in fortune regarding her and Trevor and the wake of his leaving. She wanted to savor the feeling for now, for once, knowing that disillusionment, at some point, would no doubt follow.

Okay, Cass said. You think the address . . .

I didn't mean to get your hopes up, not too high. It's where he used to live. The university couldn't say if it was current, of course. But, maybe there's someone there, a parent, relative. Maybe a neighbor he visited.

I see.

It's just another piece, a place to go and start asking. I don't think it'll be too long before I find him.

Okay . . . You know, Collis, I was thinking that I should come out there, too. I can take some time—I'm freelance—so I could come out and see him when you find him.

He was silent. Cass already thought that she might as well be out there, that she really couldn't concentrate on work, that it would make her feel better, feel as if she were doing something, taking action. Her coworkers, Tina in particular, were full of questioning looks, innuendo, pitying looks. And Cass didn't want to explain anything to anyone about her situation, except to herself and Collis Mudd. And, she hoped, Trevor.

Well, he eventually said, that's up to you, Miss Tipton.

Yes, I realize that . . . So I can get ready at least, for when you do find him. You're making progress. I appreciate it, Collis.

That's what you pay me for.

But it's more than just that, to me.

He didn't speak for a moment and she waited.

I know it is, Cass. I'm glad to help.

So, you'll call me? When you get to Cheyenne?

It's a short drive up. I'll call—though you're two hours ahead. Mountain Time here.

I'll be home. I'm working from home for a while now. You have my number.

Cass was not sure why she had mentioned the number—of course he had it. But she wanted to hear his voice just a little longer. She sensed that he wanted to hear hers.

Yes, she heard him say, I have your number.

Trevor could not sleep. There was still some light outside, low and ashen against the window shades, but he knew he should sleep, heal, not think or talk. He stayed in the bed, beneath the covers, eyes closed but listening. He could hear her padding about, hear her packing, the movement of drawers, the whisper of clothes being folded and placed, the clasping of the suitcase.

Bisma had gone out to eat, alone, but had brought back some soup and bread for him from the café. He could sip the soup though chewing bread was too painful—but at least his jaw worked, was not broken. They said little. Then she had offered him pain reliever—over-the-counter pills that she had bought—and he thanked her but did not take them. The pain was his consolation—a way to recall the humiliation, the violence of his brother. Trevor wanted to prove to himself that he could take the pain.

And so he couldn't sleep, he could only wait in bed for her. But she didn't come to bed. Eventually he heard the shower running and running and the sound of it let sleep finally overtake him.

He woke in darkness and realized that she was next to him. She wasn't touching him. Trevor understood that, because he hadn't protested her leaving, because he didn't acknowledge her rightful fear, he had hurt her. And, he realized, he had felt some hurt himself when she said that she was leaving. Still, it was for the best. It made things easier. Simpler. And, in the long run, it was an inevitable thing.

He turned in bed and studied her as best he could. He smelled the soap in her hair, the faint fragrance of her skin. She was facing away from him.

One side of his face felt weighted, as if a water balloon, or something poisonous, hung there. The pain of it drove him to get up and he went to the bathroom. He urinated, looked in the mirror and, even in the darkness, saw how his face was damaged . Yet, despite the weighted feeling, the abject pain, he was certain the swelling around his eye had diminished. He got a glass of water and drank it.

He wanted to open the window shades, to smoke a cigarette and look out on the street, at its parked cars and trees and light posts. But he returned to the bed and tried to slip quietly beneath the covers.

What did your brother mean when he said you were a killer?

Trevor wasn't so surprised that she was awake as much as that she would talk to him. Her voice was soft, though. Almost contrite. She wasn't looking at him.

You're not a criminal of some sort, are you?

No. Not a criminal.

But have you . . . Did you kill someone?

Yes. I did.

And you won't tell me about it?

No. I can't.

She raised her head from the pillow and turned to look at him. Her eyes owl-like.

Would you tell me if I weren't leaving?

No, Bisma. I wouldn't.

She closed her eyes for a moment then sat up, her knees up. She touched his bare leg with her bare feet.

Do you think you can make love? Would you want to?

Yes. I would.

It won't hurt you? With your face being such it is?

Everything hurts, in the long run.

The Powder River bus was due from Gillette at seven. After Douglas it made stops in Wheatland and Chugwater before Cheyenne. From there it went to Laramie. In Cheyenne there was a Greyhound that connected to Fort Collins. There was an afternoon Powder River bus as well, but Trevor and Bisma were there for the morning one.

Trevor was in the gift shop of the Plains Motel, waiting for someone to come and sell him the ticket. The diner—attached to the gift shop—had only a few customers. He wore the same clothes as yesterday, shirt dusty, the pants with spots of dirt from when he had been knocked down. He kept his hat down low. He could keep the eye open now, his vision no longer blurred, the swelling gone, though the bruised colors on his face were still distinct.

The Plains Motel and Trading Post's gift shop looked deficient. Its shelves only half full, the glass case had only a cash register on top, dusty souvenirs inside: plastic tomahawks and drums, toy war bonnets with dyed chicken feathers, statuettes of eagles and bears and bison. Business did not look good at the Plains.

Finally a clerk came—staring at his face but saying nothing—and sold Trevor a one-way ticket to Cheyenne.

Bisma waited with her suitcase outside on the wood porch. The air was cool and the sun seemed slow in its rise. There was light traffic. Trevor came out and handed her the ticket and a tag for her one suitcase. They stood together and waited and looked for the bus.

You should come with me.

There was a gas station across the street, a smattering of small businesses— most of them closed. Beyond that was Bartling Park, then the Interstate where Trevor could hear semis passing. The sky was tin-colored. He said nothing and then the bus came.

It was an old Blue Bird bus, flat-nosed, an oversized windshield with CHEYENNE in white letters above it, lots of aluminum. It arrived slowly. She turned and looked at him, touching her hand to his bruised face beneath the cowboy hat. She kissed him gently but he didn't kiss back.

I'm sorry, she said.

He nodded and told her there was nothing to be sorry about.

She picked the suitcase up herself and took the steps off the porch and walked to the bus. Trevor didn't move. She set her bag down and the driver took it, stowing it underneath. The driver took her ticket. She looked back once to see if he was watching her and he was. She boarded without waving.

He lit a cigarette as the driver entered the aluminum door of the bus. He could see the driver through the flat windshield but could not see Bisma in any of the tinted passenger windows. He came down from the porch as the bus was put into gear. He stood and watched as it pulled out, as it followed the bend in the road, gained distance, heading south and for the Interstate. The sun then rose unbroken above the trees of Park Hill, where the city cemetery was.

When he got back to the room he saw his jacket. It was hanging on the wooden chair by the window. He hadn't thought about it until just then, and then he did wonder if he shouldn't have gone with her. He wondered what it would be like now, without her and—he also wondered—what she was thinking at that very moment while on the bus to Cheyenne . . . But such thoughts were pointless. He would not renege on his plans, would not stop what had already begun.

And he would not let Ross scare him, push him, defeat him. The young woman—Bisma Patel—had been accidental, a mystery. It was good that she was gone.

He took off his hat and boots. He told himself he would go to sleep, shower and shave after he woke. Eat a big meal at the café. But he didn't. Anxiety was in his blood. His face throbbed. He saw the unopened bottle of ibuprofen on the table beside the bed and he opened it. Shook out four tablets. Poured a glass of water and swallowed the pills.

He went to the window and opened the drapes. He stood there and smoked and looked outside.

Collis Mudd drove the purple rental car across the railroad yard bridge and into downtown Cheyenne. He passed some old buildings, a square parking lot, saw the gold dome of the Capitol above the trees. He kept driving, turning, circling, getting a basic feel for the town. He stopped at a gas station where there was a sign for Happy Jack Road, where dry country stretched beyond it.

Inside the station he selected a city map, bottle of water and a candy bar. At the counter he asked for a pack of cigarettes—Trevor's brand.

Matches? the attendant asked.

Collis shook his head no.

Back in the car, he looked at the map while he ate the candy bar, drank some water. He found the street and general address, the one the university had given him. He already had the information on his phone, but Collis liked to hold a physical map. He also knew there were no Kallengaards listed in town, but he did not like to rely solely on lists and public information. Collis liked to do footwork—he trusted empirical evidence over what he read about, over what he was told.

Collis drove north, past the capitol, then along streets lined with large trees and older houses. He drove slow, finding the street he wanted, then the house. He sat in the car and drank some water, inspected his face in the mirror, the got out.

The middle-aged woman who answered the door said her name was Mullins, that she had lived there for over ten years and had never heard of any Kallengaards. She would not open the door beyond a crack. Collis then simply told her the truth, that he was an investigator from Florida trying to track down a man with that name who used to live in the house. He asked if she thought any of the neighbors would remember the name. She said no and he thanked her, said he was sorry for bothering her. When she closed the door he heard the her slide the bolt lock in place.

Back in the car he was disappointed but not surprised. He wondered why he had told Cassandra Tipton about the address. Normally, he wouldn't have revealed it to a client. He would have waited for the result of the information rather than the finding of it. He told himself he was only trying to reassure her.

No, I was showing off, he said to himself.

He thought of the Capitol and knew that they would have records there—plats, deeds, names of people across the state. There were not that many people in the whole state and it might be the place to try before the county or the city records. Start with a wide net, work towards the specific. So he drove back, parked in an open space in front, got out and entered the building.

Inside it was cool, quiet, the hollow echoes of footsteps and voices. The empty lobby held a musty smell. He wondered where to start—birth records, tax, real estate. He stood next to a buffalo on display and thought how he'd like to show it to James and Keena. Or to Cassandra Tipton. He quit looking at the buffalo as he was aware of being looked at himself: down the lobby there was a woman behind a glass-windowed booth.

Collis momentarily felt self-conscious. He didn't know what he would ask the woman. He knew that he was in a state not only with very few people, but even fewer of his color. So he circled the lobby's interior, past the stuffed buffalo and then a stuffed elk. There were many old photographs and documents of state history on the walls. There was a guest book. A double staircase going three stories up. He felt sleepy, uncertain, unprofessional. The clerk was still watching him as his eyes were drawn back to the guestbook.

It was a fat book on an iron pedestal, not far from the roped-off elk. He went to it and took his time examining it. He took up the feathered pen that was there and signed the book himself, leaving the space for home address and comments blank. He was the first to sign it today and it was such a big book that he thought its pages must go back weeks and moths, if not years. The lobby was so empty. Cheyenne was not a big town. Collis Mudd flipped a page backwards—just to check—and saw a few recent names and signatures. He saw the name *Bisma Patel* and then, below it and in the same handwriting, written formally was *Mister Trevor Kallengaard* . . . And whoever had written it, a woman Collis thought, by the script and name above it, had given as an address *Room 215 The Plains Hotel, Cheyenne Wyoming.*

He parked in the street, fed the meter, then walked through the doors of the Plains Hotel.

The lobby was old, antiquated, holding some of the same empty feel as the Capitol. But there was a short line of people at the front desk: a young woman and then three men who were discussing a hot air-balloonist convention. When it was his turn at the desk, he told the woman clerk that he wasn't ready to check in yet but wanted to see if his friend was still staying at the hotel—Trevor Kallengaard.

The woman looked at a list of guests.

No, he's not here.

Really . . . Could you tell me when he checked out? See if he left me a message?

I can only tell you that there's no one by that name here.

Collis Mudd reached for his wallet, withdrew the photo from it.

This is him, maybe you remember him.

Trevor Kallengaard you said?

Yes.

Oh, I remember that face. I asked Lane about him.

Lane?

Lane knew him. He's at the Wigwam.

I'm sorry?

The lounge. He works there. Lane does.

She pointed it out to him.

Trevor touched his face, letting his fingertips ride along the skin of his cheeks. Without Bisma, there was just him, the land and his brother. And now he knew what his next step should be—to find out the legal status of the ranch. With Ross, there was going to be a fight, a process, and he needed to find out about his grandfather's will, to see who officially owned what. Trevor understood that he might need a lawyer. So that was clear: find out if any of the property had been left to him. And there was a man in Douglas who would know: Aaron Stroud, Thor's lawyer. Thor's friend.

Stroud's office was downtown, not far from the LaBonte. Trevor could not imagine that it would be gone. The Stroud family had been in Converse County longer than the Kallengaards. Trevor didn't want to call ahead, to give any sense of warning or preparation, any chance for communication with Ross. He wanted to see the old man in person, if he was still alive.

Trevor walked down Walnut and turned east on Sixth. He could see the two-story building made of red brick with its granite keystones. STROUD BUILDING chiseled in wide letters in the upper facade. There were newish windows and glass doors and he walked to the doors, saw names in gold leaf, the largest proclaiming Law Offices of Stroud and Stroud.

Trevor assumed the second Stroud was a grandson of Aaron, he remembered one had studied prelaw about the same time he was at Colorado State. Aaron Stroud's only son had been a rancher, not a lawyer. There were daughters and granddaughters, Trevor recalled, but this being Wyoming, he suspected none of them had been to law school.

He went inside and saw that the office had been moved to the second floor. He took the stairs up, turned towards a solid oak door, propped open, which led to the office. Inside there was a small room with a couch and chair, plastic plants, framed prints by Remington and Russell on the walls. George Catlin. Each print had the name of a gallery in big letters beneath it—as if that were as important or impressive as the paintings themselves. Off to the side was a desk with a young woman behind it.

Trevor took off his hat and approached the desk. When the woman looked at him he saw a momentary shock in her expression and he remembered what his face looked like, what Ross had done to him.

I'd like to talk to Mr. Stroud if I could. I don't have an appointment.

She looked at him for a little longer, then asked for his name.

Trevor Kallengaard.

Trevor?

That's right.

Just a minute.

The young woman stood and walked around a half wall. He heard her open a door and then close it. Trevor walked around the wall and looked at the door, which held only the name STROUD in more gold lettering. He returned to the lobby, to the window that looked out on the street. Outside was the bright sunlight, dust moving along the curb, the leaves and branches of trees blowing, all soundless. He thought about the bus from this morning—it would have been to Cheyenne, might be in Rawlins by now. Then he thought of Bisma and wondered what she was doing, thinking, where she was and who it was that would come get her if someone was coming to get her. Then Trevor thought of Cass, and wondered who was coming to get her. He wondered if Cass had already met someone new, that men—sensing she was single, available—would be pursuing her by now. Maybe. If not by now then, no doubt, soon. The thoughts bothered him though he told himself they did not.

The woman came back out, surprised to see him by the window. She stepped to the side of the desk. Trevor held his hat in his hands.

You can go in, Mr. Kallengaard.

He went in and saw that there was another desk and another window and more western art prints. There was also a Mr. Stroud, but it was not Aaron. This Stroud was young and he stood when Trevor entered. The man put out his hand and Trevor shook it.

Sit down, please. Trevor sat in front of the desk. This is quite a surprise . . . Trevor waited . . . I'm Tom, Tom Stroud. I know your brother and I used to know you.

Yes, Trevor said but he did not really remember him. I was hoping to talk to Aaron.

My grandfather? No, he retired a long time ago. It's my practice now, though I keep his name connected to it.

Okay.

No, Trevor, this is more than a surprise, really. Your brother and I assumed that you were . . .

Dead.

Maybe, yes, deceased or missing by your own volition.

I came to see about the ranch. Thor Kallengaard's land.

That parts not a surprise, I guess.

What I'd like to know is if Aaron Stroud handled Thor's estate. If you know anything about the ownership.

There was no will.

Trevor looked at the man for a while, but the younger Stroud added nothing to the statement.

None?

Anyway, I'm afraid I can't help you because your brother is my client. Because of your mother's situation—and my sympathies—Ross became executor of her estate which is, by Wyoming law, your grandfather's ranch.

But I'm here now. I'm back.

Stroud looked out the window.

I suppose you could contest it. If you want to take the time, trouble and money. You'd have to get a lawyer to file anything and I'm telling you that Ross will fight you. I think you know Ross will fight.

Trevor did not know if Stroud was inferring his injured face, but it didn't matter. Trevor only nodded.

Let me say something you may already know, it's called primogeniture. It's an old Swedish tradition for farmers—ranchers in this case, don't want to bad mouth anyone by calling them a farmer. Stroud smiled. It's a tradition about leaving the land to the eldest son. And, again in this case, and because of the nature of your father's death, that would be the eldest grandson, your brother.

The mention of his father made Trevor want to flinch, to bend his head and no longer look the younger Stroud in the eye, but he did not.

That's not something anyone would consider, primogeniture. Not in court.

The lawyer shrugged and Trevor saw Tom Stroud openly looking at his face, at the damage done. Trevor knew for sure now that there was no real surprise in his presence, in the bruised face, because the lawyer had been expecting both.

Well—Trevor stood, put his hat on—I won't waste your time.

They didn't shake hands.

Out of curiosity, how is Aaron these days? Trevor asked.

He's fine. Still feisty.

I guess his memory is still good then?

Tom Stroud said nothing and Trevor gave him a last look before leaving the office and going down the stairs and out to the street.

The more he thought about it, Trevor was certain there was a will of some kind. Thor was too petulant about ownership, about his land, not to make sure who would receive it. He may have left it all to Ross—they were close. Ross was in many ways more like Thor's son than Trig, his father, had been. But there was a good chance that he wouldn't have left it all to his brother. In Sweden, Thor had lost out on the family land because he was not the oldest son. That was why he had come to America. And even though Trevor had disappeared, even if he had caused the death of the rightful heir, Trevor felt that his name would still be on the will. If it wasn't, the lawyer he just talked to would have proved it.

No. Aaron Stroud was still alive and he would know the truth.

And Trevor thought he knew where he could probably find Stroud, at this hour in Douglas.

Trevor stood outside the College Inn Bar with its block glass entranceway, with its cardboard signs in the windows: Tombstone Pizza, Hunting Licenses Here, No Gambling. The tavern was in the middle of the block, nondescript except for the glass blocks. It was the oldest bar in Douglas.

He went inside, into the low-lit enclosure, a world—like about any bar— purposely separated from the larger one. And the Inn was pretty much how he remembered it: the long oak bar and mirror, tin ceilings, the narrow front booths and then the tables with thin-legged chairs, the single pool table in back and then the side room where old men played poker. The neon signs were new. The video machines and jukebox as well. But most else, including the clutch of early drinkers at the bar, including the men at the poker table, were timeless.

The woman bartending looked at him in the doorway and Trevor removed his hat. He stepped further into the bar and others looked at him, the stranger, but his concentration was on the poker table. There was no music, just the sound of occasional conversation, coughs and throat clearings, boots on the bar rail, the shuffling of cards and click of plastic chips. Despite the No Gambling sign there had always been gambling at the College Inn Bar—Thor and Ross had played here, no doubt his father, Trig, had as well. Trevor walked past the bartender and the counter, made his way to the game table in back.

At the table were five men, all old and older, intent on their game of five card draw. They paid Trevor no mind as he stopped to watch them, stood silently behind the man he was looking for.

He could see Aaron Stroud's cards from where he stood: three kings, a seven and a deuce. The round's draw had not taken place. There was no hurry in the game. There were poker chips in order and disorder, there were beers and whiskey, one of them was smoking cheroots. There was a spittoon on the floor just outside the table. Trevor tried watching for a while but found himself to be impatient.

Mr. Stroud, sir, he said.

Three of Stroud's cohorts looked up at him while Stroud brought his cards in, tightly, to his chest. He turned his head and shoulders, the upper back, to see who had spoken. He took the time to look Trevor over—boots to hat, though Trevor's hat was still in his hands. There was no flicker of recognition and Stroud returned to the game without again spreading his cards.

I'll take one, he said when it was his draw.

Trevor waited this time. When the card came Trevor saw, though Stroud tried to conceal it, that it was a jack, that he probably had a full house, if the deuce was wild. The round began and Stroud saw a dollar bet, raised it another.

What can I do for you, Stroud then asked as the bets went further around. He kept his back to Trevor, his cards cupped in his hand.

My name's Trevor, I just talked to your grandson.

The old man brought his cards together but still did not turn around.

Who?

Trevor Kallengaard.

Stroud stiffened a little. He took a moment for the bet to come back around, then placed his cards on the table in a neat stack and pushed them slightly forward. Fold, he said to the table. He scooted his chair back, stood, then turned to Trevor, Trevor seeing his brown face as creased as the photos of old Indian chiefs in museums. Stroud was dressed neatly and with purpose, his jeans clean, the button down shirt ironed and tucked, large belt buckle, a string tie with an obsidian clasp. He looked at Trevor intently.

Let's us talk over there.

He pointed to the abandoned end of the bar.

There was some grumbling from the other men as Stroud left. He walked bow-legged, a little pigeon-toed, his boots old but clean. Trevor, following, realized that Stroud had to be in his late eighties, possibly his nineties. He sat with some effort on the last stool and waited for Trevor without looking. The bartender came over.

A short one, Diane.

The woman looked at Trevor as he sat.

Ginger ale, please.

She left and Trevor saw the old man taking in his discolored his face, the welts and black eye. Stroud didn't comment and remained silent until the drinks were served and the end of the bar was isolated again.

Your Trig's second boy, the one who left.

Trevor nodded.

You know, I used to teach your father in Sunday School, way back when. Your grandfather, Thor, was never keen on it but Trig's mother saw to it, even if it didn't last long.

I didn't know that. You weren't a pastor were you?

No. Not quite, but I was involved in the church. More involved in the law. Stroud took a drink from the small glass of beer, tried to straighten up on the backless stool. So I guess I ought to say I'm surprised to see you again, but in a lot of ways I'm not. And I'm thinking you're here about the land and that's what you saw my Tom about.

Your grandson told me there was no will, that everything, legally, was Ross'. He said I should go back where I came from.

Stroud looked at him with sharp eyes. Trevor felt uncomfortable. He felt as though he was snitching on the younger Stroud. The old man muttered something and shook his head.

I can't advise you on the going back part, but there was a will. I prepared it . . . Looks like I should have kept with the Sunday School teaching.

And?

Everything went to your mother. You know about your mother? Right . . . Well, Thor knew that she would be incapacitated, or already was, before he passed and so the land, purely legally speaking, belongs to both of you.

Trevor thought about asking how Thor had died—though Thor would have been very old and Trevor guessed he died like anyone else would have.

I was thinking that he would have left the house to Ross and maybe some of the land to me.

No, and that's the problem. I'll be honest, I advised him to give it all to Ross, not you or your mother. Ross' the one who lived there, worked it.

Ross was closer to Thor than my father was, really.

I know. Everyone knows that. But your grandfather wouldn't do it and then he wouldn't divide it up any, either. He could have left the Bedtick for you and the rest to Ross. I guess he figured that if you never came back, it'd all be Ross' anyway.

And if I did come back?

Aaron Stroud took another drink from his beer.

Well, if you even wanted it, I 'd like to think he aimed for the two of you to come together over it. To make peace.

That's what you'd like to think.

But what I really think, is he wanted to make you fight for it.

The two of us.

No. He knew Ross would fight. Just you, Trevor.

Trevor touched his glass for the first time. He didn't lift it or drink it.

Would you be my lawyer? he asked and Stroud laughed lightly.

I'm long retired. Tom's my grandson and I like Ross. To me, he's been on that land so long I say it's his. It may not be fair, or exactly legal, but any judge around here is going to consider that. You're not going to get Ross Kallengaard out of that house, even if the law agreed with you.

I don't want the house. I don't even need a hundred acres. I want the old homestead in the canyon, access to and from it.

Stroud played with his beer glass.

Trevor, you've been gone a long time. I'm not sure if my Tom didn't give you some sound advice.

To leave.

Now, I don't know exactly what happened to you—you may not even exactly know it yourself—but I can guess why you ran. I knew your father before he drank so much. He was a good man. He wasn't like Thor and wasn't cut out to be what Thor wanted him to be. I know you boys didn't think a lot of him, at least by the time he went to Cheyenne. But he should have left way before that. He never got to be who he wanted to be—first it was Thor, then it was the bottle and then he died. Stroud paused to look at Trevor. Even though he had you two and Anna, he never hit bottom. He didn't get the chance to rise up from the bottom, which I think he would have. You're a lot like him—resilient, troubled.

Trevor picked at his hat. He didn't tell Stroud that he already figured he was more like his father than Ross was, that his father's life was unfulfilled because he had killed him.

And I knew that girl too, Darcie. She wasn't any good for Ross, for anybody. Never going to be a rancher's wife. She was a wild girl out of Scottsbluff from a bad family, a girl that nowadays they'd say she had some psychological problem. Maybe was abused or sex-addicted and that's why she slept around so much. But that's not what my generation would call her . . . Ross must've known it. She had a hold on him even if it looked like he ignored her, even if she'd go off with about anyone. Including someone I'd never tell on, though maybe if Ross had known . . . Well. All these years and still moping.

Trevor put his hat on the bar and met the old man's eyes.

I always liked Darcie, he told Stroud.

Stroud read Trevor's face for something. Trevor gave him nothing but the old man persisted, kept looking at him until he appeared to catch the thing he had been searching for, and he turned his head and clicked his tongue.

You too, huh?

Trevor felt his blood rise. The bruised socket of his eye throbbed, his cheek. He couldn't stop his head from jerking away—an involuntary spasm—as a sign of guilt or truth or a secret revealed. He then took hold of himself and looked at the floor.

Lord.

Aaron Stroud finished his beer with one swallow then rearranged his legs so that he faced Trevor, Trevor who sat erect, his spine almost arched, arms now crossed against his chest.

Well, there was about five others that I know about and there was you and— just to put all the cards on the table—there was Thor. That's right. His own grandson's supposed betrothed. And I'm too old to hold that in anymore, to mince it or parse it, but I see it was you and Ross and Thor and Darcie and that's disgusting. And I'm not sorry I told you because I'm done with it. It's between you and yours. And if you really think that canyon, that hole in the ground, is worth it, then that's between you and your brother, too, as well as the State Park Service.

Trevor was still taking in the idea of Thor and Darcie, of others in town with Darcie, but now such thoughts were put aside.

The Park Service?

The State of Wyoming. There's some down in Cheyenne who want that parcel for a park—your canyon and that rock bridge and the right-of-way to get to it.

They've been out there over the years. And I can't tell you why Ross needs it, really needs hardly any of that land, except to hide and die on it. He won't sell it. Sure won't tolerate the government owning an inch of it.

No, Trevor said because he could think of nothing else to say.

Ross is as stubborn as Thor is dead. As your father is dead and that girl, Darcie is dead.

Trevor couldn't look at Aaron Stroud anymore. He turned to the bar and put his elbows on it and looked at the wall, at the liquor bottles and signage, the mirror. Stroud stood up from the stool and placed his hand Trevor's back.

I'm sorry. I don't like to get worked up. He withdrew the hand. If you want a lawyer, go to Cheyenne. You'll find one who'll work for you. But here in Converse County or in Casper, I doubt you'll find a soul who'll represent you.

The old man looked back to the card game, then turned to Trevor before returning to it. He put out his hand. They shook.

Good luck to you, he said. And welcome home.

The wind hit him from the west as he turned the corner and Trevor felt like he was in one of his dreams where he could not walk up a hill or could not perform a simple task. Dreams of meticulous frustration. But he kept walking, making his way back to the LaBonte. In front of the hotel, a brown pickup came slowly towards him, a Ford Lariat dirty and dinged, with a shovel pointed skyward from its bed. Ross' big face staring at him from the open window.

Trevor waited, watched his brother approach. His brother with a flat stare and hard mouth, who opened that mouth to spit onto the sidewalk by Trevor's boots—a violent stream of saliva and tobacco juice.

I know where you're at, Ross said before speeding up.

Trevor entered the hotel and walked into the empty lobby. He walked up the stairs, fishing the key from his pocket as he came to the room, half-expecting her to be there when he opened the door.

He found that he wanted someone to be there. Someone waiting for him. Willing to speak to him. Be it Bisma or Cass or Darcie or his mother. His father. But, of course, no one was.

He closed the door and didn't remove his hat. He went to the window and opened it and then sat at the table and lit a cigarette. He thought of his brother and his glob of spit. He thought of what Stroud had told him, about the land and the Park Service and eventually he let his mind come around to the subject of Thor and Darcie.

Had really known Darcie at all? Was she only a figment of his own desires—more who he wished her to be, not who she really was? It wasn't as though she hadn't told him about herself—that she had gone through a rough life in Scottsbluff and had burned her bridges when leaving, that she had gone to Portland and Seattle and Anchorage and in those places—she had hinted—she had worked as a prostitute. And then there had been Denver, then Casper. And Casper was just another stop—Trevor realized now—where she met Ross and Douglas became what was next.

Why could he not see what she was telling him? That she was only the sum of lost places and personal disaster. Except his brother didn't kick her out. And then the pregnancy. And maybe that was where she was going to make her stand—with Ross, with a child, on the ranch.

He had not understood it or her or himself.

He knew he shouldn't be surprised. Not about Darcie and her waywardness, her sleeping with many men. And he knew he should not be surprised about his grandfather. Yet, it repulsed him. Shamed him. Thor and Darcie . All of them right there on the ranch, like animals in rut. And Trevor wondered how he had been blind to it. And there, in the LaBonte, he understood finally, after all the years, that he was no more than any of the others. No different. It was only because his heart had been involved and because he had convinced himself that Darcie's heart had been involved too. She had never belonged to him. Maybe, Darcie had no heart. Trevor couldn't fathom what possessed her to seek out other men. Did she desire them as one would desire a hamburger or a cigarette? Was it, psychologically or physically, an addiction? Maybe Darcie had only belonged to herself. Or, possibly, only to Ross.

Ross was her love. The rest—him, Thor, men in town—were but entertainment. Like his father and his alcoholism, Darcie never got the chance to change. To recover. Because, like his father, she had been killed. By him.

And he lived. Lived to do what? Accomplish what? Help Cass recover from the death of Marcus—but not to give her a child, not to love her enough stay with her? He survived to return to Wyoming and do what? Build a cabin and live like a hermit?

Maybe, Trevor thought, he was the one who lacked a heart.

And that was why no one was waiting for him behind the door.

Trevor had fallen asleep at the table. His cigarette now a long pencil of ash in the plastic tray in front of him. His hat fallen to the floor. The room was dark and he wondered how long he had slept, how hard. He felt that he did not like himself, who he was, and he stood and went to the window and opened it full and looked out at the night world. He could not change what had happened, he thought, and he could not change what he had come back to do.

Then he thought of his brother: I know where you're at.

Trevor knew where Ross was at, too.

He waited until well after midnight before putting on his father's jacket and going to his truck. He drove west, lighting a cigarette as he crossed the North Platte, then followed the road as it dipped beneath the Interstate. He turned on Spring Canyon Road.

The stars were mighty in the sky, spread like rock salt above the flat crest of Table Mountain, over the Medicine Bow. He was very aware of it, the sky, the stars, and of the road and the cones of his headlights along that road.

He cut the headlights as he approached the house. Cut the engine and rolled down the slope of the drive, listening to only the smothered crunch of gravel under his tires. He closed the truck's door carefully, quietly, when he got out.

Ross' brown pickup was there, still holding the shovel in the back. Trevor withdrew it from its metal hole and carried it over his shoulder as he went to the porch where the light was not on. There were no dogs. No cattle in the pen. No horses in the first pasture that ran to the hill where his grandfather and father and Darcie were buried.

The door was unlocked. Trevor walked inside, remembering his way using the light of memory. Even within the darkness, he could see how shabby it was. Everything in need of soap or repair, the walls devoid of any trappings—no photographs or clocks or pictures. He walked forward, shovel held in front of him, seeing the scattering of magazines, the sagging easy chair with a blanket and side table with lamp, dirty plates and glasses. He turned, making his way down the black hall, looked in the first room—Thor's room—seeing only an empty bed, another recliner, the smell of ammonia and neglect. The whole house smelled of it and he did not remember it, not like this. He went further down the hall, past the bathroom, to the two remaining bedrooms—left and right. The right door shut, the left open. And inside the left was his brother sleeping.

Trevor stood with the shovel in both hands. His brother was on his back, a blanket over hips and legs, his t-shirt ridden up to expose his white belly. On the bedside table there was a lamp, a water glass and a half-pint of Old Crow, keys, a rodeo magazine and a Long Colt revolver. There was a chair along the wall next to the table—a wooden chair that Trevor recognized from his mother's dining set.

Trevor drew the chair away from the wall with one hand and set it in the center of the room, near the foot of Ross' bed. He sat in the chair, in his father's jacket, and placed the shovel across his lap. He watched his brother breathe—the slow rise and fall of the white stomach. Trevor took out a cigarette and lit it. The snap of flame in the dark room, the new coal of the cigarette.

He smoked and waited.

When his brother woke, Trevor dropped the remains of the cigarette to the floor and snuffed it with his boot. He rose from the chair and brought the shovel up high, the blade of it almost touching the ceiling. Ross blinked, sniffing the air, then saw Trevor standing over him.

Trevor shifted his grip on the shovel's smooth handle.

You better take me out in one shot, Ross said.

Trevor moved in closer, kept the shovel up high.

I want the canyon. For now, at least.

His brother shook his head slowly.

I want the canyon. I'll take you to court over the Bedtick. I can access the canyon from there, on the other side of the creek—you won't even see me.

I'll smell you.

I'll have it. Or someone else will.

Ross' eyes widened and he rose a little in the bed. Trevor kept the pistol in mind but his brother did not even glance over at it.

You'll have to sit down with me and talk—but not tomorrow. I'm going to Cheyenne tomorrow to see a lawyer. Maybe to talk to the State.

Ross sat up into a slouch, resting his back against the headboard. He pulled the shirt over his stomach. Trevor waited, feeling the weight of the shovel in his hands.

You killed her so you might as well kill me.

Darcie.

You killed her and Dad. Kill me. Kill yourself. Make everyone happy.

Trevor felt a familiar trembling in his arms, the shovel now heavy. He looked at the smug face of his older brother, who turned his eyes upon the Long Colt by the lamp. And Trevor overcame the tremble, tightened his grip, though Ross only crossed his arms. He met Trevor's eyes.

You took her from me and now you want to take my land.

It's my land, too.

The hell it is. I'll kill you or you'll kill me before it is.

Trevor then quickly brought the shovel down, only to jab it forward like a spear, sending the steel blade into the wall above his brother's head. There was a dry *foomp* as the shovel's head went into the sheetrock, missing the studs. And Trevor thrust it further into the wall, until almost half of its steel was swallowed. Then he let go, left it there like a lance directly above his brother's head.

Darcie was fucking Grandpa, Trevor said. Grandpa was fucking Darcie.

Then he turned and did not look back at his brother in the bed. He took quick steps down the hall and into the main room and out the front door. He went to his truck, started it, backed up to the road and headed for Douglas, knowing that tomorrow, he really would head to Cheyenne.

Ross drew himself up from the slouch. He reached for the bottle and took a drink of whiskey, set it back, his knuckles brushing against the Colt. He got out of bed and took hold of the shovel's handle and yanked it out of the wall, clumps of gypsum and dust falling onto the bed. He tossed the shovel on the bed.

Tell me something I don't know, he said.

Ross Kallengaard turned the porch light on then walked outside. He returned the shovel to its slot in his truck. He stood there, looked at the horseshoe of yellow on the gravel that the porch light made, looked at the shadows, the shadow of the truck, of himself, then at the darkness beyond the reach of the light's electric penumbra. He stood in his bare feet, listening for something—a car or coyote—but there was only the wind. The wind in the pines on the hill, in the cottonwoods along the draw, in the dead apple trees. Wind in the tall grass of the ditch, in the broken corral fences, broken machinery, in the barn and calving shed. The sound of wind against wind . . . He turned and looked west, where the road curved and he wondered how his younger brother knew about Thor and Darcie.

He had met her in Casper, at the Wonder Bar, and he had brought her home. She had a beautiful body but there was also something reckless, fearless, about her, that Ross had loved. Darcie had been there a week before Thor said anything about it to him: This is a working ranch and everyone has to earn their keep. And though Darcie could cook and probably spread hay and feed, Ross understood it wasn't the kind of keep his grandfather had in mind.

They had shared a woman once, in Cheyenne during Frontier Days. The woman had come back to the room with them—they were so drunk—and she had engaged both of them in a row and all three of them had fallen asleep in one of the beds. When Ross woke up, the woman was gone and he was only sleeping with Thor. He'd felt embarrassment, or maybe shame, and went to the other bed before his grandfather woke. Thor never mentioned it—about the woman, about the three of them in one bed—but it was clear that he remembered it. Thor did not try to hide his desire or expectations after the second week Darcie was living with them.

Darcie understood the situation before Ross had. Ross didn't think she was surprised—he was never even sure if she minded. Maybe it was what she expected. The first time it was a night of whiskey and cards and the radio, the three of them, then Thor told Ross to go check on the horses, that Spar—Thor's horse—was still out in the pasture. And so he went out and took care of it and when he came back neither of them were still at the table. And so he understood, sort of.

She came back to him that night. When he heard the bedroom door open he turned away from it, not yet knowing exactly how he felt about it. He assumed that he knew how he felt about Darcie, but now he realized he was probably wrong. Though he could not articulate it to himself, let alone to her. He felt her get in under the covers, next to him, felt her press her nude body against him and he said nothing. He could smell the whiskey, the cigarettes—he did not smoke—he could smell other things, too. He wanted to be angry yet he didn't feel it. He thought he should feel betrayed but he didn't, exactly. Just the heat of her body against his. And then he thought that, as long as no one else knew, as long as they didn't have to talk about it, as long as she was more his than Thor's, then he could accept it. Who was she anyway? Darcie Featherstone. Just some woman he'd picked up at the Wonder Bar in Casper.

Collis Mudd woke up with a hangover, in his room at the Plains Hotel in Cheyenne. He was not a drinker but had spent the night in the Wigwam Lounge talking to Lane Waters, the bartender, who was working a double shift. And it had taken Lane Waters a long time to warm up to him, to get over whatever suspicions or reticence he had. And that had required a number of beers and shots and tips.

Despite the hangover, it had proved fruitful. The bartender knew Trevor Kallengaard. Had seen him. Talked to him. And—eventually—had informed Collis where he would probably be able to find him. Of course it was too late to look for Kallengaard by then—and Collis was in no shape to drive—so he took a room at the hotel and did not call Cassandra Tipton.

Though now, this morning, he would have to do both: travel and call.

Miss Tipton.

Collis. I was hoping to hear from you.

I'm sorry I didn't call last night, but he isn't here.

In Cheyenne?

Right. No. He's in Douglas.

What's that?

It's a town, north of here. I was up late last night talking to someone who knows Mr. Kallengaard and he told me that's where he's from and that's where he's gone to. Douglas, Wyoming.

I've never heard of it.

Me neither, but I'm heading up there today. He grew up on a ranch around there, I was told. He has a brother there.

Lane Waters also told Collis that Trevor Kallengaard had a wife or daughter with him—the Bisma Patel who signed the guest book. But he did not reveal this to Cass. The bartender had not been that clear on the subject and Collis thought it was something *to* be clear about before he informed her.

So he's staying with his brother?

Collis Mudd cleared his throat. He sat on the edge of the bed, still not dressed. He considered that he should have showered, dressed, eaten breakfast before making the call.

My understanding of it is that they don't get along, Mr. Kallengaard and his brother. It's something I'll have to look into, if need be.

Lane Waters had strung Collis along—something Collis realized fairly soon--- releasing new information as the night went along, getting him to buy more drinks, give more tips. The bar's business was not good and the bartender, Collis suspected, was more lonely or bored, really, than trying to make money.

You're close?

Yes. I have a very good idea where he is—or hope he is. So hold tight and I'll get back to you.

You are close.

There was a momentary silence between them. He was beginning to feel better.

I believe I am, Miss Tipton.

Cass.

Cass, he said.

It was mid-morning when Trevor pulled into Cheyenne. He parked in the lot across from the Plains Hotel where the old train station—now a museum—was. He walked to the hotel's café—the Victorian Rose—and sat at the counter. There were few customers. He ordered eggs and corned beef hash, rye toast and coffee as he had not eaten yet.

He smoked while he waited for his food and thought of Bisma, knowing that she was in Colorado. He looked around the café, noticing the man sitting by himself along the window, mainly because he was African American—one of the few black people he had seen since leaving Fort Collins.

After eating, Trevor drove to the Capitol and parked out front. He was not sure who he would see about the canyon, or even if anyone would see him. But he knew their office would be here. The whole idea of the canyon and the bridge becoming a state park was abstract in his mind. Almost impossible. But it could be useful—would be useful—in dealing with Ross, whether as bargaining chip or threat.

Inside, the lobby was as hushed as before, with the same woman behind the information desk watching him. Awaiting him. He did not go to her, but walked to the buffalo and stood there. Trevor realized that he didn't want to talk to anyone, had no use for whoever might speak to him. What was there to say? Help me gain my piece of the ranch and maybe you'll get your park? But he and the state wanted the same land. He would only open a can of worms by talking to some official about it.

Trevor looked again at the buffalo and its red-lettered DO NOT TOUCH sign. He stole a glance at the woman at the desk and saw that she had given up on him, so he reached out and touched the buffalo. He felt its coarse hairs, the leathery hide of its hump. He didn't know if that was how a buffalo really felt—its hair and skin at least—or if it was only the work of the taxidermist. His idea—his plan—of owning the canyon was his birthright, as a Kallengaard—he told himself. And if that was so, then he could also dream of owning the Bedtick—even of raising bison on that land. It would not be a bad life. Then afterwards, when he was dead and gone, the state could have its park and the herd that went with it.

He withdrew the hand and felt a little foolish. He looked at the information desk, though he no longer wanted information. Trevor walked back outside to the front steps.

He stood in the sun on the steps and shook out a cigarette. Lit it. Smoked and watched what traffic there was. He felt better, determined to complete what he had set out to do.

Though Trevor very much believed in parks and the greater good, he did not want the state to take his land. Not that land. Maybe, he thought, there wasn't much difference between him and his brother, his grandfather—that his stubbornness and lack of magnanimity rose when it affected him personally, when it interfered with his own world. Probably, or possibly, the state would have helped him settle the will, could have expedited what had to be done with Ross. But Trevor did not want a lawyer or the State of Wyoming fighting his fights. No, he'd settle it—maybe as Thor wished—between brothers.

Could I bother you for a light?

Trevor turned and looked. It was the man he had seen at the Victorian Rose. The man was tall, wide, hatless and Trevor watched as he took a cigarette from a new pack and held it close to his lips. Trevor fished his lighter from his pocket and handed it to the man.

Pretty day. I've never been to Cheyenne before.

Trevor nodded and took a step away.

Tell me, are you staying in town?

Trevor looked more closely, seeing only an innocuous expression on the man's face.

I just wonder if you could tell me what to look for, what to see. Tourist stuff. Tell me where I should stay.

I'm not staying. I don't think I can help you.

Well, I was thinking of heading north a bit, maybe up . . .

Most people go to Yellowstone or the Tetons.

Thank you, but I was looking for something different. I'm from Florida.

Trevor turned fully to the man then, studied him, met his eyes. The man still held his lighter and had not lit the cigarette.

I'm sorry, I can't help you.

Okay. I guess you're headed out of town. You're just visiting like me and now you're going home.

Yes. I'm headed back.

The man nodded, handed back the lighter without ever using it. Trevor put it in his pocket and started to walk to his truck. The man called to him when he opened the cab's door.

Thank you, Mr. Kallengaard.

Trevor nodded slowly and got into the truck. He sat and looked out the windshield at the man, who was now walking away. He no longer felt better and was trying to understand how the man knew his name.

Bisma was still in Cheyenne, in her room at the Plains Hotel, talking on her phone. She was talking to the boy she had dated in Fort Collins, a young man she had broken up with three months ago. She had decided to stay in Cheyenne thinking of it as a way to ruminate on what she had been through with Trevor. *A sense of closure* she told herself, half sarcastically, though now she wasn't so sure of her motive. She now thought that maybe it was a way to avoid closure. So, this morning she did not go out, did not get breakfast or walk to the bus station, but stayed in bed and then called Andrew.

Andrew had gone home to Boulder for the summer. And after only a few minutes of talking to him over the phone, she realized that he was not the person of comfort, not the man-to-the-rescue, that she was looking for.

Yes, she said, I know I'm the one who didn't return your calls, or your texts, emails, Facebook . . . Do I have to stay in constant touch, Andrew? . . . Look, I know I'm the one who called, now. I was in Wyoming—I am in Wyoming . . . No, I don't think . . . I don't . . . Andrew, never mind. No. No, don't come get me. I'd rather you didn't . . . Because . . . I can change my mind. You know I change my mind . . . Maybe I will go to California, okay? That's the plan, isn't it? . . . No . . . No . . . No.

She hung up and turned off her phone. At times she abhorred cell phones and social media. The need, or ability, to be in constant touch with the whole world.

She sat on the bed and stared at the overhead light in her room and she thought that there was no meaning to her presence here. There was no meaning to anything she did. Writing, traveling, loving, caring, eating, breathing—what was the purpose? It did not matter to anyone else what she did or where she went or what she thought. It hardly mattered to her. If she were to die—right here, right now, in this very room—who would care? Bisma suddenly felt very light, as if a string inside herself had been pulled taut and then broken, something small and tight was now loose, and she did not like the feeling. She asked herself who could retie that string, if she could not? How could it be retied?

As he drove back to Douglas, Trevor wondered about the man who knew his name. At first he considered that the man was a State Parks employee—but he realized that was impossible. And, the man said he was from Florida . . . Trevor guessed he could have seen the plates on his truck, as Bisma had. Still, why bother to say it? The man had been in the café, then just happened to be at the Capitol? He knew his name—his last name at least.

Trevor stopped at the rest area between Wheatland and Guernsey. He used the restroom then stood outside and smoked. He watched people but saw no one he knew, did not see the man who had spoken to him. Trevor thought that, from Guernsey, he could head a little east where there was a state park: Oregon Trail Ruts and Register Cliff. He thought he could look it over, get some idea, apply that to the image of the canyon and the bridge as a park. But, no. As before, he dismissed it.

He finished his cigarette and waited a little longer, deciding that he was not being followed. He had not told the man anything specific, had not mentioned Douglas or any direction. Trevor doubted he would ever see the man again.

It was after noon when Trevor parked his truck in front of the LaBonte Hotel. He walked into the lobby and found his brother waiting for him there.

At first he thought it was a mistake, an illusion. He had not seen the brown truck out front. But he looked again at the man in the lobby and it was him, Ross, sitting at one of the small tables facing the door, drink in hand. He sat in a slouch, his eyes meeting Trevor's with an idle arrogance. Trevor thought about turning around and walking away.

You can sit down, Ross said. I've been waiting for you.

Trevor approached but did not sit.

You said you wanted to talk to me, so here I am. Sit down.

Using his foot, Ross pushed the opposite chair outward. Trevor then sat in it, not scooting it forward as Ross straightened up out of his slouch.

Good. Been in Florida I saw. Your truck at least.

I was in Florida. Part of the time.

Part of the time . . . You get married? Got kids?

No.

Trevor thought Ross would ask about Bisma, but he didn't.

Then it's us—the last of the Kallengaards. Like that movie.

What movie?

The one about the Indians.

It's a book.

Okay, a book. But I saw the movie about the last of those Indians.

Mohicans.

That's it. That's us now.

They were father and son.

Ross almost laughed, took a drink from the watered-down drink.

We don't have that problem, do we. But it's down to us, anyway you look at it, because I sure don't have any kids . And you were gone so long I figured it was only me that was left. And I liked it like that—nice and simple. Natural. The way it should be.

His brother met his eyes.

I just got back from Cheyenne, Trevor said and Ross shifted his body in the chair, quit looking at Trevor.

And you want to talk about that?

We can. You already know that the state wants the canyon for a park, that they want the bridge.

They won't have it as long as I'm alive.

That's fine with me, because I want it. If we make a deal—settle the estate—then maybe they can't touch it.

You won't have it either.

Why?

Ross appeared surprised by the question, as if it were plainly obvious why, or, that he hadn't considered Trevor would ask.

You don't deserve it. You're not family anymore . . . If I could trap you down in there, then you could keep it as your grave.

Trevor let out a long breath.

Why are you here?

Because I want you to know, for sure, that I won't give you my land. Any of it. I lived on that land with Grandpa, with Darcie, and I worked that land. I worked hard. It's mine by right—all of it. You can go hire yourself a lawyer or get the government, you can get an army, but no one will get it. And not by any law—man's law or natural law—will you get even a tiny speck of it.

Trevor took off his hat and held it in front of him and said nothing. There was nothing to be said. But then he told Ross anyway:

I'm not going away. I won't quit.

Ross finished his drink, sucking on the remainders of ice. He put the glass down and stood up, adjusting the shirt around his waist.

The land's not divisible. Either one of us or none of us will have it . . . Now, we had our talk, like you wanted. Next time I see you we'll do it my way. Can you understand that much?

Trevor nodded.

I understand more than you do.

Ross did not comment. He turned his back on Trevor and walked out of the lobby of the LaBonte Hotel.

He was parked across the street from an old hotel. Collis Mudd noted the big man who came out and watched him walk half way down the street before getting in a brown pickup and driving away.

It had not taken Collis long to drive around the town of Douglas and find Kallengaard's truck. After finding it, he'd walked up to the front doors of the hotel only to see Kallengaard through the glass, there at a table with the man who had just left the hotel. So, Collis had retreated to the car and waited.

And he waited a few more minutes before going back, into the hotel. The lobby was empty now, save for a clerk, and Collis asked the clerk if there was a Trevor Kallengaard registered.

Yes there is, the man said without searching any list. Would you like me to ring his room?

No thank you.

Found him, was the first thing Collis Mudd said when Cass answered the phone.

You saw him?

I talked to him this morning, in Cheyenne.

So he is in Cheyenne.

No. I saw him there by chance—for some reason he was there, but he went back to Douglas. And when I came up here I found him again, at the hotel where he's staying.

Cass, in Fort Lauderdale, wanted to tell Collis Mudd that she was coming out to Wyoming. But she wanted to wait, to give him time, maybe to give herself time. She would tell him the next time he called.

So you talked to him. You told him about me?

Not yet. Cass, I only said a few words to him to get him thinking, let him ease into the idea that you're looking for him. He knows it now, but just doesn't know that he knows—if you follow me. I think, in this man's case, it's best to work it a little slow, so it's not a big surprise. A shock might scare him off.

I don't understand.

Collis, who had a room at a different hotel, sat down on the bed and removed his shoes.

I can explain it better later, if that's okay. Let's just say that he knows something's going on, that I know who he is. And, eventually, that'll lead him to thinking about you.

Okay. And you're at the same hotel as Trevor? In Douglas?

No, I'm at the Best Western. Room eleven oh seven, in Douglas. Mr. Kallengaard is at some old hotel downtown. Looks like he's been there a while—the clerk knew him by name.

What's the name of the hotel he's at?

Cass, can we wait on that? I'm afraid if I give you the name, you're going to call him. And if you contact him, he might run or cut you off because he hasn't had time to think it over. I'm sure you could find it—this is a small town—but I think you shouldn't. Not yet.

Oh, she said.

I'm not trying to milk it. I don't do that. But, a day or two, he'll start figuring it out. He'll start thinking its you.

Collis stood up again in the hotel room. He thought of the name Bisma Patel and what the bartender had told him. And then there was the man who had visited Kallengaard today. This was information he wanted to sit on for now and—he told himself—would reveal to Cass when he understood it better.

Okay, Collis. I think I understand. And if he won't come back, to me, I want to hear it from him. Directly from him.

That's a deal.

Collis?

Yes?

I wasn't thinking that, about you milking it.

Thanks. That's good to know, Miss Tipton.

Cass.

Cassandra.

Now Cass knew for sure. She knew that she would fly out to Wyoming, whether it was tomorrow, or the day after, or the day after that.

In the morning, Trevor drank coffee and smoked in the café while he perused the Douglas Budget. He took the time to look at the employment ads in the back of the paper, of which there were few. He knew he needed a job. Needed money. He had seen new construction south of town and thought he could just ask there, at the job site, though he was for all purposes, an outsider, a stranger. More likely he'd have to go to Casper for work. He'd have to be more practical and commute to Casper while building the cabin on the land in his time off. Or, he could probably find oil work, in the fields no doubt, but then he'd be gone for weeks, months, and not good for anything else . . . Trevor realized that if he was going to work full time in Casper, then he might as well move there. If practicality was his motive, then he'd never build a cabin. He would end up living the way he didn't want to live.

He stubbed out his cigarette, finished the coffee and left the weekly newspaper on the counter. He went back to the room and wrote out a list on the pad of paper the hotel provided:

Drivers License.

Post Office Box

Hardware: post hole digger, Quikrete, shovel, five gallon buckets, posts, two-bys, six-bys, plywood, nails, screws, anchor bolts.

He stopped the list, knowing that he'd need more than that. He had his power tools but no power—would he want a generator? Trevor didn't think so. He had his battery drills that he could charge, he had hand tools and could get more. He needed building supplies, though he didn't need them all at once. But he'd also need a large cooler to hold water, another to hold food and ice. He needed toilet paper and utensils and plates and such, a tent. Flashlights and batteries. Firewood. A camp stove. Towels. He would need a heater for when winter came. A snow shovel. Snow tires, maybe chains, possibly a snowblade for the truck. Warm clothes.

His mind wrote lists that led to more lists and then he stopped himself. This was not what he wanted. He would build a cabin, sleep on site—this was the idea. He would get things on a need-be basis. Employment and money would have to come later, when necessary. Dealing with his brother would also come later. The same with any lawyer and litigation. Everything could wait and he would deal with it as it came to him.

Tomorrow he would move out of the hotel. He'd use the credit card to pay the bill. Use the card to pay all subsequent bills and, unless he changed it, all those bills would go to Fort Lauderdale, to the house where Cass lived. There was quite a bit of money in the account, both savings and checking, and maybe she would pay them. They had no outstanding debt—other than the mortgage on the house, which was in her name. But if he wanted her to pay the bills and promise to pay her back, then he would have to call her. And, she would know where he was.

Now on the motel stationary he composed a letter to Cass. But everything he wrote sounded flat, ill said and incomplete. He tried again, then a third time, and he saw her face as he wrote, her eyes, her hair, he envisioned her body and what it felt like, the warmth of her skin, how it felt when she touched him—a hand on his arm, a foot under the covers in bed. And then he stopped. He tore up the small sheets of stationary and dropped them in the trashcan. He felt ridiculous. He felt guilt.

The break was supposed to be clean. Irrevocable. But by writing the note, Trevor could see that it was not. He could not convey to her his current needs nor how he felt about the leaving. All he could do was apologize.

He lit a cigarette and made his mind retreat from the idea of money, the idea of contacting Cass, from Cass herself. For now he would only get his Wyoming drivers license. Purchase the most basic materials for the cabin. Check out of the hotel and use the credit card until something happened. Yes, Cass would know where he had moved to and she could send him the bills, then he would pay them as he was able.

He stubbed out the cigarette, made sure he had his keys and wallet, then, as he reached for his Stetson, there was a knock on the door. He froze, hat in hand. There were no security peepholes at the LaBonte and Trevor could only guess that it was his brother on the other side. Or, possibly, the man from Cheyenne who knew his name. But when he opened the door she was there.

She stood with her suitcase on the floor, her long black hair cleanly brushed, something different in her face—no gleam of humor, confidence, playfulness.

Trevor was uncertain what to say.

I took a bus back. Turns out they have cab service in this town, so I . . .

Bisma, he said.

. . . took a cab.

Why?

She looked straight at him. Eyes deep, limpid. She did not smile.

Because I had to. I'm in love with you.

SEVEN

The Canyon

Collis had driven back to the LaBonte Hotel and saw that Trevor's truck was still there, parked in the same space. Just checking, he said to himself and drove back to the Best Western near the river, back to his room. That was when Cass called him.

I understand what you told me, but I'm going to fly into Denver. I'll get a car and drive up to Douglas. It's not that far, right?

Miss Tipton . . .

I know, I know. But I have to. I have to see him, talk to him. It's what I should do.

Cass, I haven't even . . .

I've already booked the flight and car. It's important.

Collis Mudd touched a stuffed toy—a jackalope, a rabbit with antlers—that he had bought at the gift shop for Keena, though it would make Lakeesha laugh if he gave it to her. He knew, from the sound of Cassandra Tipton's voice, that his client would not change her mind.

Okay, he said, just tell me what time I should expect you. I'll keep an eye on him till then.

Bisma rode beside him in the truck. There was an awkwardness between them, no talk or touching. He had said nothing about her confession of love for him but had not rejected her. He had embraced her when she wanted to be embraced. But he didn't think it was true, this love. And he could not bring himself to say that he loved her in return . . . With Cass he could and would say, I love you. She would sometimes say it to him and he would return the statement, though rarely did he say it on his own initiative. Even then, in many ways, he had not fully believed it—did not think that he was capable of love in it's true sense. He was, however, certain that Cass did love him, that she was capable. After all, she had loved Marcus.

So, Trevor had held Bisma, held her and they sat silently on the bed together without talking much. And he found that he was glad of her presence, her touch, which surprised him, because another part of him wished that she had not come back. And after long minutes he told her he had things to do, that he had to get a drivers license and go to the post office in town and that she could go with him if she liked. She said yes, she said she understood what he was doing—gaining some sort of residency—because he was going to try and live on the land that had been his grandfather's.

Bisma said little and did not appear impatient as he took the written test, the vision test, then the photo before getting the license itself. Trevor used the ranch as a home address and they did not question it. His brother's name was in their records, the Kallengaard name was known in Converse County. At the same time he produced his truck title and they issued him Wyoming plates. Then, outside in the parking lot, Trevor used channel locks to unscrew the bolts and remove the sole rear Florida plate. He put that in the bed of the truck and then the new plates on, front and back.

Wyoming, Bisma said.

She stayed with him at the post office as he signed and paid for the box. They were headed for the lumber yard when, inside the truck, she turned to him and spoke of love again.

Maybe I shouldn't have said it, that I love you.

I don't know.

It's like there's something wrong between us now. I don't expect you to say it or even feel it, though I'd hope you feel something.

I can't say if there's anything wrong, anything right. But you're here. I can say that I missed you. I . . . I don't say much.

He looked at her and she turned her head from him, studying what was out her window, but he thought he saw a trace of a smile before they pulled into the lumberyard.

You're really going to build a cabin?

Yes, like I said I would.

They didn't get out of the truck after he parked.

You settled things? With your brother?

No.

Trevor...

He touched her face with his hand—her cheek, her jaw. He put his thumb against her lips. He was going to remind her why she had left before and that his mind had not changed but, looking at her, he saw that he didn't have to.

Can we stay at the hotel?

For a while, I guess, but I'm going to start living out there, in the canyon. Make do.

You don't think he'll stop you? Shoot you?

Shoot me? No, he's only trying to frighten me. I used to be afraid of him, a long time ago, but not anymore. Not now.

So if I decided to stay with you, out there...

I'm sure he wouldn't hurt you. He's not that bad. He wants to bully me. Just me.

I don't want to go back to Fort Collins, to school, to anything. I'll go camp out in the canyon with you. Tonight.

The back of the truck was full when they returned to the motel to get their things. It was long past check out and he paid for the night, for all the nights, no longer worrying about the money, about the use of the card. He would take those consequences when they came to him.

They stopped at the Texaco for gas and cigarettes and, at the last minute, Rainier Beers to add to the cooler of ice and perishable food. He drove the back way, down Cold Springs Road, around the Chalk Buttes, and into the Bedtick, a route that didn't cross the ranch house. Table Mountain was bright and clear in the late afternoon sunlight.

I still don't understand why you insist in calling that a mountain. It's a mesa, like around Durango or in New Mexico.

Trevor shrugged.

It's just what it's called.

They went past the reservoir and crossed the Pearl on Windy Ridge Road, the land fenced yet open, land carved by ancient glaciers. Trevor had noticed a car behind them at times, in the trail of dust, but as the road got rougher it had fallen back. The car had disappeared completely by the time he crossed a cattle guard and went off-road, fording Buckshot Creek with the truck.

He and Bisma traversed the blank land, bouncing and avoiding the draws and occasional outcrop of rock, until they came upon the nameless ranch road that took them to the trail that descended into the canyon.

They ate a late picnic lunch—sandwiches, apples, peanuts—beneath the cottonwoods, the sun already only half way into the canyon, yet full and bright upon the upper reaches of the natural bridge. Afterwards, he began to unload the lumber, the bags of Quickrete, a roll of Visqueen, boxes of 16d sinker nails. He had a blue tarp that could serve as a temporary roof after he got walls up, that would also be handy to keep supplies dry if it should ever rain. He had a new handsaw and axe—his circular saw, miter saw and others were pointless, unless he wanted to buy a generator, which he did not. For the time being, all Trevor wanted was a roughed-out one room cabin, a wood stove and chimney pipe, plywood flooring. One door and two windows. It would not be a log cabin. More ascetic than aesthetic, it would still be an improvement over the dirt-floored structure his grandfather had built. Eventually he could add rooms, use hand-hewed logs, add windows; he could dig a well for a pump, maybe lay pipe for inside water and a kitchen, a compost toilet of some kind.

Trevor had only a basic image in his mind: a cabin along the Pearl, in a world walled by sandstone, cottonwoods, the limestone bridge, under that singular allowance of sky. And like his grandfather's, Trevor's cabin would serve as proof that he lived here—upon the land—and not just for seven years or until Ross accepted it, but until he decided he no longer wanted to live upon it. Or could no longer.

Do you want some help?

Bisma was watching him as he methodically arranged the materials in the grass and dirt, upon the fallen leaves. The white fluff of cottonwood seeds gathering around each and every piece. Trevor stopped what he was doing—the ordering of things, the ruminating on things. He looked at Bisma as she opened the cooler and brought out a cold beer, offered it to him—it made Trevor think of Darcie.

Sure, he said and went to her and took the beer from her. I could use some help.

Collis Mudd drove past the spot where he had last seen Kallengaard then stopped. He doubled back when he saw a plume of dust behind him—the obvious trail of a vehicle on a dirt road. Turning on the small, rough road, he watched the distant dust of Kallengaard's truck , thinking it might be better just to go back to the hotel and wait for Cassandra Tipton. She was coming today and he'd have to tell her that Trevor Kallengaard was with another woman.

But Collis had promised he'd keep an eye on the man, so he drove, bouncing along and making his own trail of dust, though the truck was far ahead of him now.

Cassandra—Cass—was probably mid-flight at this moment, he thought. Then she was going to drive all the way to Douglas from Denver. He had hours— dinnertime, most likely—before he'd meet up with her. He was certain her appearance was premature. A wrong move. It wasn't that he was against her coming, in fact he admitted to himself that he was looking forward to it, had been thinking about her all afternoon, but there was another woman in the mix. Yes, this woman— Bisma Patel—could be but an innocent connection, but Collis had been around long enough to think that it was not. He wanted to catch up to them, observe them, see how they treated each other, then he'd know if they were lovers or something else. He'd considered doing a search on her, but that would turn his objective—what he had been hired to do—into something very different.

The dirt road was about gone now, the rental's low carriage scraped clumps of grass and cacti, the occasional thump of exposed rock or knobs of soil. The plume of dust that had signaled Kallengaard's truck was gone though he could see what he assumed were fresh tire tracks. He crossed a cattle guard and came to a gentle slope that led to a dry wash. He drove slower and saw four antelope up ahead. They were pronghorn with cream-colored coats, distinctive white and black markings, large-eyed. Startlingly beautiful to Collis, he stopped the car to look them over, and they turned their heads in unison to look back at him before suddenly bolting, running faster then he imagined, making their own trail of dust as they headed up the wash and over a hill and were gone.

Man, he said to himself and he thought of his children and he though of Cassandra Tipton and, without acknowledging why, he wished that she had seen the antelope with him. Wasting time, he told himself and put the car in motion once again.

There was no longer a trial now as he drove between swells of sage and dry grass, topography the same in all directions with only the distant, dirt-green mountains to the west, and a flat-topped jut of land close by, as markers for direction. Then he came to a running, shallow creek and he saw where they must have crossed it—there were tire ruts, the soil darkened where the sun had not dried them yet.

Collis pushed the car to the creek but as he hit the edge of the water he found that it was soft silt, and his tires refused to grip it. Soon, he was stuck with the front half of the purple car in the middle of the creek.

Shit.

He said it softly, as if hiding something from his children.

He tried forward and reverse, rocking and turning the wheels, only to make it worse.

He got out of the car, got his feet wet and muddy as he crossed the creek, not understanding why the car wouldn't make it when he could easily walk across. But that didn't matter. He was undeniably stuck.

Collis listened to the wind. There were no clouds in the open sky. He felt the first trickle of sweat since he left Florida roll down his neck. There was no one. There were no houses. He could hear no machinery or airplanes or car traffic— nothing like the constant din of Miami, or about anywhere in South Florida.

What could he do? He couldn't push the car out. He could see if his phone had service out here, call a tow truck—though he was uncertain about his location. Or, he guessed, he could continue on foot.

Collis Mudd began to walk.

Ross Kallengaard didn't think his brother would return to Florida. Maybe the girl that was with him had left, scared off, but not Trevor. So, he was in his truck headed for the canyon when he saw a man—a large man, a black man—come walking out of the hay field. The man saw him too and began to flag him down, which made Ross wonder just what in the hell was going on. So he stopped his pick up in the road and waited for the man to come to him, right up to his open window. But Ross spoke first.

You lost?

A little. My car got stuck in a creek a ways back.

Ross nodded his head.

You walking to town then?

I'd like to get my car out, then drive back to town.

So you staying in Douglas?

I am. Visiting.

Why?

Ross watched the man's reaction, saw him withdraw a little, take a step back.

If it's not far I guess I'll walk. Get it towed.

This is my property, so I can pull your car out. I've got some chains. You must be stuck on the Buckshot, if you've come through the field. That way.

He pointed southwest.

That's where I came from. I was out sightseeing, spotted some antelope. Got carried away.

Ross nodded and motioned for the man to get in the truck. While the man came around, he removed the flask of whiskey from the passenger seat and put it behind his own.

Only, Ross said as the man closed the door, I've got to check on something first.

Collis sat in the man's truck and looked out the windshield. Neither talked. He felt foolish and did not like to feel foolish. There was a concern, which he pushed to the back of his mind, that he wouldn't make it to meet Cass at the hotel. Though the man driving offered no name, Collis recognized him. And, if this land belonged to him, that made him a Kallengaard—the brother of Trevor.

There wasn't much resemblance, though Collis had to admit he'd only seen Trevor in person for a short period. Sometimes resemblances came in gestures and voice, in phrasing and carriage—sometimes they had the same mindsets, siblings making similar choices or how they dealt with pressure. The way they sometimes made the same mistakes.

The truck trundled along a dirt road now, a road fenced unevenly, until the man pulled over and stopped.

Just need to check on this.

He got out, closed his door, then leaned on the truck. The windows were open and he looked in at Collis.

You can come with me, if you want.

Collis did not know if it was a good idea. There was a perception of danger to the man, if he wanted to see it that way, but he thought it was something else. He got out and came around the truck.

Again he saw that the man was tall, big-boned—like himself. And there was something cagey about him, a sly and guarded intelligence. Collis Mudd felt that the man, the brother, knew Collis was holding back, that there was more to his story than a stuck car. This brother had that animal sense, just like he had sensed it about Livian before he found her out—before she had shot him.

They walked together in the dry grass which turned to sage and then brush and Collis saw how the land was deceptive, how it dovetailed to the right and there was a path that led downward. The brother kept them off the trail, wound his way between plants until they were on a ledge, the land falling away abruptly into a chasm.

Collis could see the tops of trees and a wall of orange rock. He saw a hump of stone with stunted trees and brush growing on top of it. A box canyon, was the definition that came to Collis' mind, though wasn't sure how accurate the term was. But down below, Collis saw two people, man and woman.

Collis saw that the brother was now looking at him, not the people below.

Like a little Adam and Eve, the man said.

From his vantage, Collis could now see that there was lumber and tools, that there was work in progress. And of course he recognized the truck and the man— Trevor Kallengaard. The woman, who was young, almost looked familiar. Like a girl he'd noted at the Plains Hotel in Cheyenne who'd been in line to check in before him.

Adam and Eve? Collis said, now wanting to engage the man, get the brother to talk.

Making their own garden down there—he took his eyes off Collis—thinking the snake will never show up.

You know them?

The brother regarded Collis slowly, his face inscrutable.

Do you?

No. I'm from Atlanta—on vacation.

I know one of them, my brother. She doesn't matter.

But the brother does?

They looked at each other again, Collis met his eyes.

Where did you say you were from?

Atlanta.

Just another person who doesn't belong here—like them.

I only need to get my car and I'll be on my way.

The brother of Trevor Kallengaard nodded this time. They walked back to the truck.

Ross drove slow and off-road, asking the man if this was the way he had come. The man said he thought so. Ross could not figure out who the guy was. Was he from the State, checking on the land for a park? A lawyer for Trevor? Or was he here for an entirely different reason? But Ross was sure the man was not visiting from Atlanta. There was some connection to his brother.

They found the car sitting in Buckshot Creek. They both got out of the truck and Ross took chains from the bed, a chain thick and rusted beneath the litter of grass and pine needles and some cans. It had large hooks and Ross attached one end to a metal ring at the back of his truck.

I'm going to pull you out the way you came in, then you can hit the paved road when you head west.

Okay.

Then you can drive into Douglas. From there it's southeast to Atlanta.

The man eyed him and Ross nodded, seeing that he got the message.

He had the man put the little car in neutral and then step back as he hooked the chain to the rear frame. He went back to his truck and, slowly giving it gas, dragged the car backwards out of the muck and onto solid soil.

Can I give you anything for your trouble?

Kallengaard's brother was putting the chains back into his truck.

No, except don't come out here again.

Collis gave him a tight smile but said nothing.

Collis drove only a mile or two down the Bedtick before pulling over along the empty road. He wanted to think a few things over.

He thought that he should talk to Trevor Kallengaard as soon as possible and let him know that Cass was coming, that she wanted him back. Collis would have liked to wait on it, find out about his relationship with the young woman, but that would no longer work. Between Cass coming and what he saw in the brother's eyes, he had to push things. Then again, who knew? Maybe it was best that Cassandra Tipton was coming. Maybe he was being too cautious or maybe he just wanted to leave it to fate. Let her show up, let her be rejected. He did not quite understand why she wanted the man back—she could do much better than Kallengaard, a man who had abandoned her, a man who ran away to a place like this to build a house in a hole in the ground. At least she could be free of him. But would she be? Anymore than he was free from Livian?

He knew it shouldn't matter to him why she wanted Kallengaard. Should make no difference. He was only the hired gun and his job was to find the man, which he had. He could go back to the room now, shower, put on some decent clothes and wait for Cassandra Tipton, his client, and take her to see Kallengaard. Then go back home. Get paid. That's all he had to do.

Collis Mudd waited along the road for fifteen minutes before he turned the car around. He went back to the cattle guard, crossed it and the dry wash. This time he gunned the purple car across Buckshot Creek, making it to the other side.

With a better sense of the land now, he found the trail and then the road where he had met the brother. Collis—wary that the brother was still around—went slow as he searched for the path that led to the canyon. But he didn't have to find it, because he saw Trevor Kallengaard standing alone at the top of the path, an axe in his hands.

Kallengaard watched him intently as he neared, parked and got out. He didn't look too surprised as Collis approached him.

I heard a car, thought I heard one earlier, was all he said.

Mr. Kallengaard, my name is Collis Mudd.

He put out his hand and, after a moment of hesitation, Trevor Kallengaard removed one hand from the axe and they shook.

Are you from the Parks Department?

No.

Then, besides the name, who are you?

I'm a friend of Cass'. I'm here to tell you that she wants you to come home.

Ross Kallengaard stood on the hill behind the house. The sun was in the pines, the trees' tall, narrow trunks casting shadows over the gravestones of grandmother and grandfather, of father and Darcie. Wind—cool for summer—came down from the Sheep Mountains and shook the boughs above him while he contemplated his brother's presence in the canyon. What Trevor was doing—building a cabin—was easy to understand. What to do about it, and about the girl that was with him, was different.

As Darcie was taken away from him, he could take things away from Trevor. Not the girl—this was not something he would do—but he could take a physical thing like his truck, the very structure he was assembling. And he could take Trevor's confidence, his defiance, his spirit. His hopes and plans. All that could be taken from him, just as they had from him. He would allow his little brother to believe for a while. For today at least. Then he would demolish it all. Thor would have done the same. His grandfather would not have even allowed a day.

The old man never admitted that the death of Trig and Darcie changed him, but Ross saw it. The way his grandfather quit going to auctions, the way he pushed Annie onto Gus and Frida, got her to sell the house in Cheyenne. He wouldn't let her look for Trevor—said that he would come back in due time. And, though it took a lot longer than anyone would think, he was right about that. Yes, Thor would do it the way Ross was doing it, only he'd be more ruthless.

Ross began the walk back down the hill and to the first pasture, all the while knowing that everything didn't quite add up. Because if Thor didn't want Trevor to have anything, why didn't he leave it all to Ross in the will? Why had he left it to Annie? This fact only complicated things, conflicted with what he was sure Thor would do. Unless, of course, Thor—who was certain Trevor would return—wanted Ross to earn it. To take it. To be able to say: This belongs to me and this is how I make it so.

Collis Mudd returned to Douglas. He had a message from Cass on his phone that said she was at the hotel and had a room on the same floor as him. So, when he was in his own room, he called her.

She asked to meet but Collis said he needed to shower—which was true—and that maybe they could have dinner together at the restaurant attached to the Best Western. She said that would be good and Collis hung up and he felt strange, as if things were coming a little unglued, as if his mission, the job, was not being done properly.

The very presence of Cassandra Tipton made things more difficult, Collis thought. It made him anxious. He considered the anxiety came from having to tell her about the young woman Kallengaard was with, or from having to explain about the canyon and the construction within it; possibly the anxiety emanated from the stilted dialogue with the Kallengaard brother, a man Collis was wary of, who seemed capable of violence. He wasn't sure what to tell Cass about him, either. But Collis knew he wasn't being honest with himself. He knew where the anxiety sprang from.

An hour later, when he went to her room and knocked and she opened the door, he couldn't help but to look at her: her small frame and light hair, her smile, the blue of her eyes with age lines traced around them. He had been imagining that face each time he talked to her on the phone and now she was here, in front of him, and he was pleased.

Collis.

She seemed pleased as well, maybe to see him or maybe to have come out to Wyoming by herself.

Miss Tipton.

The restaurant was spacious, decorated in peach and beige, its entrance open to the lobby and not far from the indoor pool. The hostess who seated them was formal, almost cool, putting them in a corner booth in back. They sat and looked at the menu as a young man brought water, then a plate of bread and butter. There was the sound of other diners' conversations and the echoing sounds of children laughing and splashing in the pool.

Cass felt that she had lost some of her nerve since landing in Denver and then driving all the way to Douglas. At first she was enthralled with the landscape, with a sense of her own bravery in coming to see for herself what Trevor was up to, but something about the drive further north, into the wide and barren expanse, the distant mountains, made her question herself. Now that she had gone to all the trouble and cost, she hoped it was only a temporary discomfiture. So, as soon as the waitress left with their drink orders, she told Collis: I want to see him.

Sure. Is it okay if we eat first before discussing everything? Cass nodded— she had a sense that he was not happy with her presence. I realize it's hard not to rush into it. I know you have a lot of questions or you want to reach some conclusion to all of this.

She followed his lead and made small talk about the land and the town, the weather until she just came out and asked:

Do you think I should have stayed in Fort Lauderdale? You don't seem too pleased that I'm here.

I'm sorry. I guess I'm set in my ways, but no, I'm glad you're here. It's nice to see you, Miss Tipton. Maybe this will expedite the whole situation. Maybe it will come to a quicker solution.

It's Cass, Collis.

I know. Cass.

He had steak and potato, she had chicken and rice. Iced tea for both. She reached for the bill when the waitress came with it, a woman who wouldn't look either of them in the eye. She had been curt throughout the whole meal. Collis took the bill from Cass.

Let me get it.

It'll only go on your expense account.

I think it's best I pay.

Why?

Discreetly, Collis pointed out to Cass how the waitress was watching them, how a cook from the kitchen's doorway was watching them. He told her others had been, too.

This isn't Miami. I don't think these people are used to seeing a man like me with a woman like you. And then to have you pay for the meal on top of it.

Cass didn't understand, but then she did.

Oh . . . You think?

He nodded.

Wow. So if I bought you a drink in the bar? If I invited you up to my room?

She started to laugh and Collis tried not to, but he had a big laugh. The room was silent when they were done. Even the tin-can sounds from the pool had stopped.

Whoops.

Cass felt better now and told him that she really would not mind a drink.

I didn't drank for years and years and just started again, a while ago.

I don't drink much either but, well, it's up to you.

It'll be fine. The people here will just have to get used to us.

They sat at a small table in the lounge, where they could not hear the hollow sounds of the pool. Three men in cowboy hats sat at the bar and there were a few couples at tables. The bar was done in the same peach and beige as the restaurant. The barmaid was young, friendly, and she brought them a beer and glass of wine promptly.

Collis Mudd paid for the drinks in cash.

So, I'd like to know where he is, what he's been up to.

She was in a good mood, her face bright, though she fidgeted with her cocktail napkin. She looked very pretty to Collis and he was hesitant to bring up Kallengaard and ruin her spirit. But he told himself he was not here to protect her or comfort her. He was not here to fall in love with her.

Trevor was staying at an older hotel in town, but checked out recently. He's still around though and . . . Cass, I don't think he'll be leaving this place. Her face fell a little but she kept her eyes on him. He's moved out onto some land, family property not too far from Douglas, where he's building something. A cabin, I'd guess.

A cabin in the mountains?

No. Ranch land. But it's down in a hole.

What?

Not a hole, sorry, but almost. A canyon. Out of nowhere, in all that empty land, there's this canyon. I saw him building down there.

She sat back in her chair and didn't touch the wine. Cass looked more perplexed than shocked, or saddened.

You said family land. Do you mean he inherited it or it's his brother's? Did you talk to the brother?

Collis thought for a moment how to phrase everything.

I can't say if he's inherited anything or if he's just shown up and taken over part of the property. That place isn't easy to find or easy to haul material to. It's way out there. So, maybe it was all part of a plan, why he came out here the way he did.

But the brother?

Collis did not want to talk about the brother. He was sure that that was someone Cass should not go to.

Never got the chance to see about him, but I was thinking . . .

Trev, he never told me about any land, about family.

He didn't tell you he was leaving Florida either, leaving you. He wanted to keep it all a secret—for whatever reason—and now, it looks, like he wants to hide down there. That's what I was thinking.

She looked down into her wine glass.

He never told me, never told me much. And I never asked, not really. He knew some things about me, in New Orleans, and my mother but . . . but I never told him much about myself and he never asked. I guess it was some kind of understanding between us.

Cass . . .

Collis waited until she looked up, at him.

Yes?

He's not by himself. There's a woman with him.

I see.

Collis waited, thought she might ask if the woman could be his sister, a friend, someone old, but he saw that she understood. Her face was drawn tight, her smile gone.

Cass, I talked to him today, just before I returned to the hotel. I didn't tell him you were coming to Wyoming, to Douglas, just that you wanted him to come back. To you.

And what did he say?

He said he was sorry.

Sorry? That's it?

Pretty much.

The tears came then. Small, silent, down the cheek. She continued to look at Collis then reached her hand out and placed it on top of his until he turned his palm up. As he held her small hand, Collis thought how Kallengaard hadn't asked how Collis had found him, he only put down the axe and lit a cigarette, betraying little emotion. He didn't ask what Collis' relation was to Cassandra, he remained silent and that's when Collis decided not to tell the man that Cass was coming to Douglas. It wasn't until he had finished the cigarette that he spoke again:

Tell Cass . . . Please tell her that I'm sorry. That it's too late now and, even if I did come back, it would be too late.

And Collis had said okay, that he'd relay the message and then Kallengaard wished him a safe trip back to Florida. And Collis, as he returned to his car, thought that the two brothers were alike after all.

But, before Collis could leave, with Kallengaard standing there, guarding the entrance to the canyon, making sure he was leaving, he called out for Collis to wait. And so Collis had waited while Kallengaard approached the vehicle.

Mr. Mudd, please tell Cass that I loved her. No, that I love her, too.

And Collis was surprised by that. He drove off and as he neared Douglas—knowing that Cass was already there by then—he began to wonder if Kallengaard was reconsidering, if he was realizing that he really did love Cassandra Tipton and that she was worth more than a hole in the ground.

Yet, Collis did not tell this to Cass, now that he was with her. For now, he withheld it and only held her hand. And then she withdrew the hand so that she could dry her eyes.

I want another drink, she said.

Cass told herself that she was drinking to make the hours turn more quickly, so that she would not have to think, to try to understand, what was happening to her. At least until daylight.

Be calm about all of it. I don't know the circumstances, only what I've seen.

I am calm.

I think you should slow down a little, Cass.

I don't want to slow down. I've been slow for years now, Collis. Eons and eons of slowness. I want to get drunk. I want to have a hangover in the morning so that I can wake up and say, See! At least I accomplished something.

She held up her third glass of wine.

Are you with me on this?

With you?

Are you going to drink with me, Collis? Or just tell me how to behave?

Collis studied his bottle of beer—only his second. It was a bad idea, he thought, the wrong thing to do. But, yes, there were times when the wrong thing was the right thing to do. Times when you did what you wanted to do, not what you should do. When the idea of consequence or second thoughts were for later, not the here-and-now. Which, Collis saw, was exactly what Kallengaard had done. He'd left, done it quick, cruelly and badly, but he'd left. And now Cass was acting in the moment. And himself? He was going to drink with her because, as the man said, it was too late for him to come back to Cass. And also because he could not muster up the courage to tell her Trevor Kallengaard's final words, that he did love her . . . But even those were not his final words, the final words being: No, that I love her, too.

Why the *too*? Why the *no*? It was a correction and an inclusion, *no* and *too*. And that meant, what? That he loved her. And Collis would not tell her this.

Cass, I'm with you.

The afterglow of sunset hung along the Medicine Bow, the Laramies, the Sheep Mountains, but Trevor and Bisma could not see it. The sandstone walls of the canyon had darkened to gray a while ago, the cottonwoods' trunks had turned black, their dark-leafed branches scribbled against the remainders of light.

Trevor and Bisma listened to the wind in the trees, to the steady ripple of the Pearl traversing sand and gravel and mud, still carving at the limestone of the rock. They were on their backs, looking up, next to each other in the open air, watching as the stars became luminous in the strip of sky above them.

And the night is born anew, Bisma said and Trevor only smiled.

He felt dreamy. Tired. His arms ached from digging postholes, from mixing concrete with creek water and gravel. From hammering nails. He rose his head from the bed of the truck—where they lay on blankets, with blankets over them—to see what he could of the cabin-to-be in the last of the light: the platform of two-by-fours and plywood, the studs standing for the back wall, the short stand of temporary steps he had put in at the end because Bisma had asked for them. She had said she felt dizzy climbing up and down the raised platform, thought she was catching a cold, or perhaps the flu. What he had built in the day was there, visible as shadow, like the trees. Bisma thought he was looking out of security's sake.

You're quite certain this is safe? No bears or wolves?

Trevor laid back down, looked at her in the darkness.

No bears around here. Maybe a lost cow or two.

Trevor didn't think, though, that there were any cows left from his grandfather's herd. Coyotes, which would likely be attracted to the smells of human activity and food, might venture into the canyon.

Yes, but what about . . .

Bobcats, porcupines, rattlesnakes? Possibly, but we're up off the ground.

No. I was thinking of your brother.

I doubt he knows we're here.

She said nothing and he could sense her fear, that she didn't believe him. Trevor was not sure he believed himself either. Earlier today, when she thought she heard a vehicle up above, Trevor had investigated and it had been the man who Cass had sent. But he never told her about that, or about Cass. He only said that it was not Ross. That it was nothing.

I'll deal with him when need be. Don't worry.

Trevor was certain Ross would give in eventually, that he would come to accept his presence in the canyon, his life here. They were brothers. It might take a while but it would happen and until that time of acceptance, Trevor would use the threat of giving the land to the state to keep Ross at bay.

They lay quiet for a long while, listening, everything fully black now, silent, and Trevor was sure she was asleep, was falling into sleep himself, when she spoke again.

Do you think I'm mad?

Mad? At me? No.

Not angry. Mad, as in mad as a hatter.

No.

Well, here I am with a much older man, in the back of a dusty truck in a canyon. If this isn't the middle of nowhere, then it's relatively close to it, I'd say. I mean, I'm reasonably well-educated. I could live about anywhere, on three continents at least. I could have a nice job, be married—I'm not ugly at all—be it in the States or London or Mumbai. My mother's in Mumbai and I could do all right there. I could write there—she'd understand. Or I could be off to California, as I'd wished.

Yes. You could do any of that.

And yet I've stuck myself to you and I don't even know how you feel about me. I don't know if you love me.

Trevor looked up into the sky and did not offer his hand. He felt her body shift next to him and thought she wanted to be held but he didn't do it.

Are you peeved that I brought it up? We can't talk about it? I have a right to ask, I'd think.

Yes, you do.

She raised herself up to an elbow and he turned to see her, to make out her face in the dark.

And now you're vexed? At me?

No. I can understand you wanting to know. It's a fair question.

She turned from him and remained quiet and he thought it was for the best. He understood only ambivalence—towards Bisma, towards Cass. And even if he had told the man, Collis Mudd, that he loved Cass, he could not say what it meant, exactly. At least to him. Trevor was not certain what love was. If it was what he had felt for Darcie—longing, foolishness, sex and suffering—then Trevor didn't want it. It was true, at least, that Darcie had not loved him. Yes, he had loved his mother and father, but that was a different love, almost involuntary and not romantic.

In the darkness of the canyon, he turned to Bisma.

I thought you only wanted to be lost?

She did not answer him and he decided that he was too tired for this and he let his body relax against the hardness of the truck's bed, felt the first snatch of dream come into him just as he heard her say, I believe I'm mad.

Trevor was tired and he did not respond.

She invited him into her room and he followed her, closing the door behind him. The lights were on in the room, the drapes closed. He stood by the doorway. Cass sat on the bed across from him and he watched as she slipped out of her shoes, then removed her socks.

Barefoot.

Barefoot?

If you lived here, how often could you go barefoot? I mean, it must snow a ton, must snow by September or something. If *I* lived here I'd have to buy all these new clothes—parkas and flannels, boots and snowshoes. Lots of big, heavy stuff.

They had had a lot to drink.

You're thinking of living here?

No. Though it crossed my mind. I thought of it on the drive up, Trevor and I living here, if that's what he wanted. But, no, I don't want to. I like Florida.

I do too.

She looked at him quizzically, as if for the first time seeing him waiting by the door.

Christ, Collis, come in and sit down.

There was nothing to drink in the room. They had been the last to leave the hotel bar.

He went forward to her, sat on the bed next to her, felt the mattress sag under his weight.

What do you think I should do? The woman is young, pretty—I know she is. I know it.

Collis had not said anything about Kallengaard's companion and Cass had not asked.

I think you already know what you want to do.

Do I?

She smiled, her eyes lazy yet bright with drink, her lids counterbalanced.

You want to continue to live in in Fort Lauderdale—that's one thing. You want Mr. Kallengaard, that's another. You want to talk to him, to tell him something even if it's only goodbye, so, put two and two together and they add up to a decision.

I guess so.

This time she covered her smile with her hand. She laughed.

What is it?

I don't know. I'm drunk.

The sat close together, his arm against hers now.

Cass . . .

Collis. She laughed again. Collis and Cass, it sounds like a law firm.

Like a bad television show.

Detectives. Tipton and Mudd.

Mudd and Tipton.

He smiled at her and then he kissed her.

She did not draw away from him, but pressed into him and he put his hand to her back. They both stopped for a moment after the kiss, regarded each other without speaking, face to face, then Cass kissed him harder.

Collis held her then, her slim body in his hands and arms, pressed against her as best he could while still sitting on the bed. It felt so very good to him, the kissing, the feel of her body, the warmth of a woman. She withdrew from him and began to unbutton her blouse, removed it and Collis looked at her in her white bra until she removed that and then he put his hands on her breasts, breasts whiter than the rest of her. And now she reached for his shirt, un-tucking it, yanking it, unbuttoning the top buttons and having him pull it over his head, revealing a roll of fat along his belly, revealing the scar in his armpit, a scar misshapen and hairless. She put her hand to it and asked him what it was and saw his face lose its drunken luxury.

That's where my wife shot me.

And now Collis thought of that—Liv in bed with a patrol officer. He had come home expecting something like what he saw—another man—but expecting it was much different than seeing it. He had walked out of the room and went to the hall closet and got out Todd's baseball bat . . . Livian told him, days later, that she shot him because he would not stop, that she didn't mean to hit him but he wouldn't stop. Collis didn't know how many times he had hit the other man before he felt the pain, the searing burn under his arm, on his back.

The force smoothed it out as an accidental shooting. His service revolver hadn't been used. It was Liv's gun. He was not on duty or in uniform, the other officer was not on duty. They let it go as an accidental shooting. And in counseling Liv apologized and they both went to work and took care of the kids and she finally had his attention or had her revenge for the short-term affair Collis had had years prior—if that was what she had wanted, if that was why she had had the affair in turn. Why she had shot him. So he was paying attention, but it was too late. The split had to come. But that didn't alleviate anything, really. Four children and a house and years together only meant that he missed her every day.

Collis disengaged himself from Cass, stood up from the bed.

I'm sorry. I'm sorry but we shouldn't. We can't.

Cass sat up straight, still on the bed, and put her hands on her face. She looked at him through her fingers.

I know, I know. I don't know what to say, your wife . . . Mrs. Collis . . .

It's not that. I started it. There's nothing more than I'd like to do, but we can't, Cass.

Why not?

No, Miss Tipton.

Cass flung herself back on the bed.

For fuck's sake, Collis. Even if you won't sleep with me, don't call me Miss Tipton.

It wasn't until he smelled the smoke—the odor of kerosene and treated lumber—that he heard the truck. That diesel engine, the spin of tires on loose soil, the creak of suspension over uneven ground, the truck already going up the trail and above them and then gone.

Trevor jumped out of his truck's bed and stood barefoot on rocks and grass to see the orang-flickering pyre on the cabin's platform. Firelight reflected on the creek, on the underside of the natural bridge, on trees and canyon walls. The smoke itself was visible, billowing, blacker than black, it rose almost straight up and into the wind that didn't reach the canyon floor. Trevor watched, took it in, then ran for one of the five gallon buckets.

He shoved the bucket into the creek but it was too shallow and he had to wait for it to fill and then he could not wait and ran with the half-full bucket sloshing. He flung the water into the still rising fire, feeling now the wall of heat on his face and chest and arms, his thighs. And when he returned to the creek he tried for more patience, letting the bucket fill, trying not to spill so much upon himself as he made his way to again throw the water into the face of the flame. The smoke rose even thicker, catching him, so that he had to back away coughing. But he filled bucket after bucket, each tossed into and eventually on top of the fire, until it was extinguished. He wasn't sure if it had been his effort or that it had died of its own accord.

He stood and looked at the smoldering wood. When he turned to the truck, Bisma was there sitting on the hatch, idly kicking her legs like a child would. She was wrapped in the blanket, the cloth over her head like a cowl, yet even in the night he could see her eyes, large and round and steady upon him. Only it wasn't night now, the sky was more purple, blue-gray, the first light of morning still approaching the canyon's uppermost rimrock.

Trevor, looking back at Bisma, was now keenly aware of the pain in his feet, his bare feet, where he had walked on gravel and stones and hard earth. But he didn't show the pain, would not reveal it to her or himself. He called out:

I'll have to buy more lumber.

She pulled the blanket down, covering her face.

When he woke, Collis Mudd thought of Cass. He showered, dressed and she stayed on his mind. He would see her today and he would do the job he was hired to do, as quickly as possible, and then he would be gone, having finished the job.

He did not wonder why she had done it: drank, invited him to the room, kissed him back after he had kissed her, wanted him. Just as he had not told her of Kallengaard's last words, she didn't have to explain herself. And, anyway, there were many explanations he already knew—her need to feel attractive, need for love, to feel someone else, to believe that she had not been rejected because she was not a person who was desirable, who was sexual, who could be loved. And even though he did desire her, he was not the one she really wanted. Trevor Kallengaard was.

Yesterday, when he left Kallengaard at the top of the canyon, in the time it had taken Collis to walk to his car and get inside, no doubt the man was already thinking, formulating things, maybe changing his mind—even if he thought he didn't want to—and that was why he told Collis to tell Cass that he loved her too. And Collis was sure that that statement was true, even if Collis didn't want it to be. And last night, Collis felt that he, too, could say it—that he loved Cass. Yet, like Kallengaard having to realize something he didn't want to, or maybe because of it, Collis couldn't allow himself to love her.

He did not know her well enough or long enough. Like Cass, he was lonely. He had been rejected in some way. Cass loved Kallengaard. Why she loved him was another question, one as inscrutable perhaps as to why he still loved Livian. And though he still loved Liv, he could not be with her anymore than he could be with Cassandra Tipton. And how it all ended between Cass and Kallengaard—bad or good—was not his business.

Collis sat on the bed and called the house in Opa-Locka. Lakeesha answered the phone and he talked to her for a long while before he asked to speak to Liv.

Cass woke reluctantly. She sat up in the bed and felt unbalanced, her head waterlogged with a hangover. She looked around the room—a room at a Best Western in Douglas, Wyoming—and felt an intricate sadness rise within her.

She did not want thins—the sadness, the hangover—she wanted to be full of determination, to possess an iron will, a cold optimism, but all she felt was self-recrimination and that heavy sadness that reminded her of how she felt after Marcus had died.

What must Collis think of her? And what was she thinking herself? Drinking and falling into bed with the man who was supposed to find the man she supposedly wanted?

Cass made herself get out of bed, stand up. She made a sopping sound with her dry mouth. She was in her underwear, nothing more. She looked at her bare feet and again recalled the night. At least she had taken her jeans off before going to sleep. There was a full mirror on the bathroom door and she went to it, looked at herself and decided she looked terrible, terrible.

I'm a terrible person, she said out loud.

She had not had a hangover like this in decades, not since New Orleans. Those days when she'd wake up well past noon, sometimes with Marcus beside her, other times with him already up and there'd be coffee, tomato juice, he'd roll a joint, maybe a little hair-of-the-dog to get the day rolling, to get ready for another late night of work and late night of after-work . . . But they were so young, then. Such sleek creatures. All of them could make light of the abuse they put their bodies through. And Cass remembered the humor in it, maybe even pride, some sense of either accomplishment or proof of the fun they had had. A hangover as memento. Or perhaps, in a more puritan way, there was a sense of deserving pain after a night of debauchery. But they had the whole future, the whole world in front of them, they held such power and did not even know how to use it.

For a moment Cass felt as though she was back there, again, in that last apartment on Spain Street in the Marigny, and in the feeling of it she also felt the memory of Marcus. How Marcus would always make things all right, calling her pet names, playing his guitar, loving her and making all the dullness shine, the pain evaporate or, at least, make the pain be only a small part of the life they lived. No dwelling over things, no real recrimination, contrition. Marcus. Marcus killed, leaving her Trevor. Trevor who, she knew, she continued to love.

Yes, she felt terrible. And now Trevor had a terrible woman who was chasing him down. In the room, in the mirror, Cass smiled at that.

Indeed, she was terrible, terrible, terrible and she was coming to get Trevor Kallengaard.

I smell like smoke. I'm dirty and tired and sore. I'm already sick of pissing in the weeds and I'd really like a cup of tea, maybe egg and toast, a soft bed and, you know, a toilet.

Bisma felt bad about complaining, but she wanted Trevor to see how ridiculous it all was, this living in a hole in the ground in the middle of nowhere. Not ridiculous, but outright dangerous. She wasn't even certain she wanted egg and toast—she felt queasy, achy, strange.

Trevor was already dismantling damaged boards, salvaging anything he could. He listened to her complaints but was encouraged to find that the footings were all fine and that the two-by-sixes could be saved.

Bisma pulled an apple from the cooler, looked at the melted ice and felt horrible. A soft bed would definitely be nice. She watched him and thought that he was not going to say anything, but then he did, without looking at her.

We'll have to go to town anyway. I need new lumber, supplies.

She was a little gratified to hear him speak, she felt a rise of influence.

But that costs money. Where do you get this money? Neither of us has a paycheck? Any beyond that, Trevor. Trevor? She made sure he was listening. Beyond all that, how do you think the flame started? How could it?

He stopped what he was doing and looked at her and asked how she thought it started.

I know how and I know why, but I want to hear you tell me. Trevor, tell me how it's safe to continue with this. But first, say it.

Say what?

The obvious, about the fire.

They regarded each other, Bisma now sitting on the cooler, Trevor standing among charred boards.

My brother.

Yes. He sneaks in here in the dead of night and sets all aflame. He knows and he doesn't want us here. Who says he won't shoot us?

He wouldn't.

He'd shoot you.

No.

He walked toward her. Stood in front of her. She didn't look well, the color in her face had changed, she held herself tight. It was cool in the morning but not outright cold. He thought that maybe she would stand up and come to him. He wanted to hold her, feel her and he knew that he could go to her. In just two or three steps he could go to her and take her in his arms and all would be fine. Everything would fall into place if they tried, if he held her. But neither of them moved.

I won't stay out here.

Trevor wanted to tell her that she didn't have to, that it was never his intention for her to be out here. But, things were bad enough as they were, he didn't need to add to any of it.

I'll take care of it. I'll make him understand that he can't scare me off. Ross will have to accept it.

Fine, if you can do it. But can't we stay at the hotel? If you have so much money, why can't we rent a flat and I'll look for work and we can try all of this later?

Trevor turned from her and began to pick up his tools. He placed them in the lock box on the truck.

Bisma, you're free to do what you want. You know that.

You'll stay at the hotel with me?

For tonight, if you want. I'll take care of Ross.

She looked at the canyon, at the creek and the natural bridge, at the swallows darting in and out, out and in.

I'm dubious, about your brother, but fine. Whatever . . . You can't blame me for wanting to stay at the hotel. Look around, Trevor. You can't even blame yourself.

Cass and Collis sat down for a late breakfast at the LaBonte Hotel's café. There was a measure of awkward silence between them, though Cass had apologized for the night before and Collis also. She tried to show her high spirits in the face of everything, but within her she had lost some of the bravado from the morning, from thinking of Marcus and of youth. Collis said nothing more about it, though the undercurrent of his attraction for her had not diminished.

They had checked out of the Best Western and went to the LaBonte Hotel, inquiring about two rooms and being told, yes, there were rooms but it was too early to check in. Cass and Collis had left their bags in their respective rental cars and entered the café.

Are you sure Trevor is still around?

Cass was eating light, mainly toast and coffee.

Yes. I think he's on the land, camped there maybe. I'm sure he'll be back in town, if you're willing to wait.

I can wait.

Trevor and Bisma pulled into a space in front of the hotel's lounge. They took their bags with them, Trevor's mind on the cabin and his brother. He did not see the purple car parked beneath the trees.

The lobby was cool, dark and Bisma thought of when he had first brought here to it. She tried to conjure up that sense of newness, that stimulation, and the mystery of being with him.

Ask for a big room, she said as they stepped up to the clerk.

A big room.

The clerk acknowledged him by name, welcomed him back.

They're all the same size, except the Honeymoon Suite.

The suite was available now, the clerk told them, though the price was a little higher.

Okay, the suite. One night.

Bisma looked happy, a sweet slyness in her face.

They went up the familiar steps, Trevor carrying both his duffle and the suitcase. She went in front of him and he looked at her. They had not had sex since her return to him and his desire for her seemed different. He imagined that hers for him had changed also. Something was altered between them, but whether it was a deepening or a separation of desire, Trevor was not sure.

Bisma opened the door to the Honeymoon Suite, stepped in, and was satisfied to see that it was as old and tarnished as the rest of the hotel. Cheesy. It had a king size bed, a loveseat made with leather and cow horns, elk antlers on the wall, wooden furniture and a standing mirror. Trevor came in behind her and put down the bags. He lit a cigarette.

Look at this room.

She was smiling, almost giddy. He did not speak, only smoked but she wouldn't let him spoil it. She felt much better than she had since the morning—the nausea brought on from the fire, the sleeping in the cold in the back of a truck. This was much much better.

There was a small dividing wall that made a secondary room where there was a couch and a television, then the bathroom. She stepped into the bathroom, saw a Jacuzzi tub, a glass and tile shower that had been installed incongruously from the rest of the room. She turned on the shower's water and shed her clothes. It felt good to be naked and she looked at herself in the mirror before stepping into the stream of hot water.

She washed and waited for him, certain that he would come to her. She called to him. He did not come, did not answer.

You're not out there still smoking are you?

She didn't want the room to smell of tobacco, of smoke like in the canyon. But she knew she wouldn't tell him that. She would try and not demand anything of him.

Come in the shower.

She yelled it, listened above the running of the water, but he didn't respond.

Trevor was smoking another cigarette. He stood by the window, which he had opened, and felt the warm dry air, looked at the wind moving in the trees. He could hear Bisma call, but not her exact words. There were times when she reminded him of Darcie.

He came away from the window and put the second cigarette out in the tray. Bisma was not like Darcie, he knew. Bisma was sensual, logical in her own manner. She was not about debasement or seeking acceptance, needing it. He thought she had no problem feeling good about herself. But he doubted that she truly loved him. She liked him, felt for him, cared about him and he, in turn, did care about her and liked her. But was that love? Did that grow into love? . . . Eventually, he would have to settle things with Bisma. Also, somehow, make things right with Cass.

But first he had other business that he wanted to keep at the forefront of his mind: Ross.

He couldn't let Ross bully him. Terrorize him out of the canyon, off of the land that was—legally and by birthright—as much his as Ross'. The shovel, now the burning—these acts had to be answered. Trevor didn't know how many times he'd have to respond in-kind to his brother, but nonetheless it had to be done. There was no other choice.

Trevor put on his hat. He felt his pockets for the keys to the truck, his cigarettes. He made sure he had the lighter.

Cass took her bag into the hotel by herself and was issued her room, which was on the second floor. It was a strange hotel to Cass, so old and worn out. Her room was down the skinny hall just past a lone vending machine, a leaking ice machine. She could hear the plumbing in the walls. But the hotel was inexpensive, no doubt why Trevor had stayed here. Yes, he liked old places as well. She would try to see what he saw in this hotel, in the town of Douglas, the brown landscape. And, maybe, about the other woman.

Cass didn't know how she felt about that, partly because she knew so little. Was she hurt? Jealous? Angry? Was she even that surprised? Yes, she was surprised. But overall she felt little about it. It didn't seem real, this other woman. It was abstract, more mystifying than harmful. Really, if nothing else, all she wanted to know was why he had left her. Wanted to see first-hand if there was any shame or guilt, remorse, some shred of acknowledgement that they had lived together, had taken care of each other, had had fun, suffering, love. Prior to this, Cass had never considered Trevor to be cowardly, but maybe he always had been. But . . . No. There must have been something and he was only cowardly in not explaining it to her and that's what she wanted to find out by seeing him.

Collis was not pleased with the LaBonte Hotel. He didn't like Kallengaard's taste in lodging. The Best Western was by the highway, it was clean, almost modern, easy on the eyes. This place was full of dry rot—smelled like it anyway. But Cass was his client and he still felt protective of her, still felt a need to be nearby.

Nearby in case of what? he asked himself. In case Trevor Kallengaard shows up, or Kallengaard's brother? Or, in case Cass comes to his door at night?

He wished she had remained in Fort Lauderdale, had let him handle it his way. He could have found out what the man wanted to do—return or have a final goodbye or just leave her in the dark. Collis could have worked that out of Kallengaard. And then he could return to Hialeah, to Opa-Locka, back to his kids and his divorce and the next client.

Ross parked the truck and made his way to the canyon's rim, seeing that they were gone. No truck and tools, no girl, no brother. Only the disorganization of burnt lumber, unused supplies, the smudge of worked-over dirt. But what surprised him was the feeling of disappointment within him, instead of satisfaction.

He was glad they were gone, but had Trevor given up? Maybe he'd gone back to Florida, or, only to Cheyenne to get a lawyer. Ross had to admit that his brother's return had stirred him, had brought an end to the daily ritual of whiskey and bad thoughts. It made him think of buying some cattle, finding someone to help. He could probably sell the Bedtick outright to pay for a few head, maybe he could run the remaining acres himself, but more likely he'd need help . . . And who would that help be? Of course the first person he thought of was Trevor. Run the ranch with his brother. But that was impossible. Ross tried to dislodge the thought, the idea of benevolence and forgiveness and cooperation . . . Yet, there it was.

He stepped away from the canyon and made his way back to the truck. Trevor would be back, he decided, with or without the girl. He'd return and Ross could hate him all over again. There would be another battle, he could sense that much. And revenge was a much cleaner emotion than forgiveness.

Ross, headed towards the house, but then thought about how he'd just sit in his chair with the television on, flip through one of his magazines and think of his brother. So instead, he took Spring Canyon Road west, eventually crossing Little Box Elder Creek, took Careyhurst Road, then over the Platte and to the Cattle Club Bar, near Clayton.

He did his drinking at home or at the Cattle Club. Not in Douglas. Not Casper. He no longer enjoyed the company of those who knew him the longest, knew him the best, those who had known Thor. At the Cattle Club he was still a rancher, he was Ross from down around Table Mountain. So he had a grilled ham and cheese, a beer, then whiskey. Idle conversation. He stayed well into the afternoon.

When Ross drove back home, his brother's truck was parked in the drive.

Trevor came out of the calving shed and saw Ross' truck pull up. He hesitated for a moment, unsure what to do. He looked backward, into the shed's open doorway, with its slats of sunlight revealing the rise of smoke caused by the pile of straw now aflame. He could not retreat, he could not undo what he had just done. So he walked slowly forward as Ross parked and got out.

I guess you thought you ran me off.

Ross looked at him keenly, calmly. Trevor stopped about ten feet away from his brother.

No. But you'd best. And take that girl with you. Take that black guy who's been nosing around.

Trevor was surprised. He almost asked Ross what he knew about the man, but assumed it was not much. It couldn't be.

I'm going to live here or I'll take it to court. Or, I'll sign it over to the state, make it public domain.

Ross bristled. His tall forehead full of wrinkles now.

I won't let you do that. I won't let you take anything more from me.

You mean Darcie?

Ross looked quickly away and then back at Trevor.

I'm done talking about it. You know what's coming if you stay.

No, I don't know.

One way or another, you're out. I'll do it for Thor, for Dad . . .

For Darcie.

Yeah. For her.

Trevor then looked at the calving shed, hoping Ross would too, but there was no sign of anything really amiss, not yet. He turned back, studied his brother once again, this stranger he knew as a boy. Trevor did not hate Ross, but he thought that to harm him, hurt him emotionally, psychologically, would bring a measure of satisfaction.

Darcie belonged to a lot of people, you know. By grandpa, guys in town . . .

Shut up.

By me.

Ross' milky eyes narrowed, sharpened.

She was pregnant. Also by me.

No.

You were out playing baseball, riding rodeo. You were in Rapid City, Casper, out hunting, catching cows. Who do you think she spent time with, brother? Whose baby was it? Mine.

Trevor felt unlike himself. He thought that he probably felt like Ross always had: mean, pushy, willing to hurt, liking to hurt. And he watched the upheaval in his brother's face, the blood rising, his large body tense. Then Ross suddenly came alive and charged him. He came faster than Trevor thought he could, and Trevor could only slip a little to the left before he was hit.

The blow spun him in a half-circle, but it was Ross who stumbled, who fell headlong into the gravel of the drive. Trevor's right side ached, his arm was numb. Ross picked himself up and he came at Trevor again.

Ross was more cautious this time, more deliberate, in expectation of Trevor stepping away. But Trevor met his brother's charge, and though he was knocked backwards he was not knocked down. They grabbed at each other, grunting, dirt and saliva in their mouths, like boys wrestling they tried for leverage, tried to prove who had the greater strength. Ross pressed downward on the smaller Trevor but he could not subdue him, he was breathing harder than his brother.

Ross chopped an elbow into Trevor's ribs, the same right side that already hurt, but Trevor didn't react. Trevor brought his free hand around as a fist and hit Ross in the ear and Ross stepped away only to step back in and throw punches, heavy but sloppy. Trevor returned punches with more accuracy, quicker, but then Ross caught hold of Trevor's hands and they were back to pushing each other around in the dirt and gravel.

They uttered no words, just the grunting from deep in their throats, their stomachs. Dust rose around them. Their faces red, knuckles and hands red, sweat, their hats off and on the ground. Boots scraping, sliding, losing and finding purchase. But Ross could not keep it up—he didn't have the stamina. His anger and rage weren't enough. Trevor, gripping Ross' forearm, slung his brother around in two circles, the second faster than the first, then let go and Ross slammed into the side of the brown truck with a hard, flat sound.

Ross looked at him, tried to grin but Trevor saw pain. He saw his brother trying desperately to catch his wind, his strength. Trevor went to him. Ross built enough saliva in his mouth to spit at Trevor, then took a swing and Trevor swung back, catching Ross fully on the jaw and Ross went down.

He sat in the dirt, beside his truck, a look of astonishment on his face.

Trevor's throat was dry, his breathing hard and sharp. He could not speak, but offered a hand that Ross slapped away. So Trevor stood there, working moisture back into his mouth.

It's not Darcie, Travis tried to say, it's more, it's us, there's just us . . .

Trevor did not understand what he wanted to say. He felt some visceral emotion welling up from inside him. He wanted to explain something, but could not convey what it was—or was still unwilling to. Unwilling to admit that Darcie had loved only Ross. That if she had been pregnant, it was his brother's child, not his. That he should ask Ross for his forgiveness. He knew he should say it, ask it, but then Trevor smelled the smoke.

He turned and looked to see the first flames leap from the back of the shed— and whatever emotion that was coming out of him, whatever confession or request, ceased to come out. Now there was only his brother on the ground and the calving shed on fire. The stench of cow hair and ancient manure, old wood and straw filled the air. Flames licked higher.

Trevor backed away, pointed to the fire as Ross got to his feet.

Let it burn, Ross said.

Trevor had expected Ross to care, to give a damn. He had wanted to see Ross rush to put the fire out just as Trevor had done in the canyon. He had waited a long time for his brother to come home. Fight fire with fire, an eye for an eye, do unto others . . .

Get the hose—we can still water the roof.

I'm going to get my rifle. If you're still here, I'll shoot you. I'll shoot you if you're in your truck.

Trevor watched his brother walk, stiffly, to the door of the house and enter it, not once glancing at the burning shed.

Someone will call, Trevor thought. The Palmers or Johnsons will see the smoke and call it in. Maybe Ross was calling right now. Or, maybe he was only getting his rifle.

Trevor went quickly to his truck. The calving shed crackled. He knew there was a chance it could spread in the wind, to the barn, the house, the dry land itself. He didn't think Ross would let it, but it could. And would that, in turn, become his fault too?

He drove fast down Spring Canyon Road and thought about what he had done—not just the fire but telling his brother of the unborn child, the fetus that had died when Darcie died. Yes, it could have been his, could have been his brother's, could have been someone else's. Or, it all could have simply been a lie.

He told himself again that Darcie had not loved him and, almost unconsciously, he brought the truck to a stop. Trevor, alone in the cab in the open landscape, the empty road, was certain now that Darcie had loved Ross, and Ross had loved her. But Ross couldn't display that love because of who Darcie was, or had been, and because Ross had been influenced by Thor. And for Darcie, maybe all the other men, including Thor, including himself, were either a substitute for Ross' love or someone else's love, childhood's love. Or it was just a matter of habit, addiction, subordination—possibly it was all only a thrill for her: *Kicks*. Maybe she saw no other value in herself.

Darcie could not love herself. And, Trevor wondered, maybe he could not love himself, either.

He took a cigarette from the pack and lit it. Smoked.

Darcy had not loved him. Bisma did not truly love him—or mistakenly loved him. What was love? Who did he love? If, he thought, love was a daily intimacy and not intoxication, if it was caring and acceptance and appreciation, the day-in day-out partnership mixed with human sexuality, then the person he loved would not be Darcie, not Bisma. It would be Cass. And he had run away from Cass, just as he had run away from his family, from Wyoming; all after he had killed—caused the death of—his father, Darcie, and possibly Ross and Darcie's child.

Here he was, so many years later, and he still had learned nothing. Resolved nothing. Had still not even forgiven himself or asked to be forgiven. He remained but an ignorant man.

He'd been gone a long time and she was hungry. He had come to the shower but was fully dressed, said he had to go out and set things straight with his brother, promised to come back. He had not given her time to finish showering, to even respond.

She slept after that. A nervous sleep with dreams of London and her father and then of dirt roads. When she woke she was alone in the big bed and she felt stupid. He had not come back. She dressed, brushed her hair, began to worry about Trevor, his brother, pushing bad scenarios out of her mind. Her stomach growled and she had so little money. She had spent money on the hotel in Cheyenne, on food and the bus back to Douglas.

There was still food in the cooler but all the ice had melted. Food in grocery bags but they were filled with dust. She worried some more about Trevor, then felt the resentment that comes from waiting for someone. So Bisma gathered her loose bills and coins and went down to the LaBonte Café.

Collis Mudd saw her right away. She sat alone at the counter, drinking tea, eating a sweet roll. He and Cass were in a booth along the wall, near the window that held the early evening light.

Cass.

She looked up at him. There was no more embarrassment between them, certainly no enmity.

Would you want to talk to the woman?

What woman?

The one who's with Mr. Kallengaard.

Trevor's here?

He saw how quickly she turned her head to look around.

Just her. She's at the counter, long black hair.

He knew that she had to look. And she redirected her vision to the long shelf with stools and few patrons. She turned quickly back to Collis.

She looks . . .

Indian.

Pretty. She looks young.

Bisma was now eating crackers from a wicker bowl on the counter as she sipped her tea.

She looks hungry, Collis said. I've seen enough runaways—not that she is one—to see when someone's hungry.

What should I do?

Collis thought momentarily of Cass the other night, when he had kissed her.

Well, you could offer to buy her dinner and take it from there.

Hello.

Cass sat down on the stool next to Bisma. She studied the younger woman, wondering how she should feel but, realized, she felt no rancor, no sense of competition. How could she compete with someone so young? Bisma looked her in the eye.

Hello.

Cass clasped her hands together upon the café's counter.

You're not from Florida, are you?

Bisma smiled at the absurdity of the question, at this woman's sudden appearance and her odd, almost frightened expression.

No.

You're from here then, Douglas?

No. I came from Colorado, but that's not where I'm from.

Cass noticed her accent this time. She looked back at the booth where Collis sat, watching. Bisma looked where Cass was looking.

I'd like . . . I was wondering if I could buy you some dinner and, maybe, we could talk.

Bisma was bewildered, humored, but also hungry.

Do I look that desperate?

No, no. Not at all . . . My name is Cass. Cassandra Tipton.

She unclasped her hands and watched for some recognition, as if the young woman would react to the mention of her name.

Bisma.

They both smiled a little, gently shook hands, and then Bisma wondered why the woman had mentioned Florida and the smile left her face.

Should I know you?

Cass leaned forward.

You know Trevor, don't you?

I know him, Bisma said, I know him very well. And do you?

Their eyes met, held. The sound of the cash register clicked nearby, the sound of silverware being sorted.

Yes, I do. I'm, essentially, his wife.

He came up the stairs smelling of sweat and earth and smoke. His clothes were dirty, his hands scratched, arms bruised, shoulders sore. He felt confused and deeply unhappy but held it tight within himself as he unlocked and opened the door to the room.

Inside all the curtains were closed, the late-day sun against them. No other light. No voices. He closed the door and stayed in the dark, took off his boots, removed the torn and rumpled shirt. He realized he'd lost his hat. He stepped further into the room, expecting her somewhere—the bed or in the bathroom. Though he was not hungry, he remembered that they had not eaten.

He held his pack of cigarettes and lighter in one hand as he walked, shirtless, through the spidery gray of the room, past the empty honeymoon bed, the honeymoon table and chairs, around the short dividing wall, where maybe she sat on the loveseat. Trevor didn't know what he'd say to her: that nothing was settled and he could not divine what would happen next? Only, when he looked, it was not her on the loveseat.

It was Cass.

EIGHT

A Natural Bridge

Driving west on I-25, Ross took Exit 160 and continued into Glenrock. It was almost dark when he pulled into the parking lot of the nursing home.

Inside, he strode across the white tiles to the main desk where the nurse on duty handed him the visitor's sign-in sheet.

Hey, Ross, she said as he signed his name.

He looked at her closely. A middle-aged woman, plump, glasses, her hair curled tight to her scalp.

It's Helen, she prompted him.

Helen.

They had dated twice. She had asked him out the first time and on the second date she had taken him back to her home—a trailer on Monkey Hill Road. She had a teenage son who was not there. In the trailer she'd offered him a beer and he'd asked for something stronger so she brought out a bottle of rum and they both drank the rum. The trailer was tidy, feminine. He bedded her there, in the living room, on the overstuffed couch, and she made him promise that he would call her but he never did.

He had not seen Helen, had not dated any woman, since that time—almost a year ago, now—just as he had not been in to see his mother.

I guess you've forgotten me.

He sensed both interest and contempt in her voice, but he wasn't there to talk to her.

Just came to see my mother, that's all.

There was a flush of anger in Helen's cheeks. She held the sign-in sheet in front of her instead of looking at him.

She's in her room. I guess you can remember where that is.

He looked at her, at the sheet. He stood for a moment before going down the hall.

Cass could only look at him. She did not move or give her emotions away, did not show animosity or uncertainty. She did not even say his name. But even in the husked light he looked different: skinnier, harder, shirtless but also disheveled. There was something uncontrolled, she realized. Trevor, the master of control now uncontrolled somewhere within. She decided to wait and let him say something. For once, make him be the one to talk.

So she waited but he was frozen and she began to think that he would not speak. That he'd only be a statue. Then she saw his elbows move, a slight collapse of the shoulders. She saw him raise a cigarette pack that he had cupped in one hand, hold it and shake one out and light it—the flame flaring in the bald room. He brought the cigarette to his mouth, she could hear the suck of air, the exhalation. Could smell the smoke. He drew on it a second time, this time the red coal glowing, the red coal leaving his mouth and dropping down to his side as he held it low and in his fingers. She saw that his hand was shaking.

Cass, he said.

She wanted to stand up and go to him, out of affection or despair or anger she wasn't sure. No, not anger, she realized. But she defied the urge and remained planted in the loveseat, waited for him and his quivering hand.

Cass. I don't understand.

Understand why I'm here or how I'm here?

His hand stopped, he was frozen again, the cigarette by his hip, the smoke visible in the bedimmed room.

Yes, why you're here. After the way I left you, after what I did.

She had hoped he'd understand that she was here because she loved him.

What about the young woman, Trev? What about Bisma? I've met her, talked to her—she gave me the key.

Where is she?

Cass turned her head from him.

Where is she? She heard herself say in an inflection she didn't want.

Cass made herself look at him again. The room was getting darker.

She's downstairs, maybe still eating. She's okay, if that's what you want to know. She's not alone.

Trevor nodded, brought the cigarette to his mouth. Inhale. Exhale. He inspected it then took a step forward and snuffed it out in a tray on the table by the seat. He was close enough to touch.

Unlike you, he said.

Like me?

Alone.

He fell to his knees then, in front of her. Trevor brought his elbows inward, both hands to his face. Cass could not see if he was crying, thought perhaps he was until he looked at her and his eyes were dry.

I'm sorry, Cass. I'm sorry.

Ross entered his mother's room but she was not there. He walked back out and searched for her face among the others in the community center. Old people watching television, gathered in groups, sitting alone in negligent silence. He saw her on a couch, alone, smiling. He went to her, sat next to her. His mother.

She did not acknowledge him. A few other residents stared at him and he waited until their interest waned, was gone. Ross touched his mother's arm.

Annie, he aid because he knew she still recognized her own name. Annie, Trevor's come back.

He waited to see if there was anything, any possible spark of recognition in the dementia—a vacancy that Ross was sometimes jealous of. But there was no spark and he removed his hand, leaned into a slouch. Talked to her again.

Your son, Trevor. Do you remember him?

My son?

She kept the smile on her face.

You know him?

The son of god.

No. This is Trevor, Trevor Kallengaard, the son who killed your husband.

She shook her head.

Well he's here—in Douglas. He's trying to take something from me, like he hasn't already taken enough . . . Trig. Do you remember Trig?

Trig, she said and Ross knew at least she was listening.

My father.

I'd like to meet him.

Who?

Your father.

Ross closed his eyes. He let his hand slip down to hers, gripped it, then opened his eyes. He leaned in close to his mother.

Mom. Trevor is here and he shouldn't be. He should have stayed where he was. I just wanted to tell you that, before I send him away.

They sat next to each other now, upon the loveseat. Trevor was not talking yet, he found that he couldn't explain himself, could not tell her how, why it had all happened though she asked him to.

The note, the phone call, really Trev? That wasn't enough. I couldn't let go that way. You can go, obviously, but not like that.

I didn't mean for it to be . . . To be cold like that, Cass. I thought I'd tell you, explain it after the fact, after it was too late to change it.

It was cold, she said, plainly, and waited for him.

We were miserable, weren't we? In a way. And I could have stayed and let it continue and we'd settle into our defenses. I knew you wanted things to be different—you'd said so—and I thought, maybe, by leaving I was letting you . . . leaving you free to pursue them.

Not without you, Trevor. The idea was to pursue them with you. Together. Do you understand that?

Again she waited on him. Cass next to him. He understood what she meant but he didn't understand. They did not want the same thing—at least at that time—

so how could it be done together? But he didn't say that. Like so many times, he let only the silence speak.

And because he wouldn't talk, Cass told him about Collis Mudd. She talked about what she had done and what trouble she had gone to, about flying to Denver and driving to Douglas, about seeing the woman—Bisma—and buying her a meal. Trevor nodded, listened, did not meet her eyes. Cass kept her voice low and said that they couldn't know what would happen to them—between them—unless he came back home to Florida. Then they could find out.

Was it really that bad, Trev?

He looked at her, her face, the eyes he'd looked at and into for many many years. Her hand was resting on her thigh and he reached for it, held it, twined his fingers with hers.

Ross leaned in further towards his mother, his shoulder touching hers, his face now very close to hers. She didn't draw away from him. And he thought how he could get up and go to the station and apologize to the nurse. To Helen. How he could probably wait for her and they could go get something to eat or drink and she'd probably take him to the trailer on Monkey Hill and he could stay there for days. Just him and Helen. But, that was not why he had come.

It happened long before, well not that long before, I came to New Orleans, Trevor told her. But then he stopped before talking again, now working his way backwards, because he had already told her of leaving Fort Lauderdale, of coming into Fort Collins and how he had met Bisma. He thought she wanted to hear about Bisma, how and why, and he did his best to explain it and then Trevor went back to Fort Lauderdale and tried to again explain why he had left, how he had come to commit the act of leaving and how he had been wrong.

I can see it now, Cass. I wouldn't admit it but I saw it then too, but it was in a way I'd done it before. A clean break, a slipping out into a new life. It was the only process . . .

A process?

Yes.

And that's how you came to New Orleans? You left someone in a blink of an eye?

Yes.

And this time Trevor went further back, starting with his family and the ranch and then his family in Cheyenne and then just him in Fort Collins and then he went back further and told Cass about Thor and his wife—his grandmother—about Trig and Annie, Ross. Then he told Cass about Darcie: Darcie and his brother, Darcie and himself, Darcie and others. And it was a while before he told her about Harriman Road but he did tell her, something he had never told anyone, and he told her that that was who he truly was, that was what he had done and why he had ended up to New Orleans. And she asked why he had come to Fort Lauderdale, was it because he was still running? And Trevor thought for a moment and said, No. He had come because she had lost Marcus and because he liked her and because he thought, perhaps, that he was in love with her. That was why he had left New Orleans and come to Fort Lauderdale.

And in the telling of it all, Trevor thought about his brother, the fight with his brother, the desire to hurt his brother. And he thought in the greater scheme of things, why did he want that? Why did it have to be this way? What was so important that Ross was his enemy? Which, he realized, was what he had wanted to explain to Ross at the end of their fight—but he had not been ready yet, wasn't willing yet, didn't quite know it yet.

Mom, Ross said. The whole side of his body was touching her now, he looked into her blue eyes, refusing to see that she had not forgotten who he was, who anyone was. Trevor wants to take what's mine. Grandpa would never let him do it, so I can't. Can't let him have an inch. So I'm telling you that I'll make him leave, for good this time.

Okay, his mother said, looking at him, unblinking.

He held her hand.

I mean it. I'll do it.

She appeared upset now, distressed with his distress.

Oh don't.

I have to.

Don't. Don't let it bother you.

I have to take him . . .

He'll love you. All of us love you.

Cass listened to his story, of which there was another story embedded within, and yet a third and fourth story connected to the original. She listened and no longer interrupted except to prompt him with a small question or retelling of names, places, times. And then she realized that it really was only one story. Long, convoluted maybe, but only one, and she tried to see where she came in, what role she played in the story.

She was patient. And she thought, in the back of her mind, of her own story, which was, really, the same, because there really was only one story, one with many variants and viewpoints and addenda, and she—as with everyone—was somewhere within that story.

Cass was not accustomed to thinking like this, outside the framework of herself, and had not thought this way in the longest of times, not since New Orleans and Marcus and youth. But, listening to Trevor, Cass felt that all things were similar, all creatures and all things. All things connected. You live and you die, Cass thought, you are made and destroyed. The world lives and dies everyday. And who is to say there is not a continuation of the story after the destruction? Who is to say that you, that everything, is not made and destroyed again? And again? It was impossible to know, to have certainty, and that was why it was all ultimately connected into mystery . . . Yet, knowing it was mystery did not solve the conundrum. And she couldn't adequately communicate or apply this understanding she now felt, listening to Trevor, that all things were one story. Always had been—always would be. But she would try to remember it—this feeling, this understanding—even if it only altered things only so slightly. Even after she forgot it.

He stopped at the liquor store in Glenrock before driving home under at night.

Alone at his kitchen table with the bottle of whiskey, a tall glass, a sandwich in cellophane wrapper, an apple and the Long Colt revolver, Ross could still smell his mother. The smell of her skin and hair, of the perfume she—or an aide—put on her. The very smell of the nursing home, a place he would never want to end up at. He would rather be dead than to have to live in a place that smelled like that.

He slid the sandwich aside and took the apple, bit into it. The flesh was not crisp, felt mealy in his mouth. He opened the whiskey and poured it into the water glass, neat, warm, full. He set the bottle down alongside the Colt, a gun that had belonged to Thor.

It was late when he finished talking and Cass held tightly to him on the loveseat in the Honeymoon Suite of the LaBonte Hotel.

And this is all because of an accident, Trevor.

It was my fault.

Cass thought of marriage, of the wanting a child, his running.

But it was an accident all the same.

Then they didn't talk, only looked at each other in the darkness. Looked at the faces they had both known longer than anyone else's, except their own. Cass said his name and he kissed her.

Ross woke on the kitchen table as the sun rose. His bones ached. He felt horrible. The bottle of whiskey was before him, the glass still half full. He straightened his body in the wooden chair and his gut hurt. Familiar and unwelcome, the same old stomach pains that had inflicted him for years now, that the whiskey both inflamed and cured. He put his hands on his stomach, rubbed it, then sipped from the glass of whiskey.

He looked at the table, the old table of many card games, of water rings and burns—Darcie's cigarettes, Thor's cigars. He saw the Colt pistol, knew it was loaded. He blew the air from his lungs, took another sip of tepid whiskey and thought he might vomit, but didn't.

He was shaky standing up, but made himself do it without holding on to anything. On the wall near the mudroom was the Browning rifle, the old Parker Brothers shotgun. He'd sold his other two rifles and could barely recall what they were. The Browning had been his father's, the shotgun—like the Colt—Thor's. He had shells, bullets in a drawer. Out the window he saw the clean, early sunlight on the gravel drive. He saw his truck parked awkwardly near the barn. Saw the burnt ruin of the calving shed.

What did he have left but this table and the guns, this house, his truck, the land? What did he have?

He had his word. His honor—his word was his honor—and he had his life. There was no more than that.

Bisma had traded keys with Cass and stayed in her room. That night, she had at first resisted but then looked through Cass' things. Not everything, just enough to get a sense of who she was. She had hoped to find something—gaudy jewelry, cheap clothing, a sentimental diary—some vain or tawdry thing so she could dislike the woman. Or laugh at her. Some reason to understand why Trevor had left her, why he had never mentioned her. But she found no evidence and only disliked herself for snooping. And as the time passed, as the hard darkness of night fell outside the small room and the woman did not return and Trevor did not come for her, Bisma understood where she was, or wasn't. And she slept in Cassandra Tipton's room, woke early, washed her face but could not brush her teeth or hair, had no makeup. She dressed in the same clothes and opened the door to find a large man standing in the hall, waiting for her.

Collis bought her breakfast, explained further who he was and that being outside the door was only coincidence.

But you knew it would be me and not her?

Though Collis was not surprised to find that it was her, he didn't tell her that he'd hoped it would be Cass.

I figured it could be you and that maybe you'd want someone to talk to.

She looked at him. She picked at her food.

After breakfast they went outside—Bisma did not feel well and Collis suggested a walk. They went down Walnut Street to Second Street and towards the river. She explained who she was, how she had met Trevor, how she had come to Wyoming. She was a graduate student at Colorado State. She was from some part of London, England. Collis felt for the girl, like he would feel for one of his own children, but he could not understand her. Why had she come along with a man she had just met? And then so readily relinquished her connection with Kallengaard to Cass? Perhaps there was something wrong in the relationship, something had soured, and Cass gave her a window, a way out. They crossed the railroad tracks and went down the slope to the river where they stood together with the sun on their backs. There was a park of sorts, there was a KOA campsite nearby with RVs and one tent, picnic tables and few people. The wind was blowing.

The North Platte River looked muddy. Cottonwoods and ash grew along the other bank, thickets of willow. A kingfisher sat—blue and white, barrel-chested—on a branch above the slow waters and Collis pointed it out to her. He asked if she knew what kind of bird it was.

I have no idea, she said.

The bird suddenly dropped, diving head first into the swell of water and came up with a fingerling in its beak. The kingfisher disappeared into the shadows of leaves and branches.

What do you want to do? Collis asked.

I don't know.

She was glum, confused, dismayed maybe. Collis wanted to help her. She looked at him, shielding her eyes with her hand.

Ready to go back to the hotel?

Bisma didn't answer. She played with Cass' key in her pocket.

It had been Bisma's idea to trade keys. Now she wondered if it wasn't a mistake. But there were few mistakes, she told herself, really there was only fate, the way things fell into a shape, only to eventually lose that shape until it reformed into something new, a new fate or the old one that only looked different. Fate was a process, a repetition. Some people went to great length to prevent or suppress that process.

I'll be on my way. I was going to go to California.

Where in California?

She shook her head.

You have family there, friends? In California?

No.

Collis nodded. He wondered why they all wanted to go to California.

Could you take me to the bus station? I know where it is.

Your stuff is in the other room. You do have some belongings, don't you?

Yes.

And maybe you want to talk to Mr. Kallengaard? I'm sure Miss Tipton would want to talk to you again. She's all right.

Mrs. Kallengaard.

They're not married.

Yes, they are.

No.

Yes. You can see it. I can.

Trevor, what do you want to do?

They were dressing in the sober light.

What about you? You want everything to be like it was before?

No. I can't be like that. It shouldn't be.

Trevor nodded. She sat on the edge of the bed and he watched her draw her legs up. For what felt like the hundredth time, he wondered how it could be—Cass in the room with him, in Douglas? Yet, in other ways, it made perfect sense: why wouldn't she be with him?

Honestly, do you prefer her, Trev? Or do you want me? Or do you just want to be left alone so you can build your cabin, so you can live alone?

He looked at the ceiling, then over at the desk where a lamp was on, where his cigarettes and lighter sat. He looked at his father's jacket, hung on the neck of a chair. Cass then stood, came to him. She placed a hand on his chest.

Trev, you can hide if you want to, but I don't think you can escape the world. It will always be there . . . I know what I want, and that's for you to come home. We'll take it from there. I mean, I know where home is, but I'm not so sure that you do.

Ross stood at the kitchen window watching the sunlight spread over the gravel drive. Whiskey in hand, he was waiting, waiting for something or someone. The house was so quiet. There was nobody anymore, not even himself, really. So he knew no one was coming down the road for him, no thing was waiting for him. He had his whiskey and he had his guns and he had the land.

Ross gathered up his hat and keys and the Colt revolver. He went out to the truck.

Trevor and Cass stood in the lobby of the LaBonte, their back to the front desk, while Collis and Bisma stood opposite, their backs to the sunlit windows of the front doors. Bisma would not look at Trevor.

Collis came and spoke to them.

She'd like to get her things.

Yes. Of course.

Trevor held out his key and Collis took it. When he handed it to Bisma she gave a meek thank you and glanced at Cass. She then walked past them, to the narrow stairs, Trevor watching. He then turned to Cass who looked him in the eye.

I think you should.

Trevor took her hand for a moment as she handed him the other key. He nodded, then went to the stairs where Bisma had already ascended.

Collis came and stood next to Cass, both of them watching Trevor disappear.

You got your man.

Cass didn't answer. She sat down at one of the empty tables in the empty lobby.

Collis felt the rise of disappointment within him, recognized it as simple jealousy. He suppressed it and sat down across from her.

I'm sorry. That wasn't the right way to put it.

What's she going to do?

Collis shrugged.

She says she's going to take a bus to Cheyenne this afternoon. But it's not far from here, so I can take her.

She loves him, I think. Cares about him—I can see it.

I guess. But she'll be okay. She's young.

Cass considered this, shifted her weight in the chair.

And you?

Me? I'm fine. I'll go home, back to the kids, the next case. I'll send you a big ol' bill.

He smiled for her.

Collis, I want to thank you and apologize . . .

Everything's turned out okay, Cass.

Has it?

He put his hand out, placed it on hers, gave a little pressure.

Sure it has.

Only the bathroom light was on in the room. Trevor saw her suitcase on the bed, its top open, clothes hastily thrown into it. His jacket—his father's jacket—was there, neatly folded, set aside from the case. He went to the bathroom's door, which was open and looked inside to see her. She had her back to him, her long hair shiny though not brushed. She was bent slightly, one hand resting on the sink.

She turned her head slowly, as if expecting his presence as much as sensing it, and looked at him with her black, bottomless eyes. Trevor stepped into the brightly lit room.

Bisma.

She didn't answer, ignored him. Looked into the mirror and then picked up her toothbrush, her hairbrush, other items, placing them in a pouch.

Bisma.

This time he reached out and took hold of her at the wrist. She jerked her hand free but then stopped. She leaned on the sink with both hands.

You lied to me.

He stood next to her and opened his mouth to speak but she stopped him with her eyes, looking at him in the mirror.

You lied to me about her, about who you really are.

I didn't. Bisma, I didn't know. I didn't think she would ever . . .

She raised one hand, palm flat, still eyed him through the mirror.

Do you love me?

He couldn't answer.

Do you love me?

I don't know that I love anyone.

That's not true. Who do you love?

He did not want to answer the question.

I'm sorry.

Trevor stepped closer to her. She let him take her arm, she turned towards him and she was crying now. Her eyes cat-like but crying. She put her face into his shoulder.

It was all a load of shit, wasn't it. You and me.

Maybe.

Now it will be you and her down in that dirty canyon. Not that I wanted that, to be down there, but if it somehow works out it will be you and her, not me.

I don't think so. She won't live there and I don't think I will either.

Trevor knew, now, that he would give it up—the dream, the object of his leaving. He would return with Cass. He would go home.

But I cracked you open, didn't I? You were an egg after all.

Yes, you did. And now it's done and I'm sorry. I don't know what else to tell you, Bisma. I don't know what else there is.

He held her for a while. She was done crying. She said she had to go and he released her. He asked her if she needed money and he took out his wallet, took out all the bills within it and she refused it, she asked not to be insulted and she grabbed the small pouch with her toiletries and walked past him.

He watched her put the pouch in her suitcase, close it, and pick up the suitcase. She placed the two room keys—hers and Cass'—on the table, next to the ashtray with its dead cigarettes. Bisma stopped at the door and turned to look at him in the entrance of the bathroom.

It's been quite the adventure, hasn't it? But I think I will miss you, Mister Trevor Kallengaard.

And then she was gone. There was the opening of the door and then its closing and Trevor remained where he was. He wished he could have told her the truth, that he loved her but was not capable of loving her enough, of loving her more than he loved Cass.

He did wait—two minutes, five minutes—thinking that she might return but all there was only silence, the settled air of the room, the ashtray. He looked again where her suitcase had been but it too was gone, and, he noticed, so was his jacket.

Bisma Patel stood with Collis Mudd on the porch of the Plains Motel and Gift Shop. The Powder River bus would take her to Cheyenne and from there she could get back into Fort Collins. But Bisma did not feel well. The recent nausea that afflicted her was troubling her this afternoon—brought on by Trevor, she told herself. Or by herself for, essentially, giving him away. But she had to because he did not love her.

Collis Mudd had paid for her ticket. He had given her two hundred dollars which she said she'd repay, though both of them knew that was unlikely. He was watching her now as they stood waiting for the bus.

You all right?

I feel a little sick.

I guess that's expected. A lot going on. I feel a little sick myself.

She nodded but then felt the bile rise in her throat.

Bisma hurried down the steps to the corner of the building where she vomited into the stunted weeds and gravel. She wiped her mouth as best she could with the denim sleeves of the jacket she wore. But she felt she might vomit some more. She saw Collis come to her. He offered her a clean handkerchief.

Thank you.

She wiped her mouth and he motioned for her to keep it when she was done.

Collis studied her, the paleness of her face, the eyes now sunken. He thought of home, of Opa Locka and of his kids.

Are you sure you're just sick?

The bus was pulling in now and they both turned their heads to see it. Dust rose from where it came to a stop. The dust blew across the way and overtook them.

I'm sick. She had to vomit again, wipe her mouth again. Usually in the morning but, as you can see, I'm sick now too.

Miss . . . You've been like this for a while then?

She looked up at him, standing there, judging her.

Why? Are you implying something?

He didn't answer, he only looked at her patiently until she understood.

Oh. You think I'm . . . Oh.

Collis nodded.

I don't think you should take the bus, Miss Patel.

Cass had seen her come down the stairs with the suitcase. She—Bisma—had walked quickly with diverted eyes, looking only once at Collis before going past them at the table in the lobby. And then Collis was gone almost as quick, Cass not even having the chance to say goodbye before he was out the door. Then she had returned to the room and found Trevor sitting on the couch. His legs were stretched out. He was smoking. Cass sat down next to him.

She didn't know if he had made up his mind. The young woman had left but Trevor might want to remain in Wyoming, choose to be alone. She could accept that now, now that she understood why he had left—his fear of marriage and a child; the overriding guilt for something done long ago. But she wasn't going to ask him about any decisions—he would have to tell her when he was ready.

Was it bad? With Bisma?

No.

She understood?

I think so. Maybe better than I do.

Cass wasn't sure what he meant. He turned to her.

Cass, we haven't really talked about her, what we did together, Bisma and I. I never asked if it bothers you, if it's a problem.

It's not that it doesn't bother me. It's more that there's other things—the manner in which you left, the tracking you down, last night—it's just not the main thing.

The main thing?

It's behind us, behind me. It's the past.

You can just strike it off as in the past?

I can ... Unless you keep talking about it.

Cass knew she couldn't erase what had happened—the abandonment, the relationship with another, the attention for and with another. She would always be aware of it. But, she believed she could forgive, she could put it in perspective. Which is what Trevor had been unable to do, to forgive, to put the past into perspective. Vanquish it.

Talk, not talk, Trevor said. We'll have to work on that, I guess. If that's okay.

Work on—you want to come back?

Trevor unhooked his ankles and smudged out the cigarette in the glass tray.

We can return your rental and drive back in the truck. Or would you rather fly?

Cass felt calm and elated at the same time. She didn't know how things would be, but was not fearful in not knowing.

No. I'll drive with you. But what about your mother? And your brother, Trevor. You'll want to see him, and maybe the ranch?

Trevor thought of the canyon and its walls. He thought of the cottonwoods, Pearl Creek and the natural bridge with its limestone eye. Then he considered his brother and understood that it was all ruined, he and his brother, the land itself tainted in some way, whether by mistake or spite, it was all hollow and as sad as his mother's life in Glenrock. Yet, in another way, it could never be ruined. The land and his family lived within him, even if only as dream or memory: brother, mother, father, Thor, Darcie, Gus and Frida, all of them and the ranch, Douglas, the canyon, all would continue to exist in some ephemeral way.

I've said enough to my brother. I'd like to say goodbye to my mother, even if she won't know it.

Of course. I'd like to meet her.

And I haven't been to the graves. I haven't done that.

Take me with you.

He looked at Cass carefully and nodded.

Okay. I'd like that.

Collis left her luggage in the car when they returned to the hotel. He and Bisma went into the lobby of the LaBonte then both stopped, not certain exactly what to do. He could call Cass, but that didn't seem right.

Would you like me to go up and ask him to come down? Or would you want me to tell him for you?

Bisma looked better—the color had returned to her face, her posture was erect. But she felt a great unease within her, a heavy uncertainty.

But what if it's not true? Maybe I'm just sick. A doctor . . . no, one of those tests would tell me if it's true.

And, she thought, if it was true, if she was with child, then what? What would she tell him? How would this complicate her life and his and everyone else's?

I've got four kids, and I think I know it when I see it, but it's up to you, Miss Patel.

She should tell Trevor, she thought. Even if she's wrong she should tell him. She wanted to see him, wanted to see how he would react, what he would say or not say, see what such a complication would do. But why, exactly? To bring him back to her? Bisma didn't want her to know—Cass—but why that also? She questioned her own motivations.

Maybe we could both go up. Maybe you could get her to leave and I could talk to him alone?

And now Collis wondered what this change in information, this pregnancy, would mean to Cass. Would she accept it? Even if she wanted to accept it? Cass should be told as well, but, really, that was up to Bisma Patel.

We can both go.

But at the room there was no answer to their knocks. And it was the same at Cass' room. They went back down to the lobby and then outside and Kallengaard's truck was not there, only Cass' rental. Bisma looked at Collis.

Where would they be? I think I should tell him. Not that it will change anything, but he should know. It will help me to decide what to do, I'd think.

Collis wondered what was to be gained by all of this, why he was even involving himself. If she wanted a ride back to Fort Collins, he would gladly do that, because he wanted to get to Denver and catch a flight back to Miami. She could decide on her own from there—her choice—to bring a child into the world or stop the fetus now. But he couldn't tell her what to do. Kallengaard shouldn't either—though maybe she wanted him to. And Bisma wouldn't be able to find him without Collis' help.

They haven't left town. Cass' car is still here. I should call her . . .

No. Don't.

It's the easiest, I won't tell her. They could be out to eat or to see something.

Maybe he's showing her.

Showing her what? The land?

Yes. Down there, the canyon.

Collis considered this and it seemed likely.

We could wait.

But Collis could see she that she could not wait.

Okay, we'll go look. I've got a good idea how to get there, but you may have to help me. Can you do that?

Yes.

Collis Mudd thought that everything needed to be slowed down, to be given more consideration, but wasn't sure how to do that. His instinct was to be more careful. Yet if the girl wanted to find Kallengaard in the canyon, why not? Why stop her?

Okay, but I've got to go to my room and get something. Just maybe they'll show up in a minute or two. But, if not, then we go to the canyon.

Trevor was driving Spring Canyon Road, Cass beside him on the bench seat in the Silverado. They had the windows down, the broad and spotless sky, the brown-green lumps of the Medicine Bow on the horizon. The dust and wind. He turned onto the ranch road, trying to be neither conspicuous or inconspicuous, rounding the curve to see the house.

He pointed it out to Cass, as if it were not important. Trevor saw that the drive was empty—no brown Lariat parked in the gravel. He saw the blackened mass of the calving shed, the old, still-standing barn, the hill of pines across the draw behind the house. He pulled in, parked, got out and Cass followed.

They stood together looking at the house, saw no signs of anything living. Trevor saw his hat, blown up against the remains of the old pump, caught in the weeds. It looked dirty, crushed as if on purpose. He didn't mention it to Cass, made no move to retrieve it. He pointed to the hill.

The graves are up that way.

Your brother's not here?

Doesn't look like it.

Trevor felt a measure of relief.

You want to go up there?

Yes.

They walked the littered and un-mown yard, over the hard-scrabbled dirt, to the fence of the first pasture—dead grass and clover—then down and up the wash, and up the hill through the skinny pines. The graves were at the summit.

Trevor touched his father's stone first. He saw that it was made of rose quartz—like the Oregon Trail marker on the land. He thought his mother must have picked it out but then knew it would have been Thor. His grandfather, with a touch of sentiment after all. In his head he apologized to his father and said that he missed him and said goodbye. In turn he did the same for Thor. He then apologized to Darcie and told her that he had been wrong, mistaken, had not understood and that was the best he could tell her. He touched all their markers then turned his head and saw Cass watching him. He ran his fingers through his hair, along his hatless head, and stood for a moment more.

Cass stood back, watched. She recalled the story—the many stories—Trevor had told her last night. She did not remember it all exactly, but she felt a sad affection for the moment, for the wind and the pines and Trevor at the graves. For the desolate land . She wondered if this was where he would want to be buried—a question she would ask him, at some time.

They stepped back over the fence and down the draw and across the pasture with the wind blowing steady. Cass now taking it in better, the house and corral, barn, the land.

You'll miss it, she said. But we can come back, if you want.

No. I don't think I'll want to. Even if my brother . . . I don't think so.

Will you take me to the canyon? I'd like to see it.

I wasn't sure if you would.

Why?

I don't know . . . because I left Fort Lauderdale for it. I left you for it.

Well, then I have to see it.

It's up ahead.

Cass could not see anything remarkable or different, only more of the rolling, chalky land. She looked closely through the windshield, saw a flat-topped mountain.

Is that the natural bridge?

Where?

She pointed.

No, that's Table Mountain, the bridge isn't that big.

It's kind of pretty, Table Mountain.

But then Trevor turned onto the rutted trail among the grass and prickly pear.

It's down here.

And the truck descended, circular, walls of earth rising, down into the hidden world he had left her for. And as the truck made the last turn Cass saw a place of shadow and sunlight, walled in orange and red and yellow stone, stone smooth and watery. It was a long depression of earth with trees in its center, with grass still green and water running along the far side. Leaves from the trees and white cotton seeds from the trees showered down into the grass and dirt. She was taken aback, so surprised, could not understand the striking difference from the world above yet she immediately understood Trevor's attraction to the place: an inner world, rich, mysterious, its wonder controlled in each direction. Beauty hemmed and separate from the larger, stark world above it.

He parked under the trees and they got out. Cass looked again at the striated sandstone, the waves of sleek rock, then Trevor walked her out of the trees and towards the stream and he showed her the natural bridge.

My. It's not what I expected.

And she took in the great bone of rock that was the bridge—the rock—brushy-topped and one-eyed. The sun was on its western side, casting a doughnut-shadow back into the willows and the gravel bars of the Pearl.

It's kind of amazing . . . it *is* amazing, down here.

He nodded.

It must have been hard, back then, to leave this place.

It wasn't.

And to leave it again?

Trevor took hold of her hand and pointed to the black lumber where he had started the cabin, to the bags of nails, to what he would leave behind. Then he let go of her hand. Everything was piled neatly onto the wood, all of it: the materials and trash and scrap wood. All that he had done in the canyon was stacked like a cairn upon the base of the cabin.

Trevor went to examine it, saw the empty whiskey bottle there, the only item not in place. Cass was right behind him.

What is it?

Nothing.

Still thinking of staying.

No. In the long run, it wouldn't have been like I wanted it to be.

Trevor was still focused on the empty whiskey bottle and now Cass saw it too.

Is that yours?

Not mine.

There was the distinct call of a redwing blackbird, the swallows from beneath the bridge came darting above them. Trevor turned to look and was not really surprised to see him. Ross. He came slowly out of the shadow of the stone, the Long Colt in his hand.

Cass grabbed Trevor at the elbow when she saw the man coming towards them. She moved in closer when she saw the gun.

It's okay. That's my brother, Ross.

She did not relax her grip.

Ross Kallengaard stopped a few yards from them, his eyes hooded, his hat low against the sun that fell into his face. His body, framed by the archway of the rock, looked swollen, heavy, unhealthy.

Ross, Trevor said, I'm leaving, like you wanted me to.

Ross smiled.

Doesn't look like it to me.

I'm going back to Florida . . . This is Cass, she's . . .

I don't want to know who this is, who that is, who anyone is. I told you not to come back here, yet here you are.

But I'm not staying.

You're going to bring in the state then?

No. No, you don't understand.

I understand, damn it. I understand that I can't believe anything you say. You just don't understand me. I gave you fair warning and now you're going to sneak around and tell me this and that and then you're going to sneak into my house and kill me.

Come on. Trevor could feel Cass next to him. He remained even, calm, kept looking at his brother. I wouldn't do that.

So you were fucking Darcie? I don't believe that. She never would have done that.

But Trevor could see that Ross did believe it.

Trevor, Cass's voice was high, let's leave.

He didn't take his eyes off Ross.

You go. Go to the truck.

Come with me.

I will, but you go first.

Trevor took a step backwards, trying to get Cass to let go of him, trying to get her to move towards the truck.

Hold it. Hold it.

Ross aimed the Colt at both of them.

She can go. She's not involved.

I'll say who can go.

Cass had turned but now stopped. She could not quite comprehend what was going on between the two brothers, even though Trevor had told her.

Please don't, Cass said to the brother. Please.

You. Please, shut up.

Cass had nothing to do with this, Trevor said. And it's not just Darcie, it's because of Dad, because I killed our father.

Ross' eyes widened beneath the brim of his hat. His lips curled.

Yeah, you killed him. But it's about her. It's about you coming back and getting everything all riled up. Take away what little peace I had. But it's about Darcie and about Grandpa and about the baby you say she was going to have.

The baby, Trevor said. If she was even with child.

It's about you and me now, anyway. Just us—*brother*.

Us. Trevor looked at Cass who was behind him now. He looked into her eyes and saw the fear. Us, he said again. Not her.

Okay, she can go. She'd better go. But not in the truck. She'll have to walk. This shouldn't take long, but I never know with you. She can leave her phone and walk out.

You have a phone? Trevor asked and Cass nodded. There would be no reception in the canyon, but he had her hand it over to him. He put it in his pocket.

Go on, he told her. Walk up the trail and stay on it. Douglas is east. It'll be okay, I'll catch up to you.

Cass took a few steps toward the truck then stopped. Went no further.

I won't, she said to both of them. This is impossible. Ridiculous. If I stay, you won't shoot him. You can't—he's your brother.

Ross gave a slick smile, then dropped it quickly.

Suit yourself, he said and re-aimed the Colt that had belonged to Thor at Trevor. His face turned a mallow color and he began to shake a little in his shoulders. Sweat began to roll down from beneath his hat, sweat was rolling down under his shirt. The gun seemed to gain weight in his hand and he brought his elbows in to steady it.

For god's sake he's your brother, Cass said. We're leaving. It's all yours.

He needs to tell me it's not true.

Ross was talking directly to Cass now.

What isn't true?

About him and Darcie. About the baby.

Both Cass and Ross looked at Trevor and Trevor said nothing.

Tell him, Cass said.

Trevor still didn't talk. He thought it would be easy to say the words but it was not. He could not bring himself to say it, to lie, to claim that there was nothing between him and Darcie. He was surprised that he could not do it. But he still did not want his brother to win. He was Trevor Kallengaard, from a ranching family.

Trevor. Tell him.

I'm sorry that she died, he said.

That's not what I want to hear.

Trevor knew he should say it. He should say it for Cass at least. It had to be done. But then there was the sound of a car, of gravel crackling along the trail. Ross straightened himself up, took a renewed interest in the gun in his hand. And though Trevor now said it: It was not true. Darcie had only loved his brother—She loved you, Ross—and that there was no baby, his brother was not listening. He was only looking at the dirty purple car that came down onto the canyon floor.

Shit, Collis said.

It wasn't until he had parked the car alongside Trevor's truck that he saw the situation—the body language of Cass and Kallengaard, then the brother. But he was too late to stop Bisma from exiting. She opened the door and took off for Trevor. He watched as she slowed up, then halted, as Kallengaard raised his hand and said something that Collis could not hear.

Collis gripped the wheel and tried to read it all better: Trevor Kallengaard in the middle, Cass close behind him, Bisma on the far right and further behind, the older brother there near the creek, holding a revolver with a long barrel. The brother appeared to be mainly focused on Trevor. There was time, he thought, time to diffuse it and make sure no one got hurt.

He moved his body to see if the older Kallengaard was watching him. The brother would know who he was, would recognize the car—he might be distracted if Collis remained inside. But it didn't look like the brother was watching or was too concerned what Collis was doing. At least not yet—it was hard to tell from the distance. Collis slowly withdrew his own handgun, the 9mm he'd gone back to his room for, and held it down on his lap. He took a moment to check the chamber and magazine, to be sure he was ready. Collis decided it was best to let the man see the gun, to let him know he wasn't totally in charge of the situation.

After opening the driver's door, Collis stood up with the gun in his left hand, turned it flat, pointed up. Easy to see. He stayed behind the open door for a moment.

Okay. Okay.

Collis spoke loudly, clearly, before taking slow steps toward the group. The brother was watching him now.

But the older Kallengaard did not change. Collis kept his gun in a non-threatening position while moving in closer, while finding an angle where he could shoot if he had to.

That's enough, Ross suddenly said.

Sure, Collis told him and stood the ground he had gained. He glanced over at Bisma who was almost opposite him. She was holding herself, breathing hard. We can work it out, he said. Why not let them go and you, me, Mr. Kallengaard here if you want, we can work it out.

No. No, they might as well see it, how this all works out. You too.

Collis nodded but he brought the pistol down and pointed it at the brother.

No one spoke. Bisma dropped to her knees, wrapped herself in the jacket that had been Trevor's father's. Cass stood silent, bent a little, her head at an awkward turn.

Ross, let them all go, Trevor said. He heard Cass say his name but he did not turn to look at her.

Mr. Kallengaard, let me talk to him. Let me talk to you—Collis was looking at Ross—let's you and me talk, let's put the guns down and talk a minute so that no one does what they shouldn't. Understand?

Ross did not take his bead off Trevor, but he spoke to Collis Mudd.

I've got a personal rule. If I have a gun, I'll consider things. If someone else pulls a gun, then everything becomes non-negotiable.

There was still time, Collis thought. He could hear the stream running, the birds, insects, the wind in the cottonwoods. The sky was an utterly cloudless blue. He was uncertain if the brother really wanted to shoot, if he wanted to kill, he would have done so. No doubt he wanted to scare them, make a point about who was in control. Then again, maybe the brother didn't even know himself what it was he wanted to do, which made him more dangerous.

Mr. Mudd, put your gun away, Trevor said.

Collis and Trevor regarded each other. Trevor's face was hard. If anyone knew the brother's real intentions, what he was capable of, Collis guessed it would be Trevor.

Okay.

On the ground, Ross said about the gun and Collis set it down in the dust, but within reach. Good, Ross said.

A raven, its large wings spread, circled down from above them, and settled into the trees, giving out one sharp call. Trevor watched it for a few seconds, then turned back to his brother. He'd had enough.

I'm coming over there, to you.

No. You stay put.

But Trevor was already moving.

Hold still.

Trevor walked slowly, deliberately forward until Ross shifted the aim of his gun at Bisma.

You stop when I say stop or someone else gets hurt here.

Trev, Cass called out and Trevor looked over at her, then at Bisma who was huddled on her knees and he stopped walking.

Cass said his name again and moved forward a bit, towards him, though Trevor did not see her do it. But Collis then moved quickly, running to Cass and holding her. No, he told her, stay out of the line of fire. And Bisma wondered if she should go to Trevor, to stop him, but she told herself that she couldn't and she pressed the jacket tighter around her.

Everyone go, Trevor said, without turning to his brother. Leave. You have nothing to do with it. He turned and addressed Ross: It's not true about Darcie. Not true.

That doesn't matter now. Ross' mouth was wobbly. He still had the gun aimed at Bisma. The thing is, you took her from me and maybe I should take someone from you.

No, that's not . . .

Who do you love? Ross asked and Trevor didn't answer.

Which one do you love? This one?

He was still focused on Bisma.

Or this one?

He moved the revolver quickly towards Collis Mudd and Cass. Ross smiled.

Which one of them? Which one do you love, so I can do what you did to me?

Trevor waited until he had his brother's attention then opened his arms and told Ross it was him.

You, Trevor said. He took a step forward, then another. You're my brother and I love you.

Ross' face sank and his hand began to tremble as Trevor walked towards him. He felt the Colt slip in his fingers until he tightened his grip, re-set his eyes and the grimace of his mouth.

And you love me, Trevor said.

Ross said nothing. He shot Trevor in the stomach.

The sharp pop of the revolver within the canyon brought the raven out of the cottonwoods with its rasping voice. The swallows above the Pearl made sudden shifts in flight as Trevor fell to his knees. He put a hand to the wound, so surprised to see blood pooling past his fingers, soaking the shirt he had put on that very morning. Then he settled onto his back in the dirt, knees still cocked, eyes looking only up.

Bisma was the first to scream. She collapsed further down, to the leafy ground, put her hands to her face, over her eyes. It was Cass who rushed to Trevor, breaking free of Collis Mudd though he tried to hold on to her. But she raced across the uneven earth to Trevor where she knelt and placed her own hand on his wound, trying to staunch the flow of blood. She placed her other hand beneath his hatless head, tried to prop him up but he could only bend his neck. Trevor's eyes were open but she wasn't sure he saw her. She said his name. His face was white. She said it again while she tried to keep the blood from leaving his stomach. Then his knees unfolded and his legs straightened out so that only the back heels of his boots touched the ground and his eyes rolled backwards and she thought that he was dead; but they came back—his eyes—and looked at her until he closed them. She heard him breathing, short and shallow.

Collis Mudd moved quickly back to grab his pistol from the dirt. He bent on one knee and brought the barrel up, training it on the brother who was only observing what he had done. Collis looked over at Bisma, saw her with her head tucked inside her arms, and he turned back to the brother, Ross.

Drop your weapon! Drop it!

But Ross did not drop it. He moved his eyes to Collis but did not appear to register him. Ross stood unnaturally stiff, his face neither stricken or empty, just hollow, dreamlike. His bottom lip hung low, mouth slack, open, showing yellow teeth.

Put the gun down, now!

Ross kept hold of the Long Colt, but his mouth became distorted, showed more teeth. He looked at Collis and said something but Collis could not understand it.

If you don't put it down I will shoot you. I'll have to shoot you.

Ross registered Collis then, and his mouth came under control. He smiled an impalpable smile.

I believe you would shoot me, Ross said. But, I'm going to beat you to it.

And Ross raised his grandfather's pistol to his ear and pulled the trigger and the swallows again shifted their flight.

When Collis reached Ross he could see that the man was still alive. He was breathing, blinking. His scalp was sheared to one side, the ear dangling like a leaf, the skull open, exposing his brain. Collis squatted and took the brother into his arms. Conscious of blood and other fluids, Collis hoisted Ross onto his shoulder and carried the man towards Trevor's truck.

Tailgate, he yelled at Bisma. Get up, get the tailgate!

Bisma was watching now.

For him?

For both of them. Please. We've got to get them to a hospital.

Bisma stood and ran ahead and with a second effort dropped the tailgate of the Silverado as Collis came up right behind her. With a grunt he deposited Ross into the dusty bed of the truck, head first, feet sticking out onto the open gate.

As he went back for Trevor, Collis knew that the older brother was dead.

There was only the sound of the truck's engine and the crunch of gravel as they circled upward out of the canyon. Collis drove, his face lined with sweat. They came up onto the flat earth onto the road filled with washboards and potholes, dirt and gravel. He tried to speed up, to go as fast as he dared, while heading for Douglas.

Bisma had quit crying. She sat in the cab with Collis, without the seatbelt on, doubled over and unbelieving. She did not wear the jacket—Collis had taken it and pressed it to Trevor's stomach, Trevor in the back of the truck with Cass and the brother. Bisma had only her bare arms to wrap around herself, around her belly. She told herself not to let go of it—her belly. She knew it was a delusion but still felt it acutely, that her belly was threatened, that it would somehow be cut open and she could not let that happen. She wished she could tell Trevor, tell him how she would not let it go. Argue, tease, explain. She would hold her belly and she would hold it for many months until it was time to let it go. It was what she would say, what she would do.

Cass was wedged against the spare and the toolbox, crouched above Trevor's head. She was leaning over him, keeping her hand pressed against the jacket which covered his wound. Still there was blood, but she was not crying. The brother was next to Trevor, the body only moving with the rattle of the truck on the rough road. She could not look at it, at the head of Trevor's brother. She didn't even like looking at Trevor's face anymore, a face so white, empty. She could not bear it. The wind, the dust—a land so full of dust and wind—she didn't like looking at that either. So Cass closed her eyes, kept pressing the blood-laden jacket, telling herself she was doing what she could, but did not believe it. She was not doing enough, had not done enough and she wanted to be blind to it all and she did not see when Trevor opened his eyes.

His shoulder touched his brother's shoulder. Now and then his hand touched his brother's hand with the jumbled movement of the truck. Trevor was not aware of this nor was he really aware of Cass next to him, her arm across him. He didn't really hear the truck or the wind but for a moment he recognized Table Mountain. Then he felt pain—pain that came and went, great pain and coldness as if it had snowed like in the winters of his childhood and the winters of Cheyenne. Trevor tried to lick his lips but he couldn't. He decided that he was very thirsty but he could get no moisture from his tongue or lips, his mouth or throat, he had never felt such dryness. But it didn't matter—he decided—the dryness, the cold, even the pain. He looked straight upward, into the washed sky. And this was remarkable, he thought. So clear and full of depth, layers of blue like waters along a reef. He had never known the sky, a beautiful mysterious thing. The sky something impossible to invent, to think of, if it didn't already exist—everything impossible, the blue, the black, the things that lived in it, and worlds beyond which were also all in a sky. Then pain swept over him again. Sharp, aching, clean. And Trevor decided again that he was thirsty and how much he would like to have some water. It would be so nice if someone gave him some water. He turned his head and saw Cass there, above him. Her eyes were closed. And Trevor thought about where he was and how he had come to this place, about how stupid he had been for many years, all years, and now he could do nothing about it, could not fix it . . . Cass . . . He looked at her face and knew that, possibly he could repair things, maybe repair everything, as long as he lived. All he had to do was live. But how important was that, this living? And then he saw Cass open her eyes and she looked at him and she smiled a crooked smile. She said his name. How bright her eyes were but again Trevor wondered how important it was, thirst, pain, living. He closed his eyes and it felt good to keep them closed. But then he remembered Cass there, right there above him, and the sky above her and he understood, finally he understood and Trevor opened his eyes again, wanted to see her again, the woman he loved framed by sky.